PRAISE FOR RUTH BONAPACE

"One could say many things about Ruth Bonapace's *The Bulgarian Training Manual*—that it's a 'romp,' a 'hoot,' a 'wild ride,' a 'pumped picaresque,' etc. And they'd all be true. (I'd like to add that it's the first book that ever made me see jacked biceps and six-pack abs as Freudian conversion symptoms.) Tina Acqualina, our narrator, idles high, ever alive to the world around her, deploying a homemade lingo that crackles like a cheek full of cinnamon chewing gum. One is gripped by this voice, in its clutches. What Emily Dickenson did for metaphysical conjecture, Bonapace (via Acqualina) does for obstreperous attention-seeking. For anyone who's ever entered a gym (or a bar or a real estate office or a Walmart or a church, for that matter) and asked oneself, amid the clanking and grunting and preening, is all this just some vain and ultimately meaningless exercise in pure narcissism or is there some deeper psychological, sociocultural or spiritual significance at play here? Bonapace gleefully answers: Yes and Yes!"

—MARK LEYNER, NYT BESTSELLING AUTHOR OF *WHY DO MEN HAVE NIPPLES*

"*The Bulgarian Training Manual* is inventive, surreal, and powered by the unexpected. With her lively debut novel, Ruth Bonapace takes the reader all kinds of places."

—MEG WOLITZER, NYT BESTSELLING AUTHOR OF *THE INTERESTINGS* AND *THE WIFE*

"This is a joyfully freakish story held aloft and borne along with the strength and dazzle of the legendary strongmen and strongwomen at its heart. Tina is a loud, raucous and unapologetic heroine of New Jersey and her stream-of-consciousness rings refreshingly true to life. I kept waiting for the ambitious arc of the narrative to deflate but Ruth Bonapace never wavered from her headlong rush forward… If it were a movie it would be independent, washed in acid colors and have a cult fan base with their own secret bicep-curl handshake."

—HELEN SIMONSON, NYT BESTSELLING AUTHOR OF
MAJOR PETTIGREW'S LAST STAND

"I just love the idea of *The Bulgarian Training Manual* that changes people's lives, with its hair-brained nutrition plans and strange suggestions for athletic improvement. The back-story and sub-plot of the great Eastern European strength performers is just wonderful, and hilarious. Based on careful research, the fact that these forebears of the secrets contained in *The Bulgarian Training Manual* were real people only adds to the charm and the wildly absurd nature of these 'circus performers' lives and feats, and is worthy of a Kurt Vonnegut novel. In fact, I think he would have loved this book… This is a novel that speaks with great humor of the absurdity of our media today, and how Americans will jump on money-making schemes and fads that they believe will improve their lives."

—KAYLIE JONES, AUTHOR OF *A SOLDIER'S DAUGHTER
NEVER CRIES*

"*Bulgarian Training Manual* is great! Well-done and rare!"

—BOB HOLMAN, FOUNDER OF THE BOWERY POETRY CLUB
AND ORIGINAL SLAMMASTER OF THE NUYORICAN
POETS CAFÉ

THE BULGARIAN
TRAINING MANUAL

CLASH

FICTION

To Sister Rose Matthew, CSJ, who gave me a trumpet solo in The Sound of
Music, *the horse whinny at the end of "Sleigh Ride," and ignored the spitballs
that zoomed past her podium.*

———

*To the strong women of the ages, who pursued strength and form even as
they were dismissed, mocked as freaks and relegated to circus sideshows,
paving the way for every muscular girl today proud of her athleticism.*

———

And finally, my narrator Tina, who keeps me showing up at the gym.

CONTENTS

PART III

THE BULGARIAN TRAINING MANUAL

RUTH BONAPACE

CLASH FICTION

PREFACE

A think tank, known as the Three Lombardis, was retained to choose academic and archival material relevant to The Bulgarian Training Manual for student and book club study guides. This is available in both print and Kindle editions, and selections are identified under the heading: The Three Lombardis.

The Three Lombardis are not available to Nook readers due to a dispute between the Lombardi (Jersey City) and the Riggio (Bensonhurst) families. As a compromise, the Nook version features exclusive commentary by Leonard Riggio, founder of Barnes & Noble, whose father was a professional boxer, once defeating Rocky Graziano.

The Three Lombardis is a collaborative effort among the following first cousins:

• Pietro "Pete" Lombardi: General contractor, including masonry and roofing. Gym rat with strict gluten-free, high protein diet. Drives a pickup and a Harley.

• Frankie Lombardi: Landscaper, specializing in retaining walls. After hours, he cuts a bella figura in bespoke suits. Drives a Lincoln Town Car.

• Luigi Lombardi: Botanist and operator of Bel Fiore Greenhouses in Woodcliff Lake, N.J. Personal passions include cultivation of fig trees, Italian art, and literature. Drives a red Mini Cooper.

PART I
JERSEY CITY, NEW JERSEY

BIG STEVE

Big Steve. Over there at the squat rack. Quiet. Keeps to himself. But let me tell you, that guy, he used to be one mother-fucking dude. Totally shit-faced, all the time. Tree-hugger. Hypochondriac. Gourmand of organically grown hallucinogens. Yeah, he was something else. He was also my boyfriend, sort of. We'd hook up. Smoke weed. Hang out. Chill. You get the picture.

But then, he got into bodybuilding, and it was all about tuna fish, protein shakes, rice cakes. Stuff to make muscles grow. Booze? Forget it. Steve says drinking makes your muscles shrink. Atrophy is the way he puts it. He also says muscles have memory. At my gym, other guys say they don't believe that, but Steve knows his stuff. Let me tell you. He gets all these muscle magazines, and he keeps up with the scientific research. And his connections! Talks to people you wouldn't believe. So, if Steve says muscles have memory, they got memory. Well, not like they remember names or faces or where they were. They remember how much weight they lifted. So that's why he insists on finishing every workout by lifting the heaviest weight, even if it's just for one rep, so his muscles remember for the next time. And, well, maybe I shouldn't tell you this, but just this morning, while I'm on the pec deck, Steve comes over and sticks this big stack of papers in my gym bag. Hundreds of photocopied pages in a ginormous binder clip. He tells me it's — get this — *The Bulgarian Training Manual.*

"The what?" I say, like what else am I supposed to say?

"The Bulgarian Training Manual," he says real quiet, looking around. He tells me: "It started with the power lifters. Nobody else knew about this for years. Nobody. It was all kept secret by the Communists. But it's out now, and it is going to be very, very big. It proves absolutely incontrovertibly that everything you hear in the bodybuilding world today is bullshit – a fraud. And all that stuff about not training one muscle group two days in a row? Bullshit. It's all bullshit."

"But Steeeeve," I say, "You're always telling me..."

"Read the manual," he says. "Just read the manual. And promise me one thing. Don't. Tell. Anybody."

"Not even..."

"No."

"But you told me…"

"What I said still goes – under normal circumstances. You'll understand when you read the manual. But you gotta promise me. Read the whole thing. And… don't show it to anybody. This is just between me and you."

"Uh, yeah. Sure. Are you doing it?"

"Doing what?"

"You know. What the Bulgarians are doing."

Steve looks around again to make sure nobody's overhearing. He sees Julio spotting Eddy at the incline press. Eddy's got so much weight racked up it looks like he's going to bust the capillaries in his face. Steve moves in close and tells me he's been following the program for five months and that he's made huge gains without supplements of any kind except, well, the organic ones like creatine, thiamin, coenzyme B6, and Horny Goat Weed, and that he's training three times a day, six days a week, which is contrary to everything I'd ever heard and I tell him so. And where does he get the time, even taking into consideration that he works at the gym? Mr. Big Deal Personal Trainer. Yeah, right. One obsession just rolls into another. And me? I remain, yours truly, the sidekick. The confidante. I roll my eyes.

"Goddamn it, Tina, you'll get all this when you read the manual.

It's the mental training. The Bulgarians developed special mental exercises with the lifting. Look, did you ever hear of that gymnast, Nadia Comaneci? You ever see those old pictures of her? From the Olympics?" he asks. "That look in her eyes? That's it. You can spot it. Like that! And after reading this, you'll be able to spot it anywhere, too. Trust me."

I tell Steve I'm not up on all the athletes like he is, but wasn't Nadia from Romania? Like, hello? I remember there was something about her in *The National Enquirer* and she looked fat and trashy. One of those before and afters.

Steve told me that, yeah, she don't look the same anymore because she fell into the wrong crowd and got old and shit but that back in the day the Romanians got hold of the Bulgarian manual because the two countries had the same spies, like the KGB, and they were passing information back and forth even if they weren't supposed to because one of the Bulgarian spies used to work out with Romanian KGB guys at the same gym in Bucharest, and so the Romanians ended up with *The Bulgarian Training Manual*. And Steve says back before Nadia got fat she was the best gymnast that ever lived in the whole world and very mysterious – that's the mental exercises part, he says – and very beautiful except for the black and blue marks on her legs which goes with the territory.

And Steve says the Bulgarian bodybuilders eat six times a day and that he's been eating three dozen egg whites, half in the morning and half at night. With paprika, which is recommended in the manual, and Steve says the presence of paprika is evidence proving beyond a shadow of a doubt that this stuff was not limited to Bulgaria, that it was infiltrated into Budapest and Hungary and all over Eastern Europe years ago in the Cold War, and that's why the Russians were always winning in the Olympics.

I ask Steve if that's the case, then why weren't the Bulgarians in the papers or on TV way more than the Russians? How many gold medals do they have? But Steve doesn't want to get into it. I think he's getting ticked off. Or maybe I'm just talking too loud. He tells me it's all been verified by a team of American scientists who went under the QT to Bulgaria, and they clandestinely copied everything and took it home and this is what Steve has, and now, what I have. The secrets of the Bulgarians.

But that's all I can say about it.
Like, I don't want to get sued.
Or arrested.

THE MAN FROM I.S.T.A.N.B.U.L.

I'm surprised at how dark and windy it is when I get out of the gym. I adjust my bag over my shoulder and make my way up Central Avenue to catch the bus to my apartment in Hoboken. It starts drizzling, so I zip my sweatshirt and pull up the hood. The street lights have come on, forming big yellow halos in the mist. Reminds me of those Thomas Kinkade paintings at the mall, a fairy tale scene, except for the stink of sewer gas and garbage. The big *puzza* as Grandma would say. As I approach the bus stop, I notice a guy in a gray hat staring. He takes a step toward me.

"You must go," he says.

I turn away, but not too much. I want to keep an eye on him. Thin and pale. Long wool herringbone coat, buttoned up, which is weird because it's damp, but not cold. The hat is one of those pointed shearling thingies without a brim. Round wire rim glasses. Dark curly hair flopping over his forehead in a boyish kind of way.

Reminds me of this guy I was in love with in high school. Philippe. His father worked for Air France. We were supposed to get married and live in Paris and drink Cognac and eat *parfaits*, real French *parfaits* as opposed to those gooey Hawaiian pineapple *parfaits* from Mr. Softee. I sat through French class for three fucking years in preparation for our new life. Worked on the accent so much it hurt my throat. So I wouldn't feel like an imposter. So I wouldn't embarrass myself. So I wouldn't embarrass Philippe. *Philippe*. It rolls off the tongue. *Philippe*. In tenth grade, he and his family went to France for summer vacation – they scored free tickets because his father, like I said, worked for the airline, which is the first time I really made the connection of how advantageous it could be to have a pilot or at least some kind of airline employee in the family. In fact, that might be why I am subliminally drawn to this guy Joe Fox – not the marriage part, but the airline perks. Joe flies 737s. He loves Hawaiian pizza with bacon, and he owns the real estate office where I work. Some people would not recognize the cosmic connection. It's my theory that if you look hard enough, you can connect the dots between anything and everything. I don't mean to brag, but I do it better than most people, connecting the dots, that is. Don't get me wrong. The thought of bacon and pineapple on pizza makes me gag. But the thought of Hawaii, pizza, and bacon individually are, well, happy thoughts. Like Hawaiian *parfaits* – individually, each is fine. Together, not so much.

But that's neither here nor there, because Philippe went *au revoir* a long time ago. And Joe Fox, well, he's just a pain in the ass. Charming, usually. Sexy, sometimes. But annoying, always.

So this guy at the bus stop sort of looks like Philippe, but it is obvious to me he isn't French. Just has that look... how do you call it? *Je ne sais quoi*. See? It wasn't a total waste. There's something to be learned from every relationship. Like French, for instance. So what if the douchebag went to Paris without me? I don't give a rat's ass. Maybe he drowned in the Seine. I'll bet he is losing his hair. Anyway, I digress. Lost in my thoughts. And trying to ignore this dude in the fuzzy hat who I swear is inching closer.

"You must go to Istanbul. But first, Sofia."

"Good try," I say. "But that's not my name and you know it."

"Many years I live in Istanbul. But never beautiful as Belograd-chik, Nessebar, Sofia."

"Thanks," I tell him. "I'll keep that in mind next time I'm planning a vacation."

"Sofia. We will go."

We? I look down the street for some sign of the bus. Who is this Sofia chick? He is still staring at me. I glance to the side and observe that his eyes are brown. Light brown. Almost hazel. Maybe this dude's not so bad. He's either a psycho motherfucker or an eccentric. An intellectual. A sophisticate.

"Let us go to Sofia," he whispers.

"Who are you?" I ask him, with plenty of attitude as in: "Who the fuck are you and don't fuck with me." But all I actually say is: "Who are you?"

"A poet," he says. Just like that.

"A poet," I say, nodding. What a pathetic line. I notice he has a little bit of an accent. Can't quite place it. He is not wearing a wedding ring. They say you have to kiss a lot of frogs. But I don't think I want to kiss this one, even if I am pushing 40. Well, 37 to be exact. I got time. Sort of.

He steps closer to the sign at the bus stop, the one with the charts and instructions, and squints. I decide to be helpful. Maybe he is a tourist.

"This is the Central Avenue line," I tell him.

I don't think he heard me, because he says again: "Istanbul. Must go. Now."

"No such stop," I say, a little louder. The rain is really coming down now and I'm feeling cold. I hate being cold. In my misery, something dawns on me. An epiphany, as they say.

"Hey. Where is Istanbul?" I ask him.

"Turkey."

"Is that near Bulgaria?"

"You know, then, what I am talking about."

"No. Just making conversation. Okay?"

I reach into my gym bag for some tissues and push aside Steve's manual, which weighs a ton. He looks at me and glances down at the bag. I give him a tissue to dry off his glasses, but he doesn't take it. He keeps looking at my bag, so I pull the zipper shut. I start to put two and two together as the bus is approaching.

"Look dude," I tell him, "My boyfriend loaned this to me, okay, and I have to give it back. Well, he's not my boyfriend exactly. He used to be my boyfriend, like sort of was, and I'm just trying to hit the gym and lose the muffin top. So give me a break, okay?"

I jump on the bus as soon as the door opens and head for a seat in the back. I wipe the condensation from the window with my sleeve. The guy is still at the corner, and he is taking something out of his pocket. A keychain, with a bright pink plastic egg dangling from it. I hear the bus driver arguing with somebody in the front about the fare. I pay no attention, just keep looking at this guy in the shearling hat cradling this egg thing, but what is it? He puts the egg close to his face.

A Tamagotchi?

I haven't seen one of those since I was maybe 12. Why now? Why on the Central Avenue bus? There is so much to life I still do not understand. An aura is emerging. Fashionable. Arrogant. Flirting with danger. I wipe the condensation again as the last passenger gets on. The dude is waving a red Twizzler in front of the Tamagotchi. And then the egg turns black. Of course. It could only be, I reason, Kunoitchi, the extravagantly flamboyant and cruel sister of the Tamagotchi warrior Gozarutchi. I can't believe I still remember all this.

As the bus pulls away, I think of the Tamagotchi I had when I was a little kid. The factory named it Bunbuntchi, which means Bunny Rabbit in Japanese, and I re-named it Sakesushi, which doesn't need translation. I remember how proud I felt to be entrusted with a fabled Ninja warrior.

Eventually, Sakesushi died because I forgot to clean its poop, and Grandma threw it in the trash.

As the bus pulls out from the corner I slump into my seat and put my feet on the seatback in front of me. I wonder how far it is from Hoboken to Istanbul.

And how far Istanbul is from Bulgaria.

And who the fuck is Sofia?

MORNING AT J. FOX REALTY

I crawl out of bed to pee and trip over my gym bag. Why is it so fucking heavy? Oh yeah, the manual. I pull it out and turn to the table of contents.

"The Principles of Weight Training." Duh?

"Bioenergetics." Boring.

"Recovery Through Massage." Okay. But sounds expensive.

"The Psychology of Training." I make a mental note.

"Prologue." Now, that gets my attention. I always read prologues because I find that a prologue gives me a heads up to the rest of the book and whether I should bother to go any further, or in some cases, what to look out for. Take, for instance, *Romeo and Juliet*. "A pair of star-crossed lovers take their life." When we read that in ninth grade, I was a little pissed that there was no spoiler alert, but at least I knew ahead of time that they were going to die, and a double suicide no less. And that there would in fact be a happy ending. As in "do with their death bury their parents' strife." That inspired me to read all the boring parts in between. Oh, and most important, it said right in the prologue that the play would take two hours. That's a lot of useful information. Most books don't do that. Maybe the writers don't care about giving readers what they need from the get-go. Think about it. Shakespeare is still around after all these years for a reason. That's my opinion, anyway.

In the case of the manual, I noticed there is no epilogue. Don't you need an epilogue if you have a prologue? It's just a rhetorical question I am asking myself.

Anyway, the prologue is written by a guy who claims he worked with the Bulgarian Training Federation, and he writes "great physiques are no longer limited only to those individuals with great genetics or the gifted sensory awareness of how to train." Big Steve says that I have great genetics, and if I train right, I can have an amazing bod. What does he know about my genes? I am skeptical because he also told me that I should go to church and take communion because that's one of the secrets of success in Bulgarian body-building. The wafers of strength, he said. I reminded Steve that Bulgaria was a Communist country for many years and the nuns at Our Lady of Victories told us Communists weren't allowed to have communion.

Where was I? Oh, yeah, so I'm reading the prologue, and I'm thinking this whole thing is sounding like a sales pitch, with words in bold and italics and big promises. But then I turn to the nutrition section and find recipes, but no product placement. Just the basics: Increase protein. Decrease fat. And charts that tell you what to eat depending on how many calories you need to consume every day. So, maybe it's legit.

I look up breakfast in the 2,000-calorie section: 6 egg whites. 1 yolk. 1 cup oatmeal. 1 banana.

I can do that.

It says eating six times a day keeps the glycemic index in check so you don't become catabolic - or maybe it was anabolic. I don't remember except that I had a friend who drank a lot of Coke because she said she was hypoglycemic so it kind of makes sense. Six meals divided into 24 hours would mean eating every four hours. Since I assume you're not supposed to wake up in the middle of the night to eat, I subtract eight hours for sleeping and partying. That leaves 16 hours for eating and everything else in life. I take out my calculator, divide 16 hours by 6 meals and I get 2.66 hours. This makes my head explode. If I round up to 3 hours, I'd have to get up before 8 to finish eating before midnight. I decide on every 2 hours and get it over with.

Meal 2 is 4 oz. water-packed tuna. 1 cup rice. 2 cups cauliflower. Cauliflower? Before lunch? It also says eggs should be scrambled, never fried. Ugh. I hate scrambled eggs. Especially if the white is runny. Reminds me of snot. I flip to the recipes section and fold the edge down on one that seems reasonably appealing before heading to work – "work" in my case being a euphemism. And "euphemism" being a word I like because it says so much. Euphemistically speaking.

I work in a real estate office. More specifically, I'm a Realtor at J. Fox Realty in Hoboken, New Jersey. Realtor with a capital R because it is trademarked. I don't have any hours. In fact, I don't have to show up at all since I am paid on commission, "paid" being something completely different from working. With most jobs, you put in your hours, you get a check. Put in extra hours, it's time and a half, double time on holidays. Nice. But you are stuck with ten-minute coffee breaks and a half hour lunch. Sucks, huh? Teachers have it pretty good, with summers and holidays off. But really, how much money can you really make unless you get a Ph.D.? And along the way you gotta wipe a lot of runny noses. Germ city. I wheeze at the thought.

This job gives me a lot of personal freedom. I wear what I feel like and take lunch whenever I want for as long as I want. Not that I'm one of those two-hour lunch prima donnas. I work my ass off. I sit at my desk and wait for customers. I answer the phone. I take people out in my car. I talk to people in the office. I drink coffee. I eat crackers and cheese from the gift baskets that the title companies send. I organize my leads on index cards, then copy them into spreadsheets on my laptop. I put quarters in the parking meter. I put paper in the copy machine. I answer my email. When the mortgage guys take us out for drinks, I put on my fuck-me heels and it's a party. I go to condos listed for sale and give my opinion about the decorating. If there's no one home, I check to see if there's any good drugs in the medicine cabinet they wouldn't miss.

My broker, Joe Fox, the pilot-entrepreneur-dealmaker who owns J. Fox Realty, makes the rounds at the happy hours with me when he's in town. He sticks to Scotch because he's an old fart, but I love the chocolate martinis at The Shannon Lounge. The frozen pomegranate margaritas at East LA are amazing, and The Elks bar makes the best watermelon martini with Twinkie-infused vodka on the planet. But mostly I drink red wine. It's healthy. So is Guinness, which has 126 calories and 10 carbs. Bloody Marys are high in Vitamin C, Vitamin

K, potassium, folate and antioxidants, which is why I prefer them for breakfast.

Not that I party a lot. Just some nights it's better than hanging out in my crappy apartment feeling bummed while everybody else is having fun. Going to the gym helps. So does going to the Laundromat. I like listening to the machines. I like the smell of detergent and fresh towels from the dryer. I like folding clothes. I can turn a pair of jeans into a bundle the size of a brick, and when I'm short on cash, they let me work there for a cut of the wash-and-fold. I mean, it's not a career. For now, real estate is my career, but the downside of my job is there's no steady paycheck.

It's been three fucking years since I've had my real estate license and I've made zilch. Okay, a rental here and there. But as for the big ones, all my deals fall apart. Today, I have "floor time," meaning I'm hanging out answering the phone and waiting for walk-ins. I'm on the early slot, 10 to noon. None of the agents show up that early except Deno (who I find totally annoying) and our manager Charlene (who takes her job way too seriously). Oh, and the so-called receptionist who is, shall I say, useless.

The very first day I started working here, it was Deno who gave me the office tour: a bunch of beat-up desks, worn carpet, phones with cords, bulletin boards - very low tech. When we got to the key rack, he pulled me aside and said: "Charlene watches over the keys like you wouldn't believe. Not just the hot blanks. But every single key, every dupe, doesn't matter if it's some cheap Quickset. She needs to know where they are. At all times."

I asked him what for. Deno looked and me like I was nuts. "Keys," he said, "will get you everywhere."

Anyway, today I find Deno with a couple of renters who look like rich girls, and a note that my people, as usual, have cancelled, which is why I moonlight at the Laundromat, which cuts into my gym time, and the less I go to the gym, the less energy I have and the more depressed I get, which is, what – a vicious cycle? Do you ever wonder why negative-energy cycles like this are considered vicious?

Deno says to the girls: "You young ladies are early, aren't you?" Then he says to Charlene, "How about a pot of coffee? For the young ladies." Charlene fires a look at him.

Young ladies? Come off it, Deno. He winks at the girls. "I so apologize. My previous appointment ran late." Late? It's barely 11 o'clock.

I can't stand people who are perky in the morning. Especially guys. But Deno has one redeeming quality. His family owns the diner down the street, which has the best French fries and gravy. Sometimes his mother gives me extra, no charge. And right now, bacon and eggs are calling me. I head for the door, and who walks in?

Joe Fox.

He's wearing his epaulets.

I decide to stay awhile longer.

THE FLY BOY

Now, it might not seem like a big deal, but even though Joe Fox is leaning on 55 and he can be a totally sarcastic jerk when he struts into the office with his cap and epaulets, well, there's just something about him. He flies commercial airliners: 727s, 737s, 747s, and even fighter jets back in the day.

Charlene runs the office when he's not around, which is most of the time since he is usually up in the friendly skies. Literally. And sometimes figuratively. In his private office, there are model airplanes and a mini putting range – is that what you call it, a putting range? I think so. I need to learn more about golf. At night, when he's not partying, he plays flight simulator.

A few months ago, I was working late, and Joe was in his office, eating Hawaiian pizza with bacon and extra cheese while taking a plane down the runway. He looked up at me and smiled in that little squinty-eyed way he has. I asked him to teach me to fly planes on the computer.

"Hey, Missy. I thought you wanted to learn how to play golf."

"I do," I told him. "But I saw this commercial on TV and it showed a close up of those people on the tarmac, you know, the people wearing the earmuffs or headsets or whatever they got going on, and they wave around these things that look like Lava Lamps."

"That's called marshalling an aircraft," he said.

"Yeah, exactly, and I was thinking how cool to be on the ground looking up at an airplane while it's moving. I mean, they're like so huge. You could be standing directly underneath and be okay unless you're not paying attention and end up in front of the wheels. Or you get sucked into the engine. I had a nightmare once about getting sucked into an engine. Like a seagull."

Just then, Joe got up and for no apparent reason went over to the key rack and asked, "Are any of these people on vacation?"

"How should I know?" I told him.

"Start noticing. Let me know."

Then he said, "Hey, Missy, what's on your dance card this week?"

Anyway, getting back to the here and now, these so-called young ladies, Deno's girls, are eyeing Joe up and down. He's wearing a short-sleeved shirt, so you can see his pale freckled arms and his watch, which is very big for his thin wrist. He's pulling his black wheelie bag with a smaller bag on top that has the instructions on what to do if the plane is about to crash.

One of the girls, with microbladed brows, a plunging neckline and French manicure, winks at Joe. I want to smack her.

"They're called epaulets," he tells her. "They come off."

"Back from Miami?" Charlene asks Joe.

"Nah, Phoenix." Joe opens the door of his office.

"Saw the folks," he says. "When I got there, Mom says, 'Every time I see the shadow of your plane flying over the house, I look up and I wave. And you don't even stop in to see us.' " Joe shrugs. "Same thing, every time. Same damn thing."

Charlene looks out the window and says, "They all look the same to me."

Hahaha. I forgot to laugh.

"Any messages?" Joe asks. "There's a guy who wants to build 38 condos. Where's Terri?"

Charlene points to the front desk. Terri, the sorry ass excuse of a receptionist, has her head in her arms. I think she's sleeping.

"Geez," he says. "If I'd have known I would've brought an oxygen canister from the aircraft. Instantly sober. Like that!" Joe snaps his fingers. He goes into his office, shuts the door, opens it again, and sticks his head out: "Got a deal brewing. Let me know if Murray calls." I look up at the ceiling. I grab the letter opener on Terri's desk and slam it into the wood. It sticks like a dagger. I am feeling much better.

No sooner do Deno's girls get their coffee, which Charlene has reluctantly and subserviently made, than more people start to come in. I don't know who these people are, but they sure as hell aren't looking for me. I tense up because I know what's coming. Deno's screechy nasally voice. And sure enough:

"Hi guys! You must be my 12 o'clock. You're early!"

Why is it that some people are so irritating? Do they act that way on purpose? Just to get on everyone's nerves. I open the Bulgarian manual and pretend I'm not paying attention.

Maybe I should go to the diner. Or just head right to the gym. I really should go to the gym. But then I'd miss out on the office drama. There are days when I can't make up my mind, and then it gets made up for me. This is one of those days.

I see Charlene do a little double take toward another desk. An empty desk. She picks a pair of men's gray suit pants off the floor. Everyone stops to watch.

Terri grabs the pants from her and throws them back under the desk. Then, a few moments later, I swear to God I am not making this up, this guy - this really, really gorgeous guy - comes out from under the desk, wearing the pants but no shirt. I mean, Fabio in the flesh. He looks around, finds a wrinkled dress shirt behind Terri's desk and stuffs it into his belt. Then, get this, he pulls Terri close to him and kisses her, deeply. I raise my left eyebrow. It's something not every-body can do, raise one eyebrow. Supposedly it is a DNA trait. Like touching your nose with your tongue, which I can't do. So, they come up for air and the hunk is about to walk when Terri grabs hold of his belt buckle.

"Hey, hot buns," she says, "not so fast. Just one more little thing before you go." She puts her hand down his pants pocket and pulls out a check. She shoves a pen at him and next thing you know this hung-over dude is signing papers.

I look over at Deno who writes on a pad of paper: "HE IS SIGNING A CONTRACT." Uh, yeah, I kind of figured that out.

I should quit this fucking job. Do something better with my college degree, which is worth squat. Like, hello! I am one of 90,000 psychology majors who graduate every single year. I have since learned they are also the most under-employed.

I feel like suing the university, which should've disclosed this kind of information before taking my good money for tuition. I mean, it's in the fucking U.S. Census. By the way, Ted Bundy was a psych major and a sociopath. Psych/soc? On the other hand, Monica Lewinsky also was a psych major, and so was Gloria Estefan, who went on to make a gazillion bucks.

As for me, no one cared about my college degree at any of my jobs, which were nonetheless useful and interesting: barista, admin, roadie for an alt rock band which never toured further than the Jersey Shore, seat filler at Radio City, dog walker, cat sitter, gerbil sitter (which should have been easy except they ate their babies while the owner was away), security guard at Macy's where I learned the finer techniques of shoplifting and how to get away with it, proof reader at the Journal of Particle Physics where I discovered I can spell better than these Ph.D.'s and learned corny jokes nobody else would get like: What does an atomic duck say? Quark! Quark!

It's not easy to find yourself in the world. Unless you are a member of the lucky sperm club. If you have no parents, no money, you're fucked.

Ironically, the career with the 14th lowest rate of unemployment in the country is the field of religious vocations. Nobody fires nuns. And they get great benefits. But no sex, which sucks. Would that be considered irony? I never quite figured out exactly when irony shows up and when it doesn't. They don't teach that to psych majors. Information like that you just pick up from life.

As a real estate agent, you don't need a degree, you don't have to kill anybody, and it doesn't matter if you can sing. And you not only get as much sex as you want, it's actually encouraged. The proof is in my office.

Despite those advantages, I'm thinking of asking Joe to get me a job as a flight attendant. I'll get paid to travel the world, find a rich guy in first class, get married in a cathedral in France, throw rose petals into the Seine. And stick it to Philippe. Yeah, right.

I'll just go to the gym. But first, I need to stop at the diner. Forget bacon and eggs. It's French fries with gravy.

A HOLY PLACE

I'm normally one of those people where – click – after 10 o'clock at night the brain shuts off and I can't talk. But now, once again – two nights in a row – I am exhausted, but I can't sleep. I'm reading *The Bulgarian Training Manual*, skipping around over the boring parts like the "Origins of Physiology as a Post-Corporal Discipline," checking out workout routines and recipes. There's a brief bio on the scientist who brought all this to America, Dr. Vinnie L. Capriolo Jr., a retired adjunct professor at DeVry University. He is credited with using cutting edge technology to analyze ancient manuscripts, which over the ages were painstakingly copied in root cellars by old Bulgarian women in babushkas, sipping schnapps by candlelight. Although they had wizened faces and arthritic knuckles, their ferocious rear delts and calves were the envy of the young men in the villages.

I close my eyes and I think of my own father, Gianni, known as Rusty G, who grew up in Newark and disappeared before I was born. Well, he didn't exactly disappear. He had a football scholarship to Notre Dame and knocked up mom at a bar in Atlantic City during spring break. I'd like to think he gave up a career in medicine to, well, to marry mom and take care of me, but no. He quit school to follow his dream of opening Roto-Rooter franchises throughout Texas, and my mother died of a broken heart. Or so I've been told. There is no grave. What ultimately became of dad, I'm not sure. But whenever my toilet or sink gets clogged, I think of him. Just for a minute. Like, I don't obsess or anything. I just picture a parking lot full of trucks, guys running around in overalls, snaking out drains. And there he is, behind a humongous desk, organizing it all. He is wearing a black suit, studded cowboy boots, a pinky ring, sunglasses, and a white cowboy hat. Maybe he has a wife? A daughter, not me. They live on a ranch with horses and cows and rattlesnakes and a big blue sky. Without me.

Due to this very unfortunate twist of fate, I was raised entirely by my maternal grandmother in Jersey City. Grandma drank Budweiser and watched professional wrestling on an old Zenith until she died on her living room couch, emaciated with black and blue marks on her arms and empty beer cans on the floor, during a world heavyweight bout. On the coffee table was a framed black and white glossy photo of Georg Karl Julius Hackenschmidt, the first world wrestling champion, flexing his muscles in what appears to be a Speedo and black knee socks. His head is turned from the camera, so you mostly see these enormous shoulders and quads. He appears to have been a handsome man. Grandma said that he was from Estonia, and that at one time, she was his girlfriend, that even in his 70s he would lift her over his head like a human barbell. It's hard to picture somebody using Grandma to complete a clean and jerk. But then again, this was a guy who is said to have jumped over a bench 100 times a day with his feet tied together. Grandma was probably a piece of cake, or cupcake, in Grandma's case, which brings me to the next subject: Was he good in bed? And was this before or after Grandpa died? I never asked, and she wasn't telling. There were no pictures of Grandpa on the coffee table. And Georg's is signed.

Maybe that's why I ended up with *The Bulgarian Training Manual*. A hand dealt from beyond the grave. A cosmic fate. I don't know. But that's my story, and I'm sticking to it.

I decide to get out of my head and back to the business at hand. I Google this Capriolo dude and come up empty. Maybe he uses a pseudonym for protection since he stole state secrets from Bulgaria. Or maybe he is just low-key. Steve told me Dr. Capriolo is world renowned, but not famous, which must be a bummer. If he is a real person with a fake name, why Capriolo?

The dictionary lists *capriolo* as Italian for deer, which are fast but not big and bulky. I discover it is also the name of a town in Italy and a bicycle brand. How does this all fit together: bike, deer, Italy, Bulgaria, bodybuilding? Me? And isn't *capriolo* a kind of Italian cold cut? I have nothing if not a curious mind. Always connecting A to B to C. I look up baloney and it is not a food.

It is baloney as in full of baloney or, as we say in Jersey City, "fulla shit." The cold cut is spelled bologna with a silent *g* and the *a* pronounced as *e*. I see that it, too, is a place, Bologna, a city in Italy where the *g* is pronounced *nya* and the *a* is, well, just *a*. I'm wondering whether bologna is made in Bologna, and why nobody thinks of bologna as Italian food and why there is really no mention of Italian bologna anywhere at all. I call Steve to get his opinion and he seems annoyed. I think I woke him up.

"Steve," I say. "Did you ever hear of Italian bologna?"

"I hear a lot of baloney and not all of it Italian," he says.

"No, I mean the stuff you put in sandwiches," I say.

"Stay away from that shit. It'll give you cancer," he says. "The nitrates."

"So, Steve," I say, "The Bulgarians, they invented this?"

"Uh, what?"

"The manual. I mean, did the Bulgarians invent all this?"

"Not really," he says. "They stole some of it from the Turks, who it from the Estonians. Ancient times." While he's talking, I get distracted by somebody walking past my apartment. I forgot to pull the shade down. Another disadvantage of living in a basement apartment.

"There was a town," Steve says. "A small town, where these training principles started. Probably in Biblical times. Lots of hot young men in togas."

I picture Moses on the mountain doing double bicep curls.

"Is it still there, this quote-unquote town?" I ask.

"Yes, but it's not the same," he says. "Everyone is cerebral. It's a cerebral place."

"A holy place?"

"No. Cerebral. Brainy. Nerdy. They were a great people once. The biggest, strongest powerlifters in the world."

"And now," I say, "they're what, a bunch of geeks?"

"You got it. Outsourced to the West."

"Virtual?"

"Computers," Steve says. "Games. Html. And yet, the look in their eyes. It hasn't disappeared. Not yet. It's in their souls, waiting to get out. It's like, you know, man, she was something else."

"Nadia?" I ask.

Steve gets quiet for a moment and then says, softly, "Arianna. Four-time champion. Eastern Europe. Six-pack abs and hamstrings, yeah, those hamstrings."

"Maybe it was the Horny Goat Weed," I say.

Steve's not taking the bait. He yawns and says, "Just read the manual. Do the routines. Follow the diet. Six times a day. You eat six times a day. You need to eat to lose weight. Get the metabolism up. Remember. Egg whites. You can buy them by the bucket at the bakery supply house in Secaucus."

"I'm going to lose weight eating six times a day?"

"Read..."

"Yeah, I know. I know. Read the manual. I mean this is getting, well, wow. I wonder if any of the other guys at the gym..."

"Shit. Didn't I tell you? Don't tell anyone about this. Promise me."

I notice that guy is walking past my window again. This time he stops. I dim the light to get a better look at this dude and I see the shearling hat. He looks at me, gives me a "thumbs up" and walks away into the night. The bus stop guy. It should give me the creeps, but somehow it doesn't. What's with the thumbs up? A sign of confidence? For what? My new workout routine? Or does he mean: "I'll get you and the manual and your little dog too?" Of course, I don't have a dog, but it's a figure of speech, kind of. *The Wizard of Oz* is my favorite movie. Especially the lines about the witch not being "merely" dead, but "most sincerely" dead. Really, I'd rather be sincerely dead than merely dead, if those were the only two choices.

"Tina! Promise me!"

It's Steve. I almost forgot.

"Uh yeah. Promise what?" I say.

"Jesus fuckin' Christ!! Don't tell anybody I gave you the manual," he says, sounding wide awake again.

"Don't curse God," I say.

"And what's with the Italian bologna?" he says. "Since when do you eat bologna?"

"I hate bologna," I tell him. "In day camp they gave me bologna sandwiches with butter on white bread. But that guy who wrote the manual..."

"Capriolo? You're thinking of *capicola*. Or *gabagool* as they say, a kind of salami, not really bologna," he says.

"Yeah, high in fat and salt," I say. "I don't touch the stuff. Don't worry."

"It's okay sometimes. In fact, there are times you must eat it," he says.

"But the nitrates?" I'm confused. And tired. So tired.

"On the second new moon of each year," he says. "It's in…"

"Yeah, yeah, the manual."

"Pay attention! Eat three thin slices of *capicola*, and offer one to the pagan gods of the Astral Light. On the second new moon of the year. But first dip the slices into a bowl of lemon water – Sprite's okay if you don't have lemons – and say *Semper Fidelis*. And go to church and take communion. It's good for you. And pretty soon, you'll look as sexy as Ann-Margret on a Harley."

Communion? *Semper Fidelis*? I'm sick of Steve yanking my chain. I need to get some sleep so I can get into the gym early. But I can't sleep. I surf the channels and see Rachel Ray. I can't stand that perky nitwit but there she is in front of St Patrick's Cathedral and the synchronicity is too much to pass up.

––––––

EXT. NYC STREET

RACHEL RAY and guest standing on Fifth Ave sidewalk across from St. Patrick's Cathedral. Slightly off center to show cathedral doors.

RACHEL RAY:

(smiling and holding microphone)

Hi everybody! I'm Rachel Ray and behind me is a building that needs no introduction. Yup, New York's St. Patrick's Cathedral, which draws thousands of visitors every year. It's also where we've caught up with Sister Mary Mack Trucken, a Dominican nun who lost 57 pounds in two months on a sensational new diet, inspired from heaven above: The St. Catherine of Siena Diet. *(turns to guest)* Sister Mary, tell us what your life was like before the Siena Diet?

SISTER MARY:

Fat. That's what I was. Just fat. Dear Lord, I'll say it again. Fat! I tried everything. Pritikin. Grapefruit. Atkins. South Beach. And, nothing!

RACHEL RAY:

Nothing?

SISTER MARY:

Oh, well, to tell the truth, maybe a couple of pounds came off, but nothing you'd notice.

RACHEL RAY:

So what changed it for you?

SISTER MARY:

Well, I'll tell you a little secret. One day, while helping Brother Aloysius set up for a funeral service, I looked at the coffin and thought: Do they come in size large? That's when I panicked. Yes, panicked. And I stopped. I just stopped eating. And for the better part of the week, I resisted the temptation to eat. But the following Sunday, helping prepare for Mass, I spotted a chalice filled to the brim with communion wafers. I noticed Brother Aloysius had his back turned in the Sacristy, so I made the sign of the cross and popped one into my mouth. Two, actually, well, three, to be totally honest. Then I said a little prayer of gratitude to St. Catherine of Siena.

RACHEL RAY:

Catherine of Siena, founder of the Siena Diet? The 14th Century Dominican who helped unify Italy and brought the Pope back to Rome, all the while eating her way across Europe with communion wafers? Look at this portrait of her, folks. Isn't she adorable?

SISTER MARY:

Yes, yes, and she's the patron saint, well, co-patron saint of Italy, I might add, along with, anyway, I have to admit I was a little anxious about touching the Holy Eucharist for such profane purposes, but, you know what? It did the trick! Satisfied my cravings. That smooth wheat taste, melting on my tongue, getting stuck on the roof of my mouth. Oh, I lodged it free with my tongue, very careful not to bite Jesus. The next day I went into the chapel with Sister Augustine, and we plucked out another, and--

RACHEL RAY:

-- and pretty soon, all of the nuns were scarfing communion wafers. But after a while, they start tasting pretty ordinary, wouldn't you agree Sister Mary?

SISTER MARY:

Yes, but we're still wild about them, and now some of our sisters in Missouri are busy making--

RACHEL RAY:

(*smiling to the camera*)

Hold that thought, sister. Folks at home, after the break we'll show you how to create delicious recipes from communion wafers, from party treats to desserts, in your very own kitchen. And I'll let you in on a little secret. Those chiseled hunks at the gym? Yeah, they love 'em. Serve them instead of chips when the guys are watching football, and you'll be amazed at the result.

SISTER MARY:

They're great with a little Nutella.

BLACKOUT TO COMMERCIAL

INT. STUDIO TEST KITCHEN

RACHEL RAY is standing behind the counter of the test kitchen with three guests. She is smiling at the camera and holding a spatula. On the counter there is a platter of colorful communion canopies, a plate with plain wafers and a book upright on a stand.

RACHEL RAY:

Welcome back folks. Before demonstrating how you can serve these little goodies at your next wine and cheese party – or would that be wine and wafer party? – we'll fill you in on the namesake of America's newest diet, the awesome St. Catherine of Siena. Let's give a big welcome to Father Francisco Lardo, who has come all the way from Italy with his runaway best seller *Dieting Secrets of the Saints*.

(applause)

Joining him is Stanford nutritionist Dr. Wilma Bariatros, an expert on medieval eating habits.

(applause)

Father Francisco, there are some who say that subsisting solely on communion wafers for more than thirty days is unhealthy. Yet, St. Catherine lived for more than seven years on this diet. What does the church say about the Siena Diet?

FATHER FRANCISCO:

There is no papal encyclical on dieting, per se. But there is ample literature on the spiritual benefits of fasting. Why, in the sixth century, St. Benedict said and I quote, "There is nothing so opposed to Christian life as overeating."

RACHEL RAY:

Thank you, Father Frank. May I call you Frank? For all of you watching, go to my website for examples of medieval diets. Now, I'm not suggesting you actually follow any of them to the T, because then you'd become as round as Friar Tuck! But there are some sinfully scrumptious morsels you can pick up for the holidays. Take a look at this:

(cut to image of diet on website)

<u>13th Century Friar Daily Diet</u>
   Calories: 4,500 - 6,000
   Seven pints of watery ale
   Three eggs, fried in lard
   Vegetable porridge with beans, turnips, parsnips and leeks.
   Stewed eels
   Pork chops, mutton or goose with oranges or venison with rowanberries.
   Two loaves of bread, to use as sop
   Unlimited peaches with egg flan.

(back to studio)

DR. BARIATROS:

May I interject here?

RACHEL RAY:

Doctor Bariatros?

DR. BARIATROS:

Skeletal data from bones interred at Merton Abbey indicates a medical condition known as diffuse idiopathic skeletal hyperostosis, also known by the acronym D.I.S.H., which comes from overeating. It forms a coating on the spine, like candlewax dripping down the side of--

RACHEL RAY:

Candles! Did you hear that? Candles are always a welcome addition to any dinner table and we're having a special on my website.

(cut to image of candles on webpage and back)

DR. BARIATROS:

And there's also the matter of early onset arthritis which the monks--

RACHEL RAY:

Cool beans *(winks)* So, what else, Father Frankie, can you tell us about groovy St. Catherine?

FATHER FRANCISCO:

By eating only communion wafers, not only did St. Catherine keep her trim figure, but she also attained a mystical union with God. She wrote about it in her diary.

RACHEL RAY:

No kidding! So there's a mind-body connection.

FATHER FRANCISCO:

Most definitely. Here's how she describes it: "O You who are mad about Your creature! True God and true Man, You have left Yourself wholly to us, as food, so that we will not fall through weariness during our pilgrimage in this life, but will be fortified by You, celestial nourishment."

DR. BARIATROS:
Excuse me--

RACHEL RAY:
Hold that thought, Wilma. Now, tell us, Father Frankie. Did she eat anything at all besides communion wafers?

FATHER FRANCISCO:
Sometimes a spoon full of herbs.

RACHEL RAY:
Organic?

FATHER FRANCISCO:
Of course!

RACHEL RAY:
Anything else?

FATHER FRANCISCO:
She drank the pus of the sick.

RACHEL RAY:
Eeeeewww!

FATHER FRANCISCO:
But, she survived the plague. How many of us could have—

DR. BARIATROS:
Excuse me, but evidence suggests that St. Catherine of Siena may

have been the world's first documented case of anorexia. I mean, she died when she was 33 of starvation.

RACHEL RAY:

Oh yuck, eating disorders are very serious folks, and we don't advise our viewers to eat nothing but communion wafers forever and ever. I mean, there are plenty, just oodles and oodles, of nourishing toppings I'll be demonstrating. They're also good with dips. St. Catherine was fond of herbs, as you heard--

FATHER FRANCISCO:

Catherine's writings reveal this was not anorexia nervosa, which is what most people today think of, but rather what was then known as anorexia mirabilis, translated roughly to anorexia miraculous, which we view half as a testament of her self-denial, which included virginity and self-flagellation, and--

DR. BARIATROS:

-- and half as an illness over which she had little control – just as today's insights into eating disorders recognize that the compulsion to avoid eating, or to binge eat, with or without later vomiting, over-whelmingly—

RACHEL RAY:

(close-up, smiling)
And now folks, here's where you can buy communion wafers.

(cut to webpage and toll free number and Rachel Ray voiceover)

Today's special is gluten free. No icky bloating! And we're working with nuns in Missouri on a salted caramel line. Get a batch for Super Bowl Sunday. Remember, if they survived plague and pestilence, these medieval ancestors must have been made of some pretty tough stuff. So call now and try them all: the low-cal Siena Diet snacks and the fat and feisty Monk's delight.

———

I write down the phone number and turn off the TV. These people are giving me a headache. I sink into bed and my pillow feels cool and smooth against my face. I reach out and feel the manual on the bed next to me. I'm wondering if there is any mention of communion in there.

THE THREE LOMBARDIS

Why Should We Be Strong?

Just as the man of sedentary habits and weak body possesses a correspondingly sluggish mind and lack of energy, so he who assiduously pursues physical development gains not only that desired government of his organs, but in marked degree obtains a thorough mastery of his will and, consequently, an easy and contented mind.

GEORG HACKENSCHMIDT, *THE WAY TO LIVE* (1935)

MY ABODE

I live in the basement of a house in Hoboken that I had listed for sale. No one bought the house, but the sellers appreciated my help so much they rented me the basement apartment for $600 a month, half of what it would cost if it were a legal dwelling unit, which it isn't. It's what they call a "bonus" apartment. Not that it's some kind of prize. It just means the city doesn't know it exists. Another way of putting it, a euphemism you might say, is a "mother-daughter" house, if you consider living with your mother a euphemism. Or an "in-law" suite, which is more politically correct. But it's still the same thing. An illegal apartment. A zoning violation.

It seemed like a win-win. I keep it under wraps and put up with a few inconveniences, like sharing a mailbox with the tenants upstairs and hiding my doorbell behind some plastic flowers, which I need to explain to anyone coming to see me.

The owners also warned me that there was a minuscule chance that the plumbing could back up and if it ever did to let them know. This sounded like a deal breaker, but they went on and on about their engineer and the sewer system and Nor'easters and that it could only happen during a hundred-year flood. Well, a new century must be upon us because, well, here's how it went down:

I'm walking home one night, a little buzzed, and out of nowhere there's thunder and lightning and rain coming down in sheets. I wait under a bus shelter until it slows down and then make a run for it. Fortunately, I was only a few blocks away. I fumble for my keys and jump inside – into more water. About ankle deep. Seems like the whole floor is flooded and the power is out. I call Steve and he lets me crash at his place. On the couch, because God forbid I interrupt his sleep because, yup, sleep is when muscles grow. We go back to my place in the morning, and it stinks to high heaven. There's sludge on the floor and in the tub and I'm totally grossed out. It reminds me of this documentary I saw in fifth grade about the Nile. They say when the Nile floods, they use the sludge to fertilize their farms and the people prosper. My sludge has no monetary value whatsoever except to a cleaning lady, and I think it would kill my plants, if I had plants, which I don't except, for the plastic flowers by the doorbell.

Steve points out that except for one humongous maple tree, the backyard is solid concrete sloping toward my back door. He also found some cracks in the foundation and gaps by my windows. Steve knows his trees, which is a long story, but anyway, he theorizes that when leaves get stuck in the gutter and there is heavy rain and water gets into the walls and under the door and power goes out causing the sump pump to fail – like some cosmic collision in the universe – it is inevitable that water will get in.

So, I call the landlord and he promises to clean the gutters and replace the pump and swears it will never happen again. Or, at least for another hundred years. The clean water trickling in from the outside, that is. But the backup into the tub he can't promise because, he says, it is an act of God and therefore out of his control.

Act of God my ass. I give him the finger over the phone and call my friend Choochie, who is a plumber, and he tells me the landlord should install an ejector pump. I call the landlord back and he says it is against code. And besides, he says, if they catch him putting in an ejector pump, they will see the illegal apartment and I would get evicted. A lose-lose proposition all around. It's so not fair.

But I believe in karma and shit happens for a reason. Maybe it will lead to an HGTV show. I'll get famous, cash in on my troubles. Monetize them, as they say. Then I'll spring for Yankees season tickets and a venti skim caramel mocha chip Frappuccino whenever I want.

But back to the here and now. I call Joe Fox, figuring he might know how to handle my cheap bastard landlord. He answers on the first ring, cuts to the chase and says the landlord should reimburse me for everything, including the cleanup and anything damaged.

"Joe," I say, "I know these people. Trust me, they ain't paying for nothing."

"Threaten to call the health department," he says. "They'll get fined for the illegal apartment and pay for your relocation costs. That's the law. The city will make them rip out the kitchen. Then I'll take it off their hands below market and convert the place to condos."

"I don't know, Joe. I don't want any trouble."

"A judge might even make them subsidize your new digs to the tune of six months' rent as compensation for your trouble. This could be the best thing that ever happened to you. It's a beautiful plan."

Six month's rent and a free move? There's got to be a catch.

"I don't know, Joe. I'll never find another apartment for 600 bucks. Get real."

"Look Tina, let's say you rent a place for $1,200, well, multiply that by 12. What do you get?"

"I don't know. What?"

"For Chrissake, you can't do this in your head? Where were you when they handed out multiplication tables in school?"

Ouch.

"I was a psy-cho-lo-gy ma-jor," I tell him. "Psyc/soc with a minor in French. N'est pas?" What a fucking douchebag.

"Okay, listen," he says. "$14,400 for the year – got it? Now they give you $7,200, you end up with $7,200 for the year which is – come on, think about it."

"I am."

"Which is?" he asks.

"Uh."

"$7,200. My God, Tina! $7,200 divided by 12 is $600."

"That's what I'm paying now."

"Yeah, and you wouldn't have to pump out your apartment when it rains."

"Good point. But after a year I'd be paying the whole $1,200."

"Suit yourself. I'm just trying to help," he says.

"I guess. Maybe you're right. I mean, look at me. What do I know?"

"Listen, missy. Cut the pity party. Tom Watson majored in psychology and went on to be a great golfer."

Golf? Maybe that's beside the point. Or is it exactly the point? I happen to know that Katherine Hepburn also majored in psychology, besides the aforementioned Ted Bundy and Monica Lewinsky and Gloria Estefan. All psych majors who made good in other fields. Ok. I can't act. I can't sing. I never played golf. I don't have rich parents. I'm not giving blowjobs to the president. I don't even know the freakin' president and besides, I have my principles. And Ted Bundy? We won't go there. I need to focus on my strengths.

I'm good at, well, at, I don't know – just stuff, like folding laundry. Ugh.

Truth is, I'd like to take Joe up on his idea of turning in the landlord. But the thought of walking into the zoning department or the rent board makes me depressed and nervous at the same time. And what for? Do I even want to stay here?

Lately, I feel like I'm on the edge of something big, and part of me doesn't want to get too close. I have this gut feeling, a scary feeling that's hard to put into words. Like something is going to happen. Something massive. Inevitable. But what? Maybe I need to go to the gym, get on the bike, clear my head, read the manual – and find a cleaning lady.

No. Not just a cleaning lady.

A cleaning crew. A big, badass cleaning crew.

Fuck the cost. I'll pay for it.

Somehow.

STIGMATA

"Guarda la Madonna," Grandma whispered. "She will talk to the Son. *Capisce?"*

Kneeling beside me with black rosary beads wrapped around her arthritic fingers, she pointed to a statue with powder blue robes and a gold crown. Grandma told me it was The Virgin Mary, and that she was my ticket to Jesus.

I liked the concept. A middleman to God.

The nuns at school put it differently: "The Blessed Mother has the power of intercession. She is the mother of us all. Pray to her as your mother."

But I'd never seen my own mother, and this one was made of clay.

I stared at her face for a sign that she was real, that she could see me. Was that a tear in her eye or a reflection? The nuns told us there were statues that cried, and some even dripped blood. I crept close after Mass, but I wasn't tall enough to touch her face. I thought of climbing up, but I was afraid if one of her fingers or toes broke, I'd get the shit kicked out of me. Or end up in Hell. Or both.

I don't believe in crying statues anymore. Or apparitions, but I should not say so out loud. I do know this: if you cry too much, tears come out of your nose, because there is an opening in the nasal cavity. The image of the Virgin Mary with tears is beautiful, but snot running down her face, not so much.

As for her hands, I sometimes wonder what my mother's looked like. Were her fingers long and smooth like the statue? Mine look more like Grandma's, so maybe they skipped a generation.

———

Holy Mary, Mother of God, pray for us sinners, now and at the hour of our death, which doesn't include me by the way. It's just part of the prayer. Amen. And please, send money because I need to move out of my crappy apartment. Remember, I didn't step on you in church as a kid. I could have, but I had too much respect. Well, ok, I was freaked out.

Now, if you could do me one further. Help me get my ass out of bed with the alarm so I can be at the gym when Big Steve shows up. If you do, I promise to give up sex for Lent. My jeans are tight, and I need to lose a few pounds. Five would be okay. Ten even better.

Oh, and, if you can see your way clear, help me find out who this freakin' creep is, the guy with the shearling hat who's been following me around. I'll make it up to you. I swear. Cross my heart and hope to, well, never mind. I am sorry to be asking for so many things. If I had to choose just one, well, I'll let you pick for me.

One more thing. Were you really crying that day? And if you were, why? Did I make you cry? Were you trying to tell me something?

THE FRAULEIN

Joe Fox is at lunch and his laptop is on his desk. I slip in and close the door. He was IM'ing. On AOL. Really? AOL? Need I say more on that subject? No. AOL says it all. And he is IM'ing with Ultra Luxe Fraulein. Ex-flight attendant now a ticketing agent at Lufthansa. I never met this chick, but I imagine she looks like Eva Gabor on Green Acres. I know I shouldn't, but I scroll down the page.

ULTRALUXE *Ich liebe Ihren Golfschwung.* (I love your golf swing)
J. FOX *Ihren* what?
ULTRALUXE Golf—*schwung* XXX!!!
J. FOX Oh yeah. Outta the park baby!
ULTRALUXE *Aber kannst du* putt. (And you can putt, too!)
J. FOX You noticed.
ULTRALUXE *Ich mag einen Mann, der seine Metaphern misch.* (I like a man who mixes his metaphors)
J. FOX Hey, I'm just a simple guy who likes his pizza Hawaiian and meatloaf well done.
ULTRALUXE *Ich mag meinen Sauerbraten heiß und Fett!!!!!* (I like my Sauerbraten hot and fat!!!!!)

J. FOX Sorry. Sauerbraten repeats on me. Gotta run, baby.
ULTRALUXE *Warte, mein Liebling! Mein Gestüt!* (Ok, my stud! Bless you!)
J. FOX Later baby cakes. XOXOXO.
Ugh. His generation. Not mine.

THE THREE LOMBARDIS

―――

Govern Your Thoughts

One ought to avoid all unnecessary worry and exciting thoughts, and
to cultivate a firm tranquility of mind. I have formed the conviction
that all unnecessary sorrows and cares act in all circumstances harm-
fully upon one's constitution. Melancholy reflections will in no way
influence Fate, whereas one may weaken the constitution by the waste
of energy while indulging in them. The best is to do one's duty consci-
entiously, and to leave the rest to Him who guides our destiny.

GEORG HACKENSCHMIDT FROM *THE WAY TO LIVE* (1935)

―――

WHEN THE RAIN COMES

It's the middle of the night, and I hear something far away. Sirens, in the distance, getting closer. Wind and rain hitting the house. I'd fallen asleep on the sofa while reading the manual, and now it's two in the morning. I get up and knock over the Lava Lamp I inherited from my grandmother. I look around and take in the squalor in which I live. I'd never thought of it as squalor before. I would tell myself it was, well, shabby chic. A good deal. Good enough.

But now, yes, I will say it. I so hate my apartment.

After the last monsoon, the landlord agreed to a free month's rent if I'd keep my mouth shut. I told him that wasn't enough, so they ponied up cash for cleaning and repairs. Joe was pissed because I didn't report him, so he didn't get to steal the property. I told him deals are like buses: miss one and another one will come along. And speaking of clichés, or maybe it's a truism, they say lightning doesn't strike twice, so what about a hundred-year flood? Luckily, I'm not seeing any water seepage this time.

I wrap myself in a blanket and open the door. The cool wet air calms me. From my stoop, I gaze at the lights from the new glass condo towers, just beyond the plastic flowers hiding my doorbell. I picture a lobby with shiny marble floors and rows of mailboxes and a doorman who knows my name.

A thought pops into my head, like it's being whispered into my ear:

Tina, the meaning of life is not simply to exist, to survive, but to move ahead, to go up, to achieve, to conquer.

The accent is vaguely German. I envision a tall man with wavy hair, a square jaw, smiling and tan with bulging muscles, preening on a beach. A gap between his two front teeth. Arnold? As in Schwarzenegger? I can hear him saying the words. But where did this come from? The gym? The manual? A dream? Have I gone schizophrenic? I rub my left arm and notice there are red dents and creases from falling asleep on top of the manual. Maybe I should call Steve. A very loud fire truck goes by, and I wait until it passes.

"Hey, Steve. It's me. I was wondering if I could come over."

"It's the middle of the night," he says.

Silence.

"Steve," I say. "Can you hear me?"

Nothing.

"Hello? Steve?"

"Yeah."

"Look, I know it's late, but I can't sleep here. It's making me nervous with all the rain. Like before, except this time I think the whole place might get washed away." I feel a little guilty for exaggerating.

Nothing.

I ramp it up a notch to see if he is paying attention.

"The river is right outside my door. I'll have to climb up to the roof if it gets any worse. Just unlock the door for me, and you can go back to sleep. I won't make any noise."

"Not tonight," he says.

"Listen, I really, really need you right now. I really need to talk to somebody, not just anybody, but someone specifically like you. There's this Arnold saying that you might... Steve? Steve? Are you awake?"

Silence. Maybe he's thinking it over.

"I got company," he says.

For a minute, I don't know what to say. I don't know if I am angry or embarrassed. Or both. I apologize for bothering him and hang up.

My stomach hurts. Dumbass motherfucker. Okay, he's not my guy, just my friend, so why am I weirded out by this?

I stare at the yellow glow from the streetlamps. I listen to the sirens and the wind. I breathe in the damp and the sewers. Whenever it rains a lot, especially if there's thunder and lightning, and sometimes in a snowstorm, I hear a lot of fire trucks. Maybe it's always like this, just more noticeable in extreme weather, when you are in a heightened state. Or maybe sound travels better when it's damp and dark, late at night, when there aren't so many cars and buses drowning out the other sounds, drowning being a figurative word, not related to the rain or snow. Drowning as in the feeling of being swallowed by the empty streets.

I'm tired, but I can't go back to sleep. Sitting on the stoop, I lean against the railing and try not to think about Steve and who he is... I can't say it. Even in my head. I close my eyes and feel the mist. I hear glass breaking. Glass from the bar on the corner. Must be closing time, yeah, it's got to be closing time and they are dumping the bottles into the trash. It's not a bad bar. A place for people to hang out. Together. It's easier than being alone. I notice my jeans are soaked because I've parked my sorry ass on a wet stoop. I don't care.

I am startled by a bang and jump up. A garbage truck. A guy is hanging off the side and the headlights are big foggy circles. My toes are cold, my stomach hurts and now there is a pain in my chest, squeezing down under my ribs. Maybe I have a hiatal hernia. Or a bad heart. I start to cry, and I don't know why.

Then I hear another message from Arnold:

Stop whining.

THE ICE QUEEN

I wake up without the alarm at 5:30 AM. The only thing open at this hour is the gym. I take the manual from the couch and stick it in the bag. It will give me something to read while doing cardio.

Jose is behind the desk, and I wave my card. He nods and says, "Hey, what's up. You have a fight with your boyfriend?"

I stand there and just look at him.

"Hey, I don't mean nothing. You just look like shit, that's all. Get on the bike. It'll wake you up."

I look past him and see the early light streaming through the windows. The music is pulsating and it's freezing cold. A guy racking eight plates on the bench press lets out a scream that echoes off the high brick walls. I hear metal on metal. He's right. I'm feeling better already.

I check out the bikes and treadmills and weights and I ask myself why I'm not here every morning. I forget about everything here. The crappy apartment. My lack of true friends except for Steve who is now showing himself to be a douche. The resentment over why Joe Fox hasn't flown me to Miami or Paris or Hawaii, all empty promises even though I keep my word covering for him with the keys.

Gone. All gone. Here I am in the zone, a zone with its own zip code, and I, like Billy Pilgrim, unstuck in time. An existential universe that interconnects. I think that's what is known as the order of inter-being. But enough about me.

Steve's not at the gym this morning and I prefer not to think about why.

"Jose, you ever hear of Bulgaria?" I ask him.

"Isn't that in Queens?" he says.

"Never mind."

I get on a bike. I have about 20 pages from the manual hidden inside a muscle mag to make sure nobody sees it while I'm reading.

I haven't counted, but the manual seems to be around three or four hundred pages long. No page numbers, just chapters in Roman numerals. I, II, III, IV, V, VI, VII and so on. Plus graphs and charts, a map of Bulgaria, a glossary of Bulgarian words, quotations from a monk and, of course, recipes. I'm thinking I might make the black bean protein brownies. I'm not so sure about the egg whites with blood sausage or the Bulgarian stir-fry with jellied meats, turnips and sparrow eggs. I'd probably puke. I didn't see the *capicola* and lemon ritual Steve talked about. Maybe I didn't get to that part yet, or more likely, Steve was fucking with my head.

It's mostly easy reading, except for the workout routines, which are divided into modalities and circuits and quadrants. I'll have to add a calculator to my gym bag. Three sections of workout routines divided into three weeks divided into a series of exercises that change six days a week. With music to fit the mood. And rest to recharge the soul.

It looks like this:

SAMPLE WORK WEEK

Modality 3 / Circuit 3	DAY 1	DAY 2	DAY 3	DAY 4	DAY 5	DAY 6	DAY 7
Workout 1 MUSIC	Smooth Jazz	Funkadelic	Heavy Metal	Dueling Banjos	Klezmer	Grunge	Gregorian Chant
Activity # Sets Body parts	8 HEAD 8 SHOULDERS 8 KNEES 8 TOES	8 TRICEP 8 TRAPS 8 FINGERS 6 HAMSTRINGS	3 BACK 3 CHEST 3 QUADS 3 ABS	3 CHEST 3 BACK 3 ABS 3 SPHINCTER	8 HEAD 8 SHOULDERS 8 KNEES 8 TOES	3 CHEST 3 BACK 3 QUADS 3 THUMBS	Sleep
Workout 2 MUSIC	Motown	Calypso	Black Sabbath	Bach Cantatas	Bruce "The Boss" Springsteen	Zydeco	Theme: The Shining
Activity # Sets Body parts	4 HAMSTRINGS 12 SPHINCTER	12 ADDUCTOR 12 ABDUCTOR	2 CHEST 4 BACK 6 BICEP 8 CALF	8 BACK 6 CHEST 4 BICEP 2 CALF	8 CHEST 7 BACK 6 BICEP 5 CALF	4 BACK 3 CHEST 2 BICEP 1 CALF	Sleepwalk
Workout 3 MUSIC	Classic Rock	K Pop	Bulgarian Folk Dance	Death Metal	Euro trash Techno	Reggae	Panpipes
Activity # Sets Body parts	6 BICEP 9 TRICEP 6 GLUTES 9 QUADS	10 ABS 10 QUADS	4 DELTS 4 TRICEP 4 QUADS	16 GLUTES	3 DELTS 3 TRICEP 3 QUADS	4 DELTS 4 GLUTES 4 QUADS	Mindful walking
Rest Between Sets	180 Seconds	47 Seconds	248 Seconds	95 Seconds	120 Seconds	300 Seconds	All day
Repetitions per set	Cycle A Endurance 13-15 Reps	Cycle A Endurance 13-15 Reps	Cycle B Strength 10-12 Reps	Cycle B Strength 10-12 Reps	Cycle C Power 8-10 Reps	Cycle C Power 8-10 Reps	N/A
DAILY POSITIVE SELF TALK	You never fail until you stop trying	You will achieve what you believe	Always sweat the small stuff	BE BEST !!!	Go, go, go, go, go, go, go, go, go, go, go	MOVE YOUR LAZY ASS or be annihilated	Turn on Tune in Chill out

Some of the instructions seem to be in Latin, like *in versus* and *augmentationem* and something about *Contrapunctus* XIII and *factorem caeli et terrae*. Maybe it dates back to ancient Rome. Like Steve said, Biblical times. I was relieved to find sections on yoga and workout music with the following suggestion:

On rest days, we recommend total relaxation. When physically disengaging, it is crucial to rid the brain of clanging, grunting and other sounds that have invaded the subconscious throughout the week, which trigger the workout and produce anxiety. This can be achieved through involuntary musical imagery repetition, or IMIR, also known as the "earworm" or "stuck song syndrome." Simply listen to music which, once heard, you cannot get out of your head, such as: "Have You Seen Her" (Chi-Lites), "Love Shack" (B-52s); "Sweet Caroline" (Neil Diamond); "It's a Small World" (Disney); "Who Let the Dogs Out?" (Baha Men) or any Enya recording. This will change your mood long enough to refocus your energies. Usually, a good night's sleep will break the earworm cycle, but if the song continues longer than desired, try chewing gum, reading a novel, or working on a Sudoku puzzle. If your earworm persists for more than 48 hours, consult with your physician to rule out palinacousis, which is associated with lesions of the temporal lobe. In very rare cases, earworms can last for years, influencing behavior. For example, the scientific literature shows that Jean Harris, headmistress of The Madeira School in New York convicted of murdering diet doctor Herman Tarnower, had been suffering for 33 years from acute recall of the song "Put the Blame on Mame" from the 1946 film <u>Gilda</u>.

My eyes glaze over trying to make sense of it, but I rationalize that it's better than watching the gym TV. I once bought a chicken rotisserie that I saw on an infomercial while walking on the treadmill. It was called "Set It and Forget It." Kind of a waste because I never cook, and since I want to save money so I can move, I'd rather not be tempted with consumer gadgets.

I flip to some pages that seem less esoteric:

The Bulgarians in the latter half of the 19th century commenced their training at age eight with three short workouts a day, gradually increasing time and duration to twelve brief but intense workouts a day, alternating with periods of rest where they cut back to three times a day for more extended repetitions with lighter resistance, so that by the time they were eleven or twelve their bodies could become one with the functions they performed and they retained this muscle memory for life. In other words, it's like riding a bicycle.

I get it, but since I'm 37, I'm not feeling too good about this. On the other hand, I didn't start on the stationary bike until three years ago, and I've got pretty good endurance. Which also gets you nowhere, according to the manual.

That section says the Bulgarians don't warm up. It's considered a waste of time. Practically against the law. A short stretch is tolerated, and maybe a quick sprint around the building to wake up is ok. But this business of hopping on the bike for 15 or 20 minutes before working out? Forget it. Counterproductive. I check my time on the bike. 18 minutes. I can feel the ache in my legs. Do I push on to 30 minutes? Or bag it. Do it the Bulgarian way. I don't know. I've been working my way up to 30 minutes adding increasing hills to the program each time for the last couple of months, trying to get in here three times a week.

Maybe that's why I'm not losing weight. Maybe it's not that I don't do enough cardio. Maybe I'm doing too much, as unlikely as that seems. Let me make one thing clear. I'm not fat and I don't want to look like Miss Skinnymarink over there on the StairMaster. I just have this roll under my waist, and my butt looks a little wide. "A little wide" is how Steve puts it. He measured my subcutaneous body fat with his new calipers and said it was too high at 26.5 percent. He suggested no more than 15.7 percent. He says I'm pear shaped. I'm not too thrilled, but he insists it's normal. A pear? Really?

I catch myself staring at Miss Skinnymarink, wondering what her body fat percentage is and how she would look if she had more muscle and the same amount of fat. She sees me staring and I look away as Jake, the retired butcher, and his wife arrive at the front desk. They see me and wave. It's so nice to see older people working out together. They sit on their stoop in Jersey City watching over the neighborhood when they're not at the gym. Very sweet, except that Jake has a suicide by cop fantasy and seeing them hanging out minding everyone else's business gets on my nerves.

I'm thinking about whether Jake will get himself killed eventually, and whether it will be a regular city cop, a state trooper or, as he states, an "agent of the government," which could be the CIA or the KGB or FEMA – this guy Mark who works out at my gym says his bets are on the Mossad – when the guy on the bike in front of me turns and says over his shoulder: "I hope you don't mind, but I heard you talking to Jose about Bulgaria."

"I was just asking if he heard of it, that's all."

"Just asking?" he says.

"Yeah. Why?"

"It's not in Queens."

"No shit," I tell him. "I think he was getting it confused with Astoria."

"Not necessarily," the guy says.

I'm not in the mood for this jerk. I cover the manual by turning over a few pages from the bodybuilder mag and there the page lands on an amazing picture—a woman with the physique of a man but the face of the ice queen from Narnia. Long thick flaxen hair swept back with a few carefully coiffed wisps falling over her forehead and cheek. Defiant chin. Perfectly manicured hot pink nail extensions. Anja Langer. Former Ms. Olympia contender. I've seen her in Steve's videos. (She's from – you got it – Germany. What's with these German babes?) Steve has a whole collection of Mr. and Ms. Olympia contests dating back like 20 years. Maybe more.

I remember this one night we were watching the Ms. Olympia 1988, the one where Anja came in second. We were eating pizza, M&Ms and beef jerky, his favorite foods during a three-day lull in his training. (He says you have to go off the diet once in a while, maybe even have a few beers, because it throws the metabolism for a loop and then it kind of shocks itself back and you make more progress). Anyway, I told him I thought she looked ginormous, but he said she was puny and that I could beat her easily if I put my mind to it and did some real training. Steve says I don't realize how blessed I am by my genes. Me? I could not let this go unchallenged. I asked him if I really have good genes, why am I shaped like a pear, and yet she looks like Brad Pitt on steroids? He said I might be right about the steroids, that her neck looked a little thick.

And now, here she is in the magazine, with a spotlight glinting off a barbell, her tanned physique ripped to shreds. I'm wondering when that picture was taken and why she's in the magazine so many years later. I tear it out to take home. I'll tape it to my mirror as inspiration.

I pedal faster, reading the section I dog-eared. The guy on the bike in front of me turns around again and says to me:

"They stole it from the Turks, you know. In ancient times."

"I thought this stuff was a big secret," I tell him.

"It is. Not too many of us know."

"Is it for real?" I ask. "Does it work?"

The guy stops pedaling. He rummages through his bag and hands me a thin plastic folder.

"Read this," he says. "While I'm finishing up."

"Is it from the manual?" I ask.

"No. It's a white paper, written by a panel of highly trained, independent experts who assimilate, analyze and explain stuff. It will give you the answers you seek."

ANALYSIS OF POST-MODERN ADAPTATIONS OF THE BULGARIAN TRAINING MANUAL

BY DR. WINSTON J. NEUMEISTER, PH.D., DDS, TLC

Muscle Memory = Part II
Proteins, micro-memory, and reinforcement techniques, including purposeful grunting

All astute and discerning elite athletes know of muscle memory, first given voice by the so-called strongmen of the late 19th and early 20th centuries. However, in recent years, tremendous advances have been made in scientific techniques such as genome sequencing and human clinical trials, conducted first in the Eastern Bloc by government sports federations and, more recently, funded by civic-minded Bulgarian organized crime bosses.

ORIGINS:

The proud tradition of physical culture reached a zenith in the strongmen of a century ago, whose mental concentration and profound spirituality translated into feats of strength unparalleled in today's commercial drug-ridden gymnasiums, which cater to the likes of trial lawyers and real estate tycoons who believe they can buy their way to a perfect body specimen: bikers and construction workers whose aim is not perfect symmetry and form, but biceps and pecs to show off under wife beaters; and millennial urban professionals who are under the delusion that by showing up at the gym a few times a week and faking their way through a circuit they can someday ward off The Angel of Death.

We postulate that you *cannot* ward off The Angel of Death, who will come on Her chariot for each and every person. However, the strongest among us, with a pure diet and clean mind and body, will most likely keep Her at bay the longest, and when it is time to capitulate, will do so with a dignity that will reverberate through the generations. We do not want to overstate this. We just want to present the facts, as they are.

Muscles have memory. Not only the muscles we utilize when we pose, but our internal muscle fibers connecting virtually all other internal organs. For the purposes of this analysis, we will concern ourselves mostly with the muscles we see.

THE POWER OF FORGIVENESS

Is it too late, some ask. Must we train as children? As young men and women? How late is too late? Can a person once great ever regain greatness? Are there second chances in this miserable life? We are humbled to tell you: Muscles will never forget, but they will forgive.

One commonly cited example of muscle memory is Langford Riley of Emporia, Kansas, who in 1946 was the strongest man in his regiment coming back from World War II. He was considered one of the finest specimens in the U.S. Armed Forces. A handsome war hero with severe post-traumatic stress syndrome, he then spent the next six years drinking and womanizing and was said to consume four six packs of beer with tequila chasers each day. Before retiring to bed, he would share with his random paramour of the night a double banana split with maraschino cherries, whipped cream, toasted almond slivers, walnuts, butterscotch syrup, and one scoop each of chocolate, vanilla, and strawberry ice cream, with the vanilla always in the middle. Sploshing, also known as wet and messy fetish (WMF), would often follow. Riley, although unschooled in the power of the mind, believed this pre-boudoir confection to be an aphrodisiac and by various accounts, attributed to his many conquests, his performance had been exemplary until he suffered cardiac failure and was confined to a hospital bed for four weeks.

During Riley's convalescence, he became withdrawn and socialized with no one, until he found himself sitting in the solarium with one Teddy Bernstein, professionally known as the wrestler Brocko the Belligerent, hospitalized for complications from axillary hyperhidrosis. An excessive sweating of the armpit area, this created a serious schism between Brocko and his training partners.

Brocko, who suffered from extreme shyness in high school, where he was taunted with cruel nicknames like "Teddy Bear," due to his large size, recognized in Riley a glimmer of kinship, and when the ex-soldier's hospital gown fell from his shoulder, he could see the shriveled outline of a once legendary posterior deltoid. Brocko had in his possession sacred texts cobbled together from parchments and spoken word: smuggled from behind the Russian lines; stolen from villagers displaced from Bulgaria, Estonia, and other nations; paragraphs traded on the black market for enormous sums by believers desperate for their wisdom. It is said these texts formed the basis for *The Bulgarian Training Manual*. Brocko took pity on Riley and ordered one of his minions to bring to him three pages of the muscle memory chapter, and then three more during each of the subsequent two days. Poor Riley devoured them like a parched man who had clawed his way to an oasis, chanting the passages as though they were holy verses, which they were.

In just three days – I repeat three pages, three days – remember, everything is connected to everything else, and nothing, not even numbers, pages, and days can be considered apart – Riley awakened to a new life. He flung his bedpan through the window, yanked out his IV, and stretched his arms. At once, the flimsy strings of his hospital gown popped from their seams and the entire garment proceeded to tear from the collarbone to the end of the sternum. He shouted to the stunned hospital staff, which had gathered: "Pain is not my enemy. It is my god! And I am the god of my destiny!"

A witness, Mrs. Mildred W. Nelson, R.N., wrote about the peculiar encounter in her diary, found posthumously by her children and donated to the University of Chicago, which is how we have these details today.

Conversely, it has been demonstrated that simply imagining your muscles atrophying will cause them to shrink. A thus withered musculature may trigger osteoporosis, dementia, tennis elbow, flatulence, brain lesions, nephritis, bunions, goiters, aphasia, and, in extreme cases, paralysis and death.

HEALING PROPERTIES OF ARUGULA-FED SNAILS

To demonstrate the power of the brain on physical development, researchers at Ohio State University took two sets of study participants and wrapped the right forearm and wrist of each in a cast — immobilizing their muscles for four weeks. One group was instructed to sit still and intensely imagine exercising for 11 minutes, five days a week. More than just casually daydream about going to the gym, participants were instructed to devote all their mental energy towards imagining flexing their arm muscles. The other set of participants, the control group, was told to work out at a gym for one hour per day, utilizing a combination of circuit training and zumba classes six days a week and on the seventh, two hours of Bikram yoga in rooms heated to 102-dregrees Fahrenheit. At the end of the four weeks, the mental exercise contingent was 4.6 times stronger than the control group.

Using magnetic brain imaging, researchers found that those who imagined exercise not only had stronger arms but also enhanced neuromuscular pathways. Immediately, physiologists and neurologists began weighing in.

The most cogent explanation is thus: Minute proteins in our muscles carry forward to synapses every detail of the last repetition and the precise percentage differential between exertion and total muscle failure. This information is stored completely and permanently in the neural pathways.

Later studies, utilizing the most complete copy known of *The Bulgarian Training Manual,* combined the mental and physical exercises with spectacular results. They demonstrated that when athletes perform just one rep of an exercise they previously failed to complete while visualizing each fiber, fascia and blood vessel down to cellular levels, gains were faster and more consistent, and recovery time shorter.

In addition, we recently announced a new study into the efficacy of superior nutritional aids in combination with the aforementioned mental and physical regimen. Specifically, we are interested in results produced by a new formulation currently consumed in Bulgaria, a dietary supplement said to be exponentially more effective than traditional formulae like Trenadol Enanthate, Testosterone Cypionate, or even Stanozolol.

This new supplement is made from extracts of *arugula-fed escargot*, which, when combined with ordinary communion wafers to stave off hunger, targets the primary proteins responsible for muscle memory while increasing metabolic absorption of every other substance introduced. This has been proven safe, is certified organic, and tastes like chicken.

NEVER WASTE A FREE TICKET

Like I've said, Joe Fox sometimes gets his friends free plane tickets or upgrades, even passes to the first-class lounges with free booze. Joe says he used to do this all the time, back in the day. He says before 9-11, all he had to do was flash his ID and he would get on any flight he wanted, even let his friends come along and they'd all hang out in the cockpit. But now he has to go through Ultra-Luxe Fraulein, who bypasses security. Supposedly she got caught printing Joe a couple of extra tickets to Vegas for the Super Bowl, and instead of getting fired she wound up getting a promotion.

According to Joe, Fraulein's logic was thus: 9-11 taught us that if somebody takes out the whole flight crew, even if the passengers then beat the crap out of the hijackers and tie them up—somebody must know how to fly the freaking plane. That's what the FAA concluded, too, in recommending more pilots mixed in with paying passengers, especially ex-military pilots like Joe – Fly Boys in the vernacular – who don't take crap from nobody. (BTW, there was a survey that rated Fly Boys the Sexiest Military Men for five consecutive years. Air Force rocks!)

"And in doing so," Joe said, "their balance sheet was preserved."

"Free seats for pilots and their friends are a drop in the bucket compared to the cost of replacing a plane. For example, the Airbus a380 costs $275 million, though they say you can get an end of the year model for around $210 million with 2.9 percent interest and a five-year / 350,000 mile unconditional warranty."

Yeah. Ok. My point is there are usually empty seats since people miss flights or maybe they die or end up in a coma and their relatives don't find the unused tickets until it's too late. Deno knew a guy who had a heart attack and when the family was going through his stuff to find clothes for the undertaker, they discovered a little cash, his will, and the keys to a red Saab convertible.

At the funeral parlor, the dead guy's sister found tickets in his suit pocket to a Bruce Springsteen concert. She was devastated. It was the same night as the wake.

Anyway, it's a shame when tickets go to waste, so be on the look-out. At the very least, you can scalp them.

Last winter, Joe ended up with tickets to Africa. He was going there to meet this gnarly guy, a *griot* to be specific, which is an ancient storyteller who deals in desert herbs. And, by the way, the "t" is silent. I hate mispronouncing words. And he invited me.

What sold me on the idea – I say "sold" in the figurative sense because the ticket was free – was when Joe told me that in this part in Africa, the Turkana Basin, there is a famous archeologist who had been digging up bones from prehistoric people and that there was evidence from DNA and carbon testing that they played baseball back in the day—can you imagine?—and that Babe Ruth's DNA and Yogi Berra's DNA and Reggie Jackson's DNA and Derek Jeter's DNA and Alex Rodriguez's DNA could be traced to this one place. And from this primordial genome sprung forth The New York Yankees.

Joe knows the archeologist, or maybe he's a paleontologist, from when he got out of the military. He did some work transporting organic pharmaceuticals in and out of Africa. He knew how to land in the desert, and that's where the guys were digging up the bones. He also helped them find elephant poachers, flying over the jungles and the fields. One of the things I like about Joe, besides the epaulets, is his soft spot for animals. And he knows his drugs.

Joe forwarded me a list of what to take on the trip, and we went, and we came back, and that's all I want to say on the subject. I decided right then and there I would never go anywhere with him again, never. Well, except maybe Paris. Or Miami. Someplace where you can get French fries and decent hair products.

THE THREE LOMBARDIS

Arbus saw the street as a place full of secrets waiting to be fathomed. Her subjects seem magically, if just momentarily, freed from the flux and turmoil of their surroundings.

FROM THE EXHIBIT "DIANE ARBUS: IN THE BEGINNING" MET BREUER, JULY 12 – NOVEMBER 27, 2016

HOW I MET BIG STEVE – PART 1

THE TREE

The Sciancalepores' apartments don't come up for rent very much, but when they do, they list with me. I met old man Sciancalepore my first week in real estate. I had no connections, no customers. I see Pops in front of his house in Hoboken. His wife is sweeping the sidewalk and he's sitting on the stoop smoking a cigarette. There's a "For Rent by Owner" sign in the window, so I start making small talk. The old man cuts to the chase and says he will give me the listing to a third-floor railroad flat if I promise not to bring any undesirables around because his family lives in the building. No Blacks, no Puerto Ricans, no law students. The Irish he will tolerate. He also wants somebody quiet because Mrs. Sciancalepore don't like noise. And no kids. He tells me to come back over the weekend after the current tenants move out, and at the mention of "tenants," Mrs. Sciancalepore clasps her hands and wails *"porco cane!"*

That Saturday, I go check it out. Not bad for a walkup, with plenty of sunlight because the building is not attached on one side. There are windows facing a lot with a big tree and some weeds. I'm thinking maybe I could move here myself, even if the Sciancalepores are nosy, annoying, bigoted people.

While I am surveying this bucolic scene, the door bangs open and scares the living shit out of me. I turn around and this guy's standing there, around my age, wearing blue nylon shorts, dorky black dress shoes with no socks, and a white undershirt.

"You gotta help me," he says. "They're here!"

The guy runs over to the window, jumping around like the floor's on fire and starts yelling for me to look out the window. So, I stand on my toes and look over his shoulders and there's a bunch of men in hard hats with a truck. It has a ladder type thing with a basket, the kind the electric company uses, and one of the guys gets into the basket and I watch it rising alongside the building.

"What's going on?" I ask him. I mean, really. What is this guy so worked up about?

"They're going to cut down that tree."

"Yeah? And?" I ask.

"Our tree!"

Our tree? Since when do I own a tree with this nut job?

I open the window and see the guy in the basket is already up to the fourth floor.

"They're cutting down the tree! What are we going to do?"

"Listen," I say, turning back into the apartment. "Who are you?"

"Steve," he says.

"Steve?"

"We gotta do something. They're going to cut down the tree," he says again. He seems almost in tears.

"Which apartment do you live in?"

"Two floors up." He leans out the window and looks up. "The window by the leaves. See? That's me."

Jeez, what's up with this? I want to smack him and say, "Snap out of it," like Cher does to Nicolas Cage in *Moonstruck*. Only it's a different context, and while Nicholas Cage was in love with Cher, this guy, whoever he is, isn't in love with me or vice versa. Nobody is in love with me. Sad fact. But true. At least when I die, I won't have to share a headstone. Anyway, he runs out of the apartment, down the stairs, more yelling and screaming then he comes pounding back up and leans out the window.

I yell over his shoulder to the tree guys: "Are you going to cut down that tree?"

A man in a plaid shirt, standing on the ground looking up says he is, in fact, cutting down the tree. The whole tree. Must be the boss. This is starting to get interesting.

"That tree right there?" I say, killing time.

"Yeah"

"I need to ask a favor."

"Yeah?"

"Don't cut down that tree. Not today."

Steve squeezes my arm.

"What is it, your tree?" the man says.

"My tree?"

"You related to the old man?"

I look at Steve, and he pushes me away from the window, kind of roughly to my annoyance, and yells: "You're damn right I am. I told you!"

I ask Steve what old man? He says it's his father. I put two and two together and figure dad must be Mr. Sciancalepore and this is the Stefano that Pops was talking about in his broken English. I wonder why I've never seen him in town.

Steve leans farther out the window. I tell him to be careful.

I hear the man in plaid shout: "Listen kid. He paid us to cut down the tree. Wants it down by the time he gets back."

Steve looks at me. His big blue eyes are wide. He's sweating. He seems scared. I want to fuck him on the spot. I come to my senses and push away the thought.

"Talk to them! Please. Tell them to stop!"

"Why? What's the big deal?" I ask.

He is pacing the room, saying: "Oh my god oh my god oh my god."

I decide to take this into my own hands. I lean out the window and yell: "Stop!! Now!! Or I will call the police." I grab one of the branches and pull on it to get their attention. I hear a chainsaw kind of close and I let go, the branch snapping back into the yard.

"Listen," I tell Steve, "You better talk to your father."

The boss yells to the guy in the basket. "Hey, watch out with them branches at the top."

"Maybe you can talk to him," he says.

I really can't get in the middle of this, otherwise his father will never list another apartment with me and he'll call my broker to complain. I do a preemptive strike and call the office for advice. Maybe somebody knows the tree guy. Terri answers, and when I tell her what's happening, she puts me on hold and the next thing I know, Joe Fox is on the line.

I run though the predicament, and no sooner do I give him the address than Joe tells me to wait right there, don't do anything. He'll be right over. I've never seen him volunteer for anything that fast except maybe an orgy. Meanwhile, Steve is leaning out the window, trying to reason with the foreman down below.

"I have a very serious respiratory ailment," Steve is saying. "The tree, it, it cleans the air at night."

"Yeah. Sure." The guy turns his attention back to the man up in the basket who is lopping off branches with the saw. "Hey! Over more to the right. Yeah, that one."

Steve is not giving up.

"The tree takes away the carbon and turns it into carbon dioxide and then changes that into pure oxygen, which it then releases into my room so that I can sleep."

As ridiculous as this sounds, I feel bad for him and try to think of a solution.

"You could buy a sonic air purifier," I suggest. But Steve seems distracted. He resumes screaming out the window.

"If you remove the tree, I will not be able to breathe while I am sleeping. I can only sleep in that room because of the tree. There is nowhere else for me to sleep. If I stop breathing at night for too long, I could die - or wake up with brain damage."

Then he looks at me with those big bedroom eyes that say trust. A shared destiny. Intimacy.

I nod. "That would be a shame," I say.

"A shame?"

"To wake up with brain damage."

"Easy for you to say."

"Listen, I know what you mean," I tell him. "I wake up with anxiety every day. But brain damage would be much worse. Better to die in your sleep."

"Are you fucking with me?" he says.

"I just mean compared to brain damage," I explain. "To end up a vegetable because they cut down the tree would be, well, I think that would be irony. I would be afraid to fall asleep knowing that either situation would be a possibility." I want to ask Steve if he thinks it would be ironic, too, but I'm not sure how smart he is.

Steve says he's going to call the cops and have the tree guy arrested. He dials his phone and talks to the dispatcher. I'm thinking he better hurry because these guys are working fast, and they've got most of the top branches off. A big one hits the side of the building, scrapes against the window.

"I just called the cops," Steve yells to the guy on the ground. "I'll have you arrested." He holds the cell phone out the window to show them.

The foreman doesn't seem impressed. He waves for the chainsaw guy to stop, and it quiets down.

"Hey kid," the guy says. Steve smiles at me and give me a little high five.

"You want the chips?"

"Chips?" Steve asks.

"Some people like to keep 'em for mulch. Otherwise, we'll take 'em away. Either way, no charge."

Just then I see Joe Fox. He is walking over to the foreman. I squeeze next to Steve and lean out the window so I can hear them.

"Listen bud," the foreman says. Then he stops, takes off his hardhat and says, "Hey. Don't I know you?"

"I don't know. You fly to Florida much?"

"Yeah, I been there. Two weeks ago."

"Maybe you saw me at the cabin, on the way out of the aircraft."

"You a… what do they call them now… a flight attendant?"

"Try again."

"Male stewardess?"

"You're getting cold. Real cold."

"You work at the airport."

"You might say that."

The guy steps back and takes a better look at Joe, who is wearing the epaulet shirt and cap.

"Pilot!"

"Bingo! You're good. So now, about this situation we have here."

"Do you fly them airbuses?"

"I prefer the 737s, when I can."

"That's what we had I think when we went to Florida, took the wife and kids. Wait till I tell them!"

"See, what did I tell you? Now my friends here, they seem to like this tree in the yard, and I want to find out –"

"I got a question," the tree man says. "Can you get me a ticket? Or maybe an upgrade?"

"How about drinks on me? Scotch on the rocks? Now, about the tree."

"Nah, nah, nah. I got a job to do. C'mon guys, we gotta be outta here by 11, we got two more jobs today." He motions for the chainsaws to resume.

A police car comes up. Joe talks to the cops and they drive away. Then he spends more time talking to the foreman, but with the chainsaws revving up I can't hear a thing. Then Joe walks away and enters the building. He comes into the apartment.

"Who's your friend?" he asks me.

"Steve. He lives upstairs. His father owns the building, and the funny thing is, I never talked to him until today when he—"

"Do something!!" Steve pleads.

"Hey, kid. What are you so worked up about? It's a nice tree but…"

"He needs the tree to breathe at night," I explain. "It cleans the air. His father wants the tree down and…"

"Get an air filter."

"Air filter?" Steve says.

"Yeah, Home Depot. Plug it in and forget about the tree."

I tell Joe that's not the point – that Steve needs the tree.

"Why exactly do you need the tree?" Joe asks him.

"I work for the sanitation department," he says.

"And I work for an airline," Joe says with a cool sarcasm only he can pull off. I feel bad for Steve. Sort of. Because when the word *sanitation* registers, I say, "You're the garbage man? You know what I want to know? Why do you guys come in the middle of the night? I get woken up every time and then I can't get back to sleep."

Steve makes air quotes and says, "I am not 'The Garbage Man.' I work at the landfill, the waste transfer station."

OMG. So this guy works at the dump? He is beginning to lose his attraction, bedroom eyes or not. Joe and I look at each other. Meanwhile, the tree guys have the whole top off and the branches all the way down to the third floor.

Steve runs to the window. Grabs his phone and dials 911 again.

"Hello? Hello? Emergency! Send somebody. 701 Bloomfield Street. Hoboken," he tells the dispatcher. "Hurry!! I can't hear you. What? Can you speak louder? The noise? Chainsaws! Yes! Chainsaws. They're, oh my god, they're getting close! Too late. I think we're too late."

I tell Joe maybe we need to call 911 and get this guy into a strait-jacket. I also ask him what happened with the foreman. Why didn't they stop?

That's when Joe tells me he didn't ask them to stop. In fact, he told them to take the tree down and not pay any attention to Steve or me because the tree is on a building lot he owns with his partner Murray. They're planning to put up six condos down the block. But they need a variance. And Steve's dad would agree to the variance only if they let him take down the tree because the tree roots are undermining the structural integrity of his foundation wall. And if Joe and Murray don't get their variance from the zoning board, because old Pop Sciancalepore objects, they lose a ton of money.

I'm thinking maybe Joe's wings are losing their luster, too. Does he have no heart?

Steve is slumped on the floor by the window. He throws the phone across the room and puts his head in his hands.

"It's over," he says. "The pure oxygen from the trees cleanses my lungs. The methane, the carbon dioxide, carbon monoxide, all the carbons."

"Like I said, kid, get an air filter," Joe says.

"Or a job with the tree company," I suggest, trying to be helpful. "Like those guys. In the trees all day. You'll feel great."

Steve's not buying it. I hear footsteps and the tree guy walks in with some papers for Joe to sign. He sees Steve on the floor and nods over to him, looking at Joe, like asking if he's okay. Joe shrugs.

"During the day, at work, I notice that my heartbeat is faster, and I have to take deeper breaths," Steve says. "I feel like I've run a marathon sometimes. This is caused by the methane and carbon dioxide, but I know the tree protects me. When I wake up in the morning, I no longer feel that way. I have increased oxygen in my lungs."

"Hey, I know what you mean," the tree guy says. "A few years ago, I went away with the wife for an overnight trip. We went to my aunt's funeral in Cleveland, and we stayed at a Holiday Inn. There were no trees outside, just shrubs. I got like, nausea, nausea and fatigue. I threw up. Couldn't keep nothing down."

"And eventually you lost consciousness right?" Steve says.

"Yeah. But nothing a good night's sleep couldn't handle."

Steve looks at me. His eyes are watery. He reminds me of Bambi. I want to give him a hug, but not in front of Joe and the tree guy.

"You ever go on vacation?" I ask him. He shakes his head.

"You're always here?" I ask.

"Except to go to work," he says.

"At the dump?"

"The landfill."

"Right."

The tree guy says: "Look, kid. Pop's paying the bill. He wants the tree down, it comes down. You want any chips?"

"I can't eat when I'm upset."

"The chips from the trees, the wood chips. Maybe you can use them. No charge."

I tell Steve, he might as well take them. They're free, and they smell nice. He could put them in his room. It'll be almost like having the tree outside the window. Maybe better. Joe tells Steve smelling woodchips cures a hangover, which I never knew. And that people pay good money for wood chips. Steve doesn't know what to do, so Joe tells the tree guy to just leave the chips, he signs the papers himself, and the guy leaves.

Then, Joe sits down with Steve.

"What you should be worried about, kid, are the trace amounts of nitrogen, ammonia, sulfides and hydrogen at the landfill," Joe says. "I'm telling ya, some of these are known to be more than trace amounts. Studies were conducted by the state, but not released to the public, showing these chemicals can be present in up to ten percent of the air. Maybe more, in my opinion. These cause coughing and eye irritation in addition to breathing difficulties."

"You know your stuff," Steve says. He is starting to look better already. I'm glad Joe is able to help, shows his sensitive side, even though he was in cahoots with Mr. Sciancalepore to get rid of the tree in the first place, which I'm not about to bring up at this point.

"I know my pharmaceuticals," he tells Steve.

"I heard India is amazing," Steve says. "The hashish."

"Morocco, better in Morocco," Joe says.

"I don't believe in drugs," Steve says, "except the natural kinds." Wow. I think Steve and I are kindred spirits. Natural, organic, all the way.

"In the Amazon, there's this tribe which makes a liquid by mixing psychedelic plants," Steve tells us. "Ayahuasca. Used in traditional ceremonies."

"You sure you never left your room?" Joe asks.

"Just to go to work."

"At the landfill." Steve shakes his head and smiles.

"The city dump. Listen. It is what it is."

"You're OK, kid," Joe tells him. With all this talk of drugs, I ask Joe if he has any on him. I mean, this apartment is empty. We've got nothing to do so...

"Nah, I'm on my way out. Can't bring 'em on the aircraft." He winks at me and adds, "You'd have to go to Amsterdam with me. How about it? Loved that route. Had it for years. But Miami is okay. Better golf."

"Too many pesticides," Steve says. "Especially on the greens. That's why I don't go near them."

"Pesticides? *Pesticides*? You work at the dump," Joe says.

"I know. I know," Steve says. "My eyes get very red on the job. My throat hurts all day long. When I get home, I go to my room and I open the window and I look at my tree and lay down for about a half hour. And I feel better. My mother brings my dinner to my room because she knows how important it is for me to be near the tree and to allow nature to clean my lungs. My father does not agree."

"Did you try talking to him about the tree?" I ask.

"He is not a reasonable man. He says the tree is too close to the house, that the roots are growing right through the foundation and he doesn't want the house to fall down. He is incapable of reasoning."

I hear footsteps again, and I think maybe Mr. Sciancalepore is home. But it's the tree guy again.

"Hey Joe!" we hear from the hallway.

"The executioner's calling," Steve says, showing he has a sense of humor, morbid though it may be.

"Hey kid, you want us to grind the stump?"

"Three hundred dollars and we grind out the stump. You can plant grass on top, like it was never there. Or we can leave the stump."

"What would anyone want a stump for?" Steve asks.

"I don't know, use it as a bench. Put a flowerpot on it. Do whatever the hell you want. You want us to grind the stump?" Steve says nothing. The tree killer rolls his eyes and Joe shoots me a look that seems to say, "What the fuck?" Then they leave, and I can hear them talking as they go down the stairs.

Suddenly, it's quiet. The apartment is totally empty, except for us. The noise outside has stopped except for some muffled voices, and I no longer care what they're saying. Here we are, me and this wacky guy who I feel like I've known for a long time. A kindred spirit. Alone. Different. It's not often you meet a guy and in an hour you get a whole life of fears, anxieties and passion for, well, a tree. I break the silence. I tell Steve he would be better off without the stump. Erase the past, start over, no more reminders of the tree and the whole traumatic day. I point out it's like a breakup, like keeping pictures of an old boyfriend or girlfriend around the house, a daily reminder of what used to be, what could have been. He slumps to the floor and leans against the wall. I sit next to him, and then realize maybe he's never had a breakup, this babe in the wood. We both stare at the ceiling.

"I woke up last night," he says. "There was a full moon and it was so bright, almost as though there was a light on, shining right into my room. I could see the leaves, like they were dancing, yeah, dancing on the walls, and the air was clean, cold and clean."

"Crisp," I interject, to show I'm paying attention. People in crisis need empathy.

"Crisp. Yeah. Crisp. I took a deep breath, and I listened to the tree branches," he says. "In the wind." For some reason, I am very interested in this. "It's like they were sending me a message, whispering to me."

"To give a voice to something?" I suggest.

"Yes, exactly. Like it was telling me something. I don't know. I know it's weird."

"About today?"

"Yeah. Now it's done."

"Nothing we can do now," I say. "It's gone."

"Nothing," Steve says. "It's over."

"Um, well, no. I didn't mean that exactly." I tell him. "What I mean is, you should come to the gym with me. It will help. It will, well, alleviate stress."

"Maybe one of these days," he says. "I'll think about it."

"No, you have to. You must."

Steve looks at me. I'm a little embarrassed. I hardly know him.

And maybe it's not safe to be too close to him, what with the chemicals on him from the dump. Maybe he's radioactive. I'll deal with that later. I feel like kissing him, but I don't.

"My mom has strawberry *parfaits* in the freezer," he says. "Would you like one?"

I am thunderstruck.

"You ever been to Paris?" I ask him.

"No."

"Me neither. There are trees on the Champs Elysees. I knew this guy…" I stop, thinking maybe I shouldn't tell him about Philippe. Too much information. "I knew this guy, a friend of a friend of a friend, who went there and told me people eat *parfaits* under the trees in Paris." Whew. Good save.

"What kind of trees?"

"Uh, I don't know," I say. "Trees are trees. Leaves are leaves."

"No," he says. "I saw the Champs Elysees. On the news, on TV. They are horse-chestnut trees. I'm sure of it."

"No shit," I say. *Horse* chestnut? What the hell kind of tree is that?

"If I go, will you go with me?" he asks.

"You buyin'?" I ask.

"Plane tickets? I don't know. I don't have too much cash."

"No, the *parfaits*," I say. "I'll take care of the tickets."

"You can't."

"I've got friends in the business," I tell him.

"I don't know," he says, "I mean, the air on the plane, the recycled air, no trees, I just don't know."

"Look, just chill, okay?" I tell him "Forget Paris. Forget planes. Forget the *parfaits*. Just go to the gym. Supreme Physique in Jersey City. That's where I go when I feel bummed out. Look, I gotta go. I've got customers waiting at the office."

What a lie.

HOW I MET BIG STEVE – PART 2
THE LETTER

Unbeknownst to me at the time of the tree incident, my manager Charlene had a letter in her possession from Steve, which she showed me after I told her about the tree guy. I was particularly impressed by his neat handwriting. Very tiny letters in blue fine-point ink, all spaced equally and slanted at a 45-degree angle, which, in my opinion, points to Catholic school cursive.

Dear Miss Charlene:

Your real estate office has a "SOLD" sign on the house next to mine. I do not know how to reach the new owners, so I would like you to convey my message to them. As the real estate broker, you are in a position to intervene for the public good – and maybe save a LIFE (mine).

I see they are renovating the property, which I have no problem with. It's their right. However, the contractor told me they plan to remove the tree from the side yard to create a driveway, and this crosses the line into a violation of MY rights. "Why?" you may ask. Excellent question!! You see, I report to the sanitation department very early in the morning, directing trucks at the landfill. The pure oxygen I receive from the tree <u>during the night</u> cleanses my lungs of the noxious gasses I inhale <u>during the day,</u> and thus it protects me from all dangers to my health and well-being on the job except for an explosion, and since I don't smoke, that is unlikely.

Also, in my bedroom I feel at peace. I listen to the sound of the branches swaying, and I watch the shadows they cast on my walls in the moonlight. My mother brings dinner to my room because she knows in her heart that we must allow Nature to do its work. My father, he does not agree.

My father insists he wants the tree removed. Killed!!! Destroyed!!! Just because its roots are growing into our basement and undermining the foundation. He keeps a Zastava M76 sniper rifle in the kitchen pantry. It was smuggled from Serbia through Italy and into Hoboken. He showed it to the contractor, and they shook hands. I fear my fate has been sealed and you are my last hope to prevent this catastrophe.

Please help me!!!!!! I know the tree needs me as much as I need my tree. It is depending on me. No one understands the whispering of its leaves except me. Even my mother is oblivious.

Do not allow my father's threats of lawsuits and hideous violence to influence you. Understand just how urgent this is!!!!!!!!!! I walk by your office every day and peer in the window observing you. I know you will do the right thing.

Most sincerely,
   Stefano "Steve" Sciancalepore

HOW I MET BIG STEVE – PART 3

THE GYM (THE DETAILS ARE NOT IMPORTANT. OR ARE THEY?)

Well, just goes to show that no good deed goes unpunished. After the tree went kaput, I got Steve to quit his job at the dump, get out of the house and into the gym. I convinced him his respiratory ailment was the psychosomatic result of an overbearing Sicilian father and an enabling Napolitano mother who in bouts of severe depression fed the child canned Franco-American SpaghettiOs. She also secretly gave her little Stefano ballet lessons, a little-known fact that to this very day he will refuse to admit.

I was so proud when Steve ventured out to his first dive bar (with me), his first hookah lounge (with me), and his first dance club (with me). He quickly found his stride, flying to South America three times in six months (by himself). Told me he got a gig importing nutritional supplements involving cousins on his father's side in Argentina. An emerging market. I was skeptical but rationalized he needed space after his liberation from the landfill and pent-up sexual energy after years of deprivation. Turned out, he really did get into pharma and as his vitamin business grew, so did his physique.

I wanted to try the vitamins, but he said they were just for guys, that if I took even one, I might grow hair on my face. I asked if he was dealing in roids but he said no, just powerful organic substances never tested on women.

Within months he made massive gains and stopped socializing

completely. No drinking. No weed. No sex, which put the kibosh on whatever fantasies I had of this turning into love, marriage, and a baby carriage. The allergies disappeared and people started calling him "Big Steve."

A healthier version of his former fucked up self.

Steve told me his new goal in life was to win the New Jersey all-state bodybuilding championship, so he could strut back to the dump and show the guys what he's made of, to get the respect he never had from his father and blah blah blah. Omigod, do people really need to over-justify every fucking thing they do? I told him so, and he didn't speak to me for a week. I finally apologized, because friends are friends and he had some tough breaks growing up, which I could relate to being raised by an alkie grandma and a violent ignorant grandfather. In Steve's case, he suffered with a mother who served him dinner in his room. We all have our crosses to bear. And some lasting scars. To this day, he avoids walking under trees whenever possible. I think it's PTSD.

But, as I said, Big Steve knows his shit about training. And when he says follow the manual, I suspect he must be on to something.

Something big.

TICKET TO RIDE

The phone rings, and it's "Blocked."

It is against my principles to answer blocked calls. I answer it anyway.

"They need the manual." It's a man's voice with a familiar accent. "It has been lost. The art has been lost."

"Aren't you the guy from the bus stop?"

"Listen," he says. "The art has been lost."

"Was that you walking past my apartment?"

"I have a ticket," he says again.

"Look," I say. "I don't know you from Adam. What is your name?"

"Jerry," he says.

"Bullshit," I say. "Nobody from Istanbul or Bulgaria or wherever the hell you are from is named Jerry. And why do you wear that hat?"

He repeats that he has this ticket, a ticket to Istanbul, for me. I start thinking that I may not have as much money – yet – as some of the people in my office, or as nice of an apartment as some of, most of, any of my friends – yet – or a fiancé – yet. But nobody else I know gets offered as many free tickets as me. That's got to count for something.

Still, tickets or no tickets, this is making me uneasy.

"Istanbul is in Turkey," I tell him, taking command of the situation.

Silence. I hate silence. Finally, he says, "I have been in the prisons and the cafes. I have walked with my grandfather by lamplight at Ramadan." Uh, okay.

"Since you are obviously well-travelled," I tell him, "maybe you can help me with this. It's something I've wondered about since I was a kid. But I never met anyone from Turkey until now. Do they have Turkish Taffy in Turkey? I mean, they have French fries in France and Belgian waffles in Belgium, but do they have Turkish Taffy in Turkey? The little genie guy on the package. Is it..."

"The candy?" he asks.

"No shit, fuckwit." Did I really say that? I'm thinking I should apologize for being rude. Screw it. No apologies in order.

"There is an ancient tradition," he starts to say when I interrupt.

"Do you like the banana? I think the chocolate, it tastes, well, I think it's like a chocolate soda, but how do they get the banana so yellow. Is it artificial?"

"I've never had banana taffy," he says.

"I thought you were Turkish!"

"I don't know. I think..."

I cut him off.

"You don't know?"

"No."

"If you are not Turkish, then what are you?"

"I am Turkish!"

Good. The best offense is a good defense and I have him on the defense. Or is it the other way around? He's squirming.

"I don't, well, banana, banana candy, taffy. I don't know how they make it. I never had it. I don't remember if I saw."

"Never mind," I tell him. "It's not important. It's just been bugging me. Hey, where are you calling from?"

"I will guide you," he says. "Let us meet."

Maybe he's like that guy from The Karate Kid. The one who looked like a rat and taught, no, wait, those were the Ninja Turtles. I can't think straight. The intensity is too much. So I say the first thing that pops into my head: "You don't look like a bodybuilder."

"I told you," he says, "the art has been lost. The great gyms that once dotted the Balkans have vanished. There are but two that remain, and only one carries the honor of the ages. The other is a fraud. A petty-bourgeois den of debauchery, mixed metaphors, and corrupted syntax. The Ancient Gym of righteousness is in a little town that has no name, in the mountains just beyond Sofia. Reached with the aid of a wizened coyote from Turkey. It is covered by brambles and brush. Inside there are two bench presses, one flat, one incline. A few dumbbells. Not much more. I remember. I remember… an image. A feeling. A perfect French press. Seems like a lifetime ago. Many lifetimes"

"At my gym," I tell him, "we don't use the term French press. We call them skull crushers. Oh, and 'dotted the Balkans' is like saying 'dotted the landscape.' It's cliché. You can do better."

"Dappled?" he suggests.

"Too fah-fah. Need something more solid."

"Spattered? Carpeted? Strewn?"

"You're striking out dude," I tell him. "Try 'great gyms that once anchored villages across the land, the gyms that burst forth from the sinewy hands of ancient peoples, gyms that thrived, prevailed and multiplied until recent yadda yadda yadda.'" He does an "ahhh" that seems to connote he is impressed, and I feel a little uneasy. Since when did I become such a wordsmith? Did I swallow one of Big Steve's "vitamins" by mistake? In the background, I hear the faint sounds of clanging metal and thuds. Murmur of voices. Moaning. Grunts. Was that a scream?

"Are you calling me from the gym?"

"No," he says.

"So, if you are not at the gym, where are you? I mean, what's that sound in the background?"

"What you hear are the sounds of the dead poets and power lifters. At one time, in the ancient lands, these voices were as one."

I'm not getting it, but I notice the sounds are getting louder, and it's creeping me out.

"What the fuck are you talking about?" I shout. "What is this?"

He says I am too young, grown up too late, but there is a song they are singing, if I listen closely. I listen.

One two three four,
Can you rack a little more?
Five, six, seven eight nine ten
I'll spot you.

"You know, it sounds familiar," I tell him.

"Listen!" he says sharply.

Oooh, you pretty things.

Don't ya know you're driving the Weiders insane?

"Beatles? Bowie? But not."

"Smart girl," he says.

"Do I win anything?"

"They usually stick to the public domain but..."

"Let me try one," I say. I'm feeling invincible.

Here come big bicep.

He come, lifting up slowly.

He one roided user.

He got abs ripped, wraps on the knees.

Holds you on his shoulders you can feel his neck freeze.

Pump more iron.

Right now.

Over me.

"Catchy tune," the guy says. "But a little derivative."

"What?"

"It's getting late."

"Listen, you're the one who called me, Buddy." I'm getting really creeped out now.

"The name's Jerry."

"Asshole. Your name's not Jerry. It's probably, I don't know - Gus."

The dude is clearly annoyed and lectures me how Gus is not a quintessentially Turkish or Bulgarian name, that he is 100 percent Turkish except for a small Estonian wing of his family, plus a few Germans, a Scot, and three Bulgarians. All of them poets, musicians and masters of physical culture. Then he riffs and rants about Greeks and coffee and New York street gyros. So I tell him a famous archaeologist, Richard Leakey, had a theory that all New York Yankees first basemen, past and present, can trace their DNA to the Turkana Basin in Africa, which has nothing to do with Turkey, as I have come to learn, and that there was a cave found there with remnants of ancient pinstriped cloth. He says I am wise, but time is running out. He needs to tell me about the Ancient Gym. I suggest we meet up at EZ's Bar down the avenue where we can do tequila shots and gab. He declines my offer, and I am not sure if I should be insulted, depressed, or relieved.

"The Ancient Gym," he says, "was first destroyed by Alexander the Great and the invading armies that followed, and over the last half of the century waves of imperialist corporate raiders devoted to Ayn Rand turned a population of power lifters into slaves and scribes. The lost sacred manual holds their truth."

"What's in it for you?" I demand.

He seems taken aback, stammering some gibberish about snails and arugula and worldwide development rights.

"Where did you get this from?" I ask.

"Big Steve," he says, and hangs up.

I try to dial back but – it's blocked.

TAZ

Bulgaria. Turkey. New Jersey. Forget it. I'm thinking me and Big
Steve should go to South Florida and open a gym based on the
Bulgarian training. We'd have a niche in the market. Could be the
next Venice Beach. Sure, the Bulgarians might not like us capitalizing
on their secrets. But seriously, how would they even know?

I can see myself scouting beachfront locations in the morning,
then sipping mojitos by the pool at sunset.

In between, I'd look around for any iguana rescue farms. When I
was a kid, I had an iguana named Taz. He grew too big for his cage, so
I put him in the cellar where the furnace could keep him warm. I fed
him romaine lettuce and tofu and made him a nest from old towels.
Then one day, Taz was gone. Grandma told me she sent him to an
iguana farm in Florida.

My grandmother supposedly sent all my pets to farms. Gerbils,
ducks, mice, butterflies, geckos, tadpoles, iguanas, parakeets. In Florida, she said, there are farms for all of them. I imagined her carrying
them to the FedEx store on Central Avenue while I was at school.

Eventually, I came to suspect Grandma killed Taz. Assassinated
him in his sleep. Maybe she murdered all my pets. If I wind up in
Florida, I'm going to do a little detective work in the infinitesimal
chance that I might find Taz. After all, iguanas live a long time. And
then I could restore my faith in Grandma's kindness.

Sunshine, oranges, my own gym, a high-rise with a big terrace overlooking the ocean, Taz. I don't know. This also makes me uneasy. What if there's a hurricane? What if Steve flakes out? What if Taz really is dead? What if the Bulgarians find us? What if we can't pay the rent?

What if? What if? Like I've said, things can get out of control. Once something starts, who knows where it leads.

Case in point. I owned a house for about five and a half minutes. Bought it when I first got my real estate license. I was thinking positive: reinvention, be my best self, think and grow rich, power of now. Then, one thing led to another which led to another and so it goes and here I am. I bought it, I lost it and now I live in a shithole. Literally. I told everybody that house was not meant to be, which gave it a spiritual quality. Declutter, downsize, delegate. Divest. Let the bank unload the fucking house. Everyone agreed it was a smart thing to do.

Everyone except for Larry, the mortgage guy at my real estate office, who seemed a little freaked out. Gave me a card with a lawyer to call in case the FBI comes around. He said don't worry, but don't divulge any details. I'm cool with that.

After all, Larry's a chill kind of guy. Brings donuts to the office on Saturdays. Good to hang with when I'm bored. Gives me a few bucks on the side when I throw him business. Anything else I can say?

It started when he was talking to us in an office meeting about how anyone can buy a home, even people who get paid off the books or hide cash or have lousy credit. Sounded interesting, but still out of my league. I said this out loud, and Charlene shot me a look and told me – in front of everybody – I should broaden my horizons, expand my thinking. And that, in fact, there was a seminar coming up called, not so coincidentally, "Expanding Your Thinking."

Charlene then asked us all what we would like to change about ourselves. I told her I wouldn't change a thing. I liked my life exactly the way it was, with some exceptions. So, on her recommendation, I found myself sitting in a poorly ventilated, crowded room in Midtown where I was supposed to have a breakdown and a breakthrough. I didn't think I needed any more breakdowns than I already had in my life, but she was sure it would be good for me.

For three fucking days, I watched people cry and get spectacular insights into their lives. Except me. I felt like a failure. When I went home, I was so exhausted and depressed that I fell asleep for maybe

15 hours. When I finally opened my eyes, it happened. I had the breakthrough. I will buy a house in Jersey City where I can live and convert the basement to a coin laundry. I'd never run out of quarters for the parking meters. Broaden my horizons. Expand my thinking.

I punched the air. I was psyched. An hour later, I met Larry at the office. It went like this:

He asks for my latest pay stub. I'm not sure when I got paid last, so Charlene helps me find one in her file cabinet. Larry looks at it and gives it back. $15,000, he writes on the application.

"Hey Larry," I say, "I know I'm not a big producer, but I make more than $15,000 a year."

"Don't worry. It's per month."

I like that. Put your goals in writing, they say.

"How about bank statements?"

"Bank statements?"

"Yeah, to show how much you have."

"I saw on TV…"

"Yeah, don't believe it. Those TV ads are just scams."

He writes down "Citibank: $150,000."

"I don't have $150,000."

"That's ok, you don't need it. We just need to state something."

"How much do I need for the down payment?"

"Nothing."

"Closing costs?"

"Nothing. We'll do a seller concession and roll them into the loan."

"I thought you said the TV ads are wrong."

"They are. This is how you do it."

"You mean I can do no money down anyway?"

"Yup."

"Good. So, what's the payment?"

"Including taxes and insurance, $3,200 a month."

"That's too much. Forget it."

"We'll do interest only – make it $2,800 a month."

"Nope. Can't swing it."

Larry's thinking about something. He pulls some papers out of his briefcase.

"Gotta check the guidelines." He makes a phone call. I wait. He hangs up.

"Okay, here's what we can do. $1,800 a month with neg am. We'll put you on a biweekly plan so you will pay it off in no time. The rate is higher, and there's three points, but we can raise the purchase price to cover the points and closing costs."

"I don't know. What if something goes wrong later, like if the basements floods? I mean just suppose the basement floods – not that it would – but if it does and knocks out the furnace, I would need at least $1,000 to fix it, not to mention gas and electric since I've got that covered in my rent now."

"What do you want, everything? Come on, Tina."

"No, I just need some extra money for emergency."

"Okay, if we increase the price another ten grand and get the sellers to give it back to you under the table, will they go along?"

"I don't know, I'll ask."

"But they can't tell their lawyers – a lot of lawyers won't do it because they could get disbarred."

"What about my lawyer?"

"Who are you using?"

"Marty Trauma."

"Did he ever find a new office?"

"I don't know. I think he works out of his car."

OBJECT LOVE

Did you ever notice how people get attached to stuff? For example, in my office, the only thing Terri seems to like better than sex is her stapler. She brought it with her from the last office she was in and she pets it when she is on the phone and holds it in her lap when she talks to her boyfriend Sandy. She points it at people, and she once threw it at Charlene and almost hit her in the head.

It's nothing much to look at. Gray, metal, ordinary, not one of those girly girl staplers that come in candy colors. She seems more attached to it than she should be. Deno has a nameplate that he says his (invisible) girlfriend (probably his mother) gave him, with his name in gold letters on a black background. Joe Fox has a golf trophy next to his single malt. Jose at the gym won't give up his metal water bottle even though it's scratched and dented and seems very unsanitary. He strokes it while he is on the phone, which grosses me out. One of the guys yelled over to him "You like that bottle so much, why don't you *marry* it?" Yes. That's immature. We know that. But it *is* possible, in theory. I saw on TV there was this chick who loved an object so much she did marry it, sort of. There I was watching the sports channel with Big Steve when this archery expert comes on. Boring, right? I stand up to get a beer when the announcer says: "Erika LaBrie shot an arrow into the air and ended up in a formal commitment ceremony with the Eiffel Tower." Wait, what?

As I open the refrigerator I say, very nonchalantly: "Hey, Steve, I think getting married at the Eiffel Tower would be cool, don't you?" I am convinced Steve can become a multi-dimensional person, eventually. He's got a great bod. He is gainfully employed. And smart in his own idiosyncratic, idiot-savant way. He just seems to have very little interest in sex or travel, except to bodybuilding shows.

"I don't think she got married at the Eiffel Tower," he says.

"That's what it sounded like to me."

"I don't know," he says, "maybe they'll explain it after the commercial. While you're up, get me a Gatorade."

While you're up. Guys always say that. Then the TV announcer says, "Welcome back, and here we are with our guest Erika LaBrie, now known as Erika Eiffel, who has a very special relationship with the famed monument."

"What the fuck?" Steve says.

Not at, in or *on* the Eiffel Tower, like Tom Cruise proposing to Katie Holmes. But as in, "Do you, Erika, take thee La Tour Eiffel" kind of affair. The ultimate destination wedding.

"I mean, how do you do that?" I say to Steve, who keeps staring at the screen while twisting the top off the Gatorade. I pop open a Corona.

The TV guy says, "Erika's love affair came on the heels, or should I say the footings, of her previous romance with the Berlin Wall, which, as it turns out, was already spoken for by a Swedish woman who is now, sadly, a widow, but whose love shines eternal on her webpage. Now, Erika, maybe none of us will ever hitch our wagons to anything as spectacular as a national monument or an F-15 fighter jet, but I'd say most of us have fallen at least once for something without a pulse. Wouldn't you agree?"

Blah. Blah. Blah. Love on the rebound. Unrequited. Oblivious. Made of steel. My life exactly.

"My theory is," Steve says, "emotions run a gamut starting with fondness or the 'just friends' kind of attachment." He looks at me. I look at him. Just friends? *Just?* "Did you ever have something, not *somebody* but some *thing*, that felt like a friend?"

"I had a Raggedy Ann doll. I wrote my name under her heart with red ink. I think I was five or six."

In that split second, I could once again feel her pinched little joints, knots connecting her bodily parts like links of sausage. I don't like thinking of her as links of sausage because there was a cartoon I saw when I was little where a dachshund turned into links of sausage, and I was terrified it could morph further into a child-flesh-eating avatar that would turn me into a series of links like Raggedy Ann. To this day, if I buy a string of sausage at the supermarket instead of separate ones, I stick my fingers in the plastic and rip it open, slashing each link from the next and then separate them before putting the package in the fridge so they can't recombine into a hideous smiling hound. I know. It's one of those things.

My Raggedy Ann always seemed calm, maybe too calm. Didn't matter if I flipped her flaccid joints back and forth, or shook her, or wiped bloody boogers across her chest after picking my nose. She'd just stare with her button eyes and painted smile. Sometimes I'd wonder if she was demented, and I would try to trick her, to see if she would blink or frown, even turning the light on and off in the middle of the night to try to catch her in mid-blink. It was then that I realized that some forms of communication could not be explained by the natural world.

Raggedy Ann and sausage dog disappear as Steve pulls me close to him on the couch. I run my hands over his shoulders. Maybe he is the real deal. Maybe after all these months of nonstop training, day after day after day, he is finally coming around. I nuzzle my face to his neck. He reaches across and puts his hand on my shoulder. A good sign. Usually, he doesn't caress anything but a barbell. I wrap my leg over his. He leans in and says in a quiet and sexy voice: "Tina, I once knew a guy who had an affair with a motorcycle."

"What do you mean?" I ask, jumping back.

"He was jacking off with this thing, polishing it, never left it out of his sight. A hundred fifty bucks for a saddlebag, top of the line Weatherall cover. Red. Yeah. It was red. Decals, polish, the whole nine yards. I used to fuck with him so bad. I'd yell things like, 'Hey, get a garage!' But now this gets me thinking. Maybe the guy felt like the bike loved him back. And at the time, I thought he was just weird. But I've discovered psychologists have a name for this obsession. A name!"

"Everything has a name," I say, unsure if he is gaslighting me. Then again, he did have a thing about that tree when we met.

"It's called, get this," he says, "*objectum sexuality.*"

I take this as a signal that he is, in fact, an all-American macho horn-dog. I stretch and give him a come-hither look.

"Are you making fun of me?" he asks, looking way too serious.

"No," I tell him. "I think it's perverse, but interesting. I get it. Like the blood pressure gizmo at the doctor's, where you squeeze the little bulb and your arm turns numb. Then you release the pressure before you get gangrene. Some people try this oxygen cut-off stuff on the throat, claiming it enhances the sexual experience. I prefer the arm, where the margin of error is easier to control."

"So, did you keep it?" he asks.

"Keep what?"

"The Raggedy Ann. Do you still have it?"

"Kaput. Deceased. R.I.P."

"Dead? How could a doll be dead?"

"Grandma threw her in the washing machine. The arms came out separately and the body was empty and there were cotton balls all over."

"Like road kill?" he asks.

"Yeah. I wanted to close my eyes, but I had to look."

"Like I said, road kill."

"Stop it."

"Yeah, I guess it sucks, huh," he says. "Did you get another one?"

"Yeah. She bought me a supersized Raggedy Ann. At first, I thought it was my old one, reincarnated."

"Maybe it was," he says.

"No. I peeked under her dress to find the heart, but my name was not there."

BACK FROM THE DEAD

Telling Steve about Raggedy Ann in the washing machine reminded me of the time I sent a letter to this doctor who wrote a book about people who came back from the dead. I was hoping maybe he would include my own brush with the afterlife in a future edition. Then we could appear together on TV. I never heard back. Turns out, he was busted for killing somebody in a failed attempt to bring that person back from the brink. I then discovered other people have written best sellers about near-death experiences, so I figured why not pitch it on my own. I didn't get any takers, but it's worth revisiting. So, here's the original letter. Any suggestions would be appreciated, but don't steal my idea.

Dear _____:

I died and came back to life.

It was similar to (but better than) the book, _____,
which I found on a seat of the Central Avenue bus. God works in strange
ways, don't you think? My friend Big Steve believes that my near-death
experience was just brain chemicals on overdrive. I disagree.

It was August 12th, 10:34 pm, give or take a few minutes. I'm hanging in
the vicinity of the Dunkin Donuts, smoking weed and talking on my phone
when this guy, let's just call him This Guy, comes out with This Other Guy

screaming stuff like "Shut the fuck up man. You're fucking useless." Sorry about the language, but I want to be 100 percent accurate. Then I see This Guy pull a gun on This Other Guy, so I run across the street and get hit by the No. 42 bus and next thing I know I'm heading to the other side. And I don't mean the street.

I was sucked through a tunnel filled with a bright light and beautiful music. First, I heard Red Hot Chili Peppers. Then Coldplay. Aerosmith. The Beastie Boys and Radiohead. One after the other.

At the end of the tunnel there was a picnic table covered with cans of Orange Crush, taco chips and guacamole. To the right, waiters were handing out Prosecco. I think I saw a case of Stella Artois and what seemed to be pulled pork sliders. If it's important to know the exact menu, you can hypnotize me and we will figure it out.

The next thing I noticed was Charlie, the dog Grandma poisoned when she was hungover and he was barking too loud. I decided it would be best to avoid him.

In the bar area, I saw Grandpa with a clean shave and a babe under each arm. I was suddenly conscious of my pear-shaped body. I couldn't check my hair or makeup because there were no mirrors. I floated over the picnic table, watching everyone with golden tans and small waists and broad muscular shoulders strutting in tank tops. That's when I spotted Grandma descending on a cloud with biceps bulging under her stained cotton housedress. I watched in amazement as she adopted a karate stance, kicked Grandpa in the balls and vanished.

It then occurred to me that my mother must be there, but since she died when I was a baby, I didn't know what she looked like. Then again, wouldn't she recognize _me_? Aren't people in Heaven supposed to watch over you forever? Maybe I just landed in the wrong celestial neighborhood. Or, maybe she had forgotten me. After all, it was a long time ago and Heaven did seem like a really happening place.

I went back to the bar and picked up a margarita on the rocks with salt. I was about to ask the bartender where I might find my mother when I hear Big Steve: "C'mon baby, come on back."

I didn't want to go back. I wanted to hang out and meet Mom and see who else was around, find famous dead people like Kurt Cobain, Amy Winehouse or even Mr. Rogers, not to mention some saints. I mean, what the hell? I hadn't even seen St. Peter, who is supposed to greet you at the gate. By the way, you should know, there isn't any gate. You just get dropped off at a picnic. Like getting out of an elevator. An escalator might be more accurate.

I hear Steve again: "Tina, I got tickets for the Yankees, me and you, right over home plate." It felt like he was whispering right in my ear: "C'mon baby. Cracker Jacks. Bazzini nuts. Chili dogs."

Next thing I knew, I was sliding back through the tunnel, with so much wind in my face I couldn't hold on to my drink. And I came back to life, just like the people in the book.

If you publish my story, I think we can spin off the picnic scene to the food network. We could also do a book about pets in Heaven. People would pay good money to know what happens when their pets die. You don't need to pay me a dime until it is published and we get on TV. What do you say? Do we have a deal?

Sincerely,

Cristina Acqualina Bontempi

PS – After it was all over, something was still bothering me. Why were they playing Radiohead in Heaven instead of John Lennon or Hendrix or Prince? Could it be that's just part of being in Heaven? You get to hear what you want?

EYE CANDY

I buy a ticket to my first bodybuilding show, for inspiration. Big Steve says the guys on stage will be tan and naked except for Speedos. Do I really give the impression that I'm trolling for guys? That is so not me.

I'm going for the same reason he's going: to check out the competition.

"At this point, you don't have enough muscularity to place in the bodybuilding section," he told me. "But keep it up and soon you could enter the women's fitness competition that precedes the main event. That's what gets a lot of guys in early, seeing all the girls in sparkly bikinis and high heels. I bet with a little pre-show dieting you could get up there."

I act unimpressed, but truth is I've already seen changes in my bod since I've had the manual, and I don't work out in an oversized tee anymore. Steve says my back looks like a Christmas tree when I do pull-ups. I think it's a compliment. Better than a pear.

The morning of the show, I pull on my new gray and pink Spandex capris, a tight black tank top, a snug denim vest, and check myself out in the mirror. Good to go. Sort of. Honestly, days like today I feel like I have a long way to go. I dread standing next to fitness chicks in stilettos and with fake boobs.

Me, yeah I could be more consistent. I don't work out three times a day like the manual says, and I'm not on the juice. I tried doing this thing where, what do they call it? Double split/triple vertical three on/one off routine. Or maybe it was triple split/double quadrant. No, double split. That would be two times a day. Yes, that's what I'm doing, just not every day and sometimes two times and sometimes once and I don't take every fourth day off, though in the manual it says rest time is very important, but I seem to be getting traction even without that. If I work out once a day for six days, is it the same as working out twice a day for three and taking the fourth day off? I'm thinking that maybe even if you don't follow this stuff exactly, as long as you get the same number of workouts in during the week, it doesn't matter what order. Steve says I got it totally wrong because the level of intensity during the high intensity sessions makes a difference and that you need to have low intensity intervals for contrast, to shock the body. Whatever. All I know is when I was in the mall the other day and I saw my reflection in the window of a shoe store, it was kick-ass good. Or maybe it was a distorted reflection. I'll take what I can get.

Steve says the secret is to create an optical illusion, so if I stand straight and have stronger shoulders and upper back, specifically if the side lats are wider, my entire back will look like a V, which means my waist will appear smaller than it is.

V as in the shape of the letter, being the shape of my upper body. I get it.

V as in Victory. Velocity. Vincenzo. (Jose's dog.)

So even if my waist doesn't shrink, it will at least seem smaller. Trim. Slim. A beautiful illusion. Except for the little muffin-top still spilling over my waistband. I worry, though, about creating humongous shoulders just to make my waist look smaller because then, holy shit, I'll just look so weird, like my head will seem too small. But Steve says, no, everything will sculpt out in proportion.

Sculpt. I like that.

Sculpt. So hands on. Sophisticated. The Gates of Hell. I saw it in the mall, at the museum store, a 3D refrigerator magnet in amber glass. The mind, the subconscious, connects things in strange ways. I looked to see if they had any Michelangelo. I figured there must be a David magnet somewhere but – not, which is ok. I don't need that naked dude on my refrigerator. And I really didn't want the Gates of

Hell on the refrigerator either. I get the feeling that the universe is testing us all the time.

Anyway, I go to this bodybuilding show, right? It's at a grungy old movie theater with sticky wood floors. I pay ten bucks for a morning ticket and look around for a seat. In the aisle straight ahead, a guy with a shaved head is taking pictures of a little boy doing a double bicep curl. The kid grits his teeth and growls. I pivot to the other side and sit down.

Some chicks with muscle shirts and fabulous tans are in front of me. One is slumped in her chair texting and the other is sitting on the armrest with a big camera. I like her sneakers. Black Reebok high tops. They're not in style anymore, but she pulls it off.

"Am I in your way?" Reebok girl asks, shifting on the armrest. She puts the camera down and takes a Tupperware out of a paper bag. I tell her not to worry because the show hasn't started yet.

"My boyfriend is in the light heavyweight division," she says, opening the Tupperware. I smell tuna. Ugh. She rips a pack of chocolate protein powder, sprinkles it in and mixes.

"Nice tan," I tell her, ignoring the stench. "Were you on vacation?"

The two look at each other and make a face. The chick on the arm rest points to a tote bag and the other one lifts it from the floor. She reaches in and takes out a pink card and gives it to me.

"Hypno-Tan," she says. "Kills two birds with one stone."

I'm a little put off by the dead bird cliché, but I take the card.

"Ask for Dr. Sadlyer. He's the best." I put it in my bag as the lights dim. "Look, some people are photogenic, others are hypnogenic," she says, lifting her camera. "I happen to be both. And tanogenic, too." The chick slides off the armrest and into the seat. She turns around one more time.

"All of the beds look pretty much the same. But when they give you the headphones, if you don't make a special request, you just get some random person and most of them suck. Dr. Sadlyer is the only one you want."

Her friend whispers something. She nods, looks at me and shrugs.

"Ask about the telepheromones. Costs extra, but it's worth it. I mean, the way I see it, might as well get the most bang for your buck."

I slink down and take a candy corn from my pocket. I eat the white part and save the yellow and orange for later. The chicks in front of me keep bobbing up and down in their seats, which is very annoying. I'm beginning to wonder where Steve and the rest of the guys are when I feel a tap on my shoulder. It's that creep with the shearling hat from the bus stop. Weirdly, I do not fear this man, even though he is behaving like a stalker. I have this sense that there is a purpose behind him, a mission of some kind, and I am determined to find out what that is. I look him in the eye. He immediately averts his gaze, as if he's not talking to me. Only he is. And it's an old trick. The old beady eyed sotto voce. I saw it on TV.

"The Dukan Diet became the world's most talked-about diet book after Kate Middleton used it to drop two dress sizes before her wedding," he says in a quiet drone. "The diet lists hundreds of foods, of which dieters are allowed to eat as much as they like, based on medieval eating patterns. However, these ideas may not be all that new, as primordial man was not so different in that respect."

"Listen wise ass," I say, "I happen to know medieval diets. Parsnips and turnips cooked in lard, sopped up with loaves of bread, washed down with ale. My uncle Louie used to eat that. He called it the Robin Hood brunch." Wow. Can't believe I invented that on the spot. Thank you, Rachel Ray.

"Mutton with gruel?" he says.

"Posset of eggs," I shoot back.

"Stewed eels."

"Venison with prunes and bacon." I feel myself gaining momentum.

"Goose with rowanberries and figs."

"Goose liver whipped with suet and pored over polenta." I'm totally in his face now. "Six thousand fucking calories a day. Hello? Friar Tuck? Monastic life was a piece of cake."

He leans back in his seat and sighs. I think I got him.

"Diffuse idiopathic skeletal hyperostosis," he says finally. "Also known as D.I.S.H."

What the fuck? No fair! Someone's been coaching this dude.

"Where is it?" I demand. He looks at me like he doesn't understand the question.

"The Tamagotchi," I say. "It's feeding you intel."

He gets out of his seat, heads toward the aisle, then stops.

"No," he says. "I know my physiology. And the Tamagotchi is dead."

We look at each other, as if time has stopped. He appears to be anxious, searching for words. Finally, he says: "Rachel Ray."

I'm about to tell him Rachel Ray is a nitwit, but he puts an index finger to my lips, very gently.

"You have been watching Rachel Ray," he says. "There is no shame in this. Finish the candy corn. Yes, I know. There are three more in there, plus the one you started. Two for today. One tomorrow. The day after, only the yellow. And then, *Dietus Mirabilis*."

With that, he rushes up the aisle and out the door. From my seat, I can see Steve with Jose in the lobby, picking up their tickets. Steve pats Jose on the butt and they head inside. I move away from the bobbing chicks, sink into another seat and settle in for the show. I put my hand in my pocket. The candy corn is still there. All three and a half of them. Three and two-thirds, to be accurate, and I decide that from now on, accuracy will be words I live by. Or more accurately, the word to live by, since it's only one, until I find more.

DEEP BREATHING

I am at Hypno-Tan. 30 percent off the first visit with the discount card that chick gave me at the show. I lay down, my bare ass on glass. I adjust the goggles and turn the little knob to Channel 5, just like they said at the desk. I hear panpipes and waterfalls. I pull down the cover and the lights go on. I feel nice and toasty, blissfully baking in bright lights, melting *mozz* with goggles. I close my eyes and drift.

I'm almost asleep when I hear a voice, a woman's voice, raspy with a nasally accent. Jersey? Not quite. Queens? Long Island? All of these, and yet none.

Long-term trends are coming to a favorable point for you, Aquarius. This is a good day to examine them and step forward in pursuit of your goals.

That voice. It is from the headphones, but it seems so here and now. Is she in the room?

There's a great deal of energy working in your favor. Get out of bed early this week and get moving. But first dial 1-877-224-MIND. Your personal psychic will be standing by. All major credit cards accepted.

A commercial? I paid good money to lay here and listen to a fucking commercial? The New Age music resumes, and I berate myself for wasting twenty bucks. But since I did, I may as well relax, get a little tan and never admit to coming here.

I'm dozing off again when I hear another voice, a man's voice, deep and calm.

Tina, all your thoughts, your feelings, the images, the accomplishments, and achievements in your life are deeply, completely, personally, positively, powerfully and permanently associated with, connected with, and reinforced by the word "Sunshine."

"Oh fuck!" I hear myself say, maybe too loud. Another commercial. An infomercial. I reach up to lift the cover, get my clothes on and get the hell out, but I hesitate. That baritone voice. I wonder, if I masturbate in the tanning bed, would anyone notice?

Tina, please focus. Every time you connect with your word Sunshine in any way, Tina, whether you see it, say it, think it or feel it or hear it or write it—however you connect with it in both the conscious and self-hypnotic states, it sends all of these very powerful, personal, positive and permanent reinforcers to all parts of your body, that this is who you are, from this moment on, for the rest of your life.

Wait, what? How does he know my name?

Omigod this must be the hypno dude. Sadlyer himself. I open my eyes, squinting, hoping I don't go blind from the infrared rays, to see if there's a swinging watch that I'm supposed to be looking at. No watch, just the fluorescent tubes. The panpipes get a little louder, and then the guy talks again. I close my eyes and try to relax, waiting for him to say, "you are getting sleepy." He keeps talking but he doesn't say anything about getting sleepy. How am I going to get hypnotized without that? Maybe I missed it. Maybe he said it and I didn't notice.

Tina, all these good things that you now associate with the word "Sunshine" are a part of you. A warm, calm, clear, blue-sky kind of day, lots of energy. The perfect summer day. Limitless possibilities and energy. Exhilarating and uplifting. A feeling that says everything is okay and, especially, that you're okay...

I drink in the soothing voice. I feel the sunshine. I feel the love. I feel the universe unfolding. A drop of sweat is rolling down my left temple. It tickles. I hope he doesn't make me do anything stupid, like run around the place naked while hypnotized.

And, Tina, if you find there are little bumps along the way, you just take a deep breath and know them for what they are, little bumps. You organize. Prioritize. You simplify, and you feel like you are one step ahead. You feel good about this huge transformation you're undergoing.

Transformation? Is he fucking kidding me? All the crap I go

through every day with these douchebags at my office, with Deno and Charlene giving me shit and Joe acting like I don't exist and Steve with his food and yadda yadda about the fucking manual and meanwhile there's this chick and, oh man, obviously this dude has never been to my apartment.

Imagine you, a little you, looking up at Deno, Charlene, Joe and, who is it you said, Steve?

How does he know about Deno and Charlene? And Big Steve! Is this guy listening to my thoughts? Is he reading my mind? I'm lying on the warm glass bed, wondering if he can see me naked and exposed, and if so, I should have gotten a pedicure and a wax before coming here, coming being only an expression because this sexy voice is now just freaking me out. I start to sweat again, but this time a cold and clammy sweat. I listen. Nothing. Not even the panpipes. Then it starts again.

Remember the image of the little you looking up? Now, imagine you have the big you, looking down. And you do deep breathing, those deep, revitalizing breaths...

I breathe. I don't know what the fuck is going on, but I breathe.

Feel the relaxation moving from your toes to your ankles to your knees. Breathe. Filling the lungs, and exhale deeply. Like Steve with his tree, only this will live on.

I breathe. With my eyes closed, I make out the glow of the tanning tubes, and I feel warm again. The panpipes return. I hear water swooshing. I hate the sound of water swooshing. Reminds me of my apartment. Reminds me of Roto-Rooter, things from my past, things I don't want to think about.

Now Tina, take everything you don't want to think about, and come up with another image.

Holy shit. This guy really is reading my mind. But right now, I'm too mellow to care, like I took a few hits on a bong.

Maybe you picture little balls of dust bunnies, and maybe you sweep them into a box, and burn the box, and see the little balls turn into smoke and disappear into the sky. Higher and higher, into the sky.

I breathe.

In and out.

In and out.

Ommmmmmmmm.

THE THREE LOMBARDIS

While powerlifters are concerned with lifting massive amounts of weight with perfect execution and pay little or no heed to their physical appearance, bodybuilders are judged solely on appearance and not on how much weight they lift, which is merely a means to an end, the end being a perfect Adonis-like physique. Therefore, while in training, many bodybuilders eat enormous quantities of food to gain mass, but with equal zeal before a contest, they follow cutting-edge diets to shed fat and subcutaneous water to achieve a "shrink-wrapped" look that displays each striation of muscle. Here are a few examples we found from the literature:

———

As seen on www.bodybuilding.com:

Feeding Tube Diet/Nasal Drip Diet/K-E Diet

Your food is delivered through a feeding tube connected to a bag of nutrients. It goes in the nose, down the esophagus, and into the stomach. The fluid bag is filled with a high-fat, high-protein, low-carb mixture, sending your body into ketosis. It's advertised that through this diet, you can lose 20 pounds in 10 days. There are also a few nasty side effects that can occur from having tubes shoved down your throat for so long, including halitosis, nasal drip, cough, and infection.

Baby Food Diet

The basic plan calls for eating baby food. All day. Fourteen jars of delicious, liquidy peas. The theory is that bland, mushy baby food in portion-controlled jars will prevent you from overeating, or from really enjoying your food for that matter. Fourteen servings of baby food equals approximately 1,000 calories. With such a large caloric deficit, you should drop a few pounds.

Virtual Diet

Ah, the French. Instead of actually chewing and swallowing crepes, croissants, and boeuf bourguignon, with this Parisian diet you pretend to eat. It was inspired by a Dolce & Gabbana campaign that featured images of Madonna holding food to her mouth, but not actually eating. So, enjoy your cup of steaming chicken noodle soup: smell it, feel the warmth, put it to your lips, just don't ingest it. Once again, this isn't a long-term plan, but rather a super-low-calorie crash diet meant to shed poundage quickly.

ADAPTED FROM "DIETS FROM THE EDGE" OCTOBER 29, 2012

———

SPECIAL DELIVERY

When I get home, there's a package at my door. Plain brown wrapper. Not too heavy. I look at the label and it's from Clyde, Missouri. Can mean only one thing. The Congregation of Benedictine Sisters of Perpetual Adoration, makers and distributers of low-gluten communion wafers. The unconsecrated host. Next best thing to buying Jesus himself. As Rachel Ray put it, the Lo-Cal snack of the saints. I'm psyched.

I carefully take the box inside and unwrap it on the coffee table. The thin white wafers are in a clear cellophane bag, like taco chips. Amazingly, none are broken. The nuns really know how to wrap these suckers. Or maybe it's because of, well, what they are. *Dietus Mirabilis*. The thought makes me uneasy. I wonder if I should open the bag carefully, respectfully. I tug at it gently in various angles and nothing's happening, so I yank it with my teeth. The wafers tumble onto the table. I find a plate and stack them in concentric circles, higher and higher. I take the one off the very top, place it slowly on my tongue and it immediately sticks to the roof of my mouth.

While trying to dislodge it with my tongue, I read the instructions that came inside the bag. They are printed in English, French, Spanish and Bulgarian.

"For optimal absorption, sublingual administration is the preferred method. Place in contact with the mucous membrane beneath the tongue,

where a profusion of capillaries will diffuse the host directly into the blood-stream, thus reducing the risk of degradation by salivary enzymes and the harsh environment of the gastrointestinal tract."

For some reason, I feel like I've seen this before. Could it be in the nutrition chapter of the manual, the part I skipped over while attempting the recipe for black bean brownies? I vow to look it up, but first, I try another. This time, I put it under my tongue and let it melt.

At first, I feel nothing. Then, the light in my apartment seems a bit brighter, rays coming through the window. Colors are amplified. The music is amplified. Music? I didn't remember turning on my iTunes. Maybe it is from the street. A booming bass, loud, louder, pulsating through me. I smile and start to sway with the beat. I get down on my knees, put my hands to the floor, and feel compelled to do 30 pushups, which I execute effortlessly, reciting a line of the Hail Mary with each. I feel strong. Happy. Invincible. A wave of warm content-ment washes over me. I am rolling.

RETURN TO SADLYER

I return to Hypno-Tan even though this time I have to pay full price. Again, I ask for Dr. Sadlyer, and the receptionist tells me I'm in luck, he's in today.

"You mean he's here, in the office?" I ask her. She looks at me with a blank expression.

"Where is he?" I repeat, a little louder.

"Who?" she asks. I try to keep my cool and not pull her hair out of her head. After all, I am here to relax.

"Dr. Sadlyer," I say with just the right touch of sarcasm. "You said he's in today, and I'm asking you where in this place, in this office, this building, is Dr. Sadlyer located."

"He's not here," she says.

"You said he's here. I specifically asked for him."

"He's in today," she says. "Just not here. He's someplace else. I don't know where, but he's on duty. He's just not here, here. You want my supervisor?"

"No, forget it," I tell her. I breathe.

I go inside, get into the bed like the last time, turn the dial to Channel 5, the lights pop on and I wait for the panpipes and waterfalls. I had a toy kitchen when I was a kid, and it came with packages of cake mix, small doll-sized packages, and I would add water to the cake mix and put it in a little plastic oven with a light bulb to bake.

The things that come to mind while relaxing are unbelievable. Haven't thought of that since I was maybe five or six. Expanding the mind, clearing the thoughts, waiting for the panpipes and the sexy baritone voice of Dr. Sadlyer, I hear a very slight call of a panpipe, wind rustling in the leaves. I picture a rainforest, big leaves and warm mist. Just when I least expect it, I am startled by a huge crack of thunder, and I hit my head on the top of the bed. Is it raining? Not a cloud in the sky when I came in, and now, a downpour? I think of my apartment and what I might be coming home to. Then, the rain stops, and the panpipes get louder. The nasally woman's voice comes on again. Shit. The commercial. It's worse than going to the fucking movies. At least the trailers are interesting.

A bit of conflict never did anyone any harm, Aquarius, and that is why you will be happy for the dispute that suddenly brings a bit of life to a relationship on the point of extinction. Having something to argue about can keep a partnership alive. Today, be grateful for your differences. But first dial 1-877-224-MIND. Your personal psychic will be standing by. All major credit cards accepted.

I am trying not to pay attention, but I want to punch this lady's lights out. Why is my horoscope always negative? I'm waiting for: "Today you will come into a great deal of money." Yeah, right. I try to relax again as I wait for Dr. Sadlyer's silky, sexy voice.

He doesn't disappoint.

STOP AND COP

A car slows down as I get off the bus. It's been following me for a good half a block. The window rolls down and there are two guys inside with clerical collars and ghetto caps. The guy in the passenger seat leans out and holds a small round white wafer in his hand.

He whistles. "Hey chicky. Got an Altoids box here going for a buck and half. For you, 120." He shakes the box. "Cash and carry."

I quicken my step and the car is still following. "This is the real thing, baby. Missouri. Fresh baked."

I make a run for the gym door, swing it open and slide my pass under the bar code reader. I catch my breath, nod to Jose and head to the locker.

"What's up, Tina?" I hear him say. "Looks like you seen a ghost. Lighten up."

IN THE NEWS

CLYDE, MO. (Reuters) – Roman Catholic parishes across America report that attendance at Mass has skyrocketed over the last two months, resulting in widespread shortages of communion wafers.

The Congregation of Benedictine Sisters of Perpetual Adoration, who supply most of the nation's Catholics with communion wafers, were reportedly working around the clock to meet demand.

"The poor sisters are exhausted," according to a source close to the contemplative convent, who wished to remain anonymous because she was not authorized to speak. "We have gone from two million a week in production to five million and we still have at least 30 million orders pending. They say it's related to a show on the cooking channel. Since we don't watch television, we could not have anticipated this."

While they normally bake the hosts in custom-embossed designs and FedEx the sacred cargo in air-tight metal containers, demand has forced the nuns to stuff plain wafers into Ziploc bags with bubble wrap, using USPS for no-frills delivery.

"For heaven's sake, we've been so busy with communion, there's no time left to dust the holy relics," she added wearily, a reference to the convent's collection of 550 scraps of human body parts and related ephemera, known as relics, considered to be the largest of its kind in the United States.

While demand is extraordinarily high for the wafers in general, it is the gluten-free line that has seen the greatest uptick.

"We started making them for celiacs a few years ago," the convent source said, "having received special dispensation from The Holy Father to reduce the amount of wheat to less than .001 grams. We've had a small but steady clientele, with a typical parish priest going through maybe 8 to 10 gluten-free hosts per week. Now, I don't know. It's anybody's guess."

Rev. Michael O'Sullivan, 68, of Our Lady of Mt. Carmel parish in Los Angeles, reported the line at his church for gluten-free wafers last Sunday was at least 20 times as long as the regular communion line.

"Usually, we just get kids and their parents coming to the 9 o'clock Mass, but last Sunday most of the people at the altar were these humongous guys in gym clothes. While we don't have a dress code, this was still very unusual," said Father O'Sullivan. "And the stench! Oh, my Lord, the stench. An elderly deacon became nauseous and fainted at the altar rail."

Bruce "Hot Stuff" DiTestarone, manager of Gold's Gym in Venice Beach, about a mile from Mt. Carmel, confirmed that last Sunday most bodybuilders left after their early morning workouts without stopping for a shower.

"They were talking about getting to the church on time," DiTestarone said. "I thought they were joking."

There were reports of a bodybuilder who went to the altar rail at Our Lady of Czestochowa Church in Jersey City, N.J. three times before a priest recognized him and refused to serve him.

"Instead of returning to the pew, he just kept going to the back of the line," said Father Joseph Ferrari. "After speaking to other parish priests this week, we concluded this was not an isolated incident. We are thinking of starting a support group, modeled on the AA and Al Anon programs already in place at the church."

It isn't just Catholics who have noticed the rocketing demand. Episcopal, Methodist, and Lutheran congregations have also reported sharp, though less extreme, increases.

Although the nuns in Clyde, whose vows of silence increase efficiency in the workplace, produce most of the wafers used in Catholic churches across America, the leading secular manufacturers that sell to mainline Protestant churches have also reported widespread shortages and have asked employees to work overtime. The only churches reporting a drop in attendance, and in communicants, were denominations that used ordinary bread loaves, such as Presbyterians.

What does this mean for the parishes - and the nuns who toil to produce this manna from heaven?

"It's been good for the collection plate, that's for sure," said Father O'Sullivan. "We've been closing in on our budget deficit these past weeks and if it keeps up, we'll initiate a capital campaign."

While the church does not charge for communion, Father O'Sullivan said he can count on even the most penny-pinching attendees to pull at least a dollar from their pockets.

"You'd have to be a small man indeed to take the very body and blood of Christ and then run out without even so much as a wee contribution," he said. "And these fellas, trust me, were not small men, oh, not for a minute."

The Cavanagh Altar Bread Co. in Rhode Island, which boasts "a special baking process that prevents the product from touching human hands," reported a wave of inquiries for distributorships.

In Canada, where the communion product is sold in supermarkets, grocers report empty shelves and supplies backordered for at least a month.

Meanwhile, at the convent in Clyde, where the assembly line has been cranking 24/7, Sister Rose Matthew, 79, was admitted to a local hospital with heat stroke, high blood pressure, and severe dehydration, triggering an investigation by the Occupational Safety and Health Association (OSHA).

"We have received complaints of repetitive stress injuries, asthma from inhaling flour dust and burns from the oven racks," said OSHA spokesman Guy Amato. "We discussed the situation with the Mother Superior, who is cooperating and agreed to lift the vow of silence and arrange for group therapy after vespers."

Meanwhile, Mother Superior, in an exclusive interview, said her marketing consultant predicts the imminent demise of the convent's long-time revenue stream.

"We have intel that competitors are using counterfeit product," she said. "Communion wafers are being manufactured in Bangladeshi slums, cottages along Norwegian fjords, even little villages in Bulgaria, and then repackaged with our name."

HIGH TEA

It is 4 o'clock when I finally finish up at the gym. My biceps are pumped, and my legs are a little wobbly. It's the feeling I've come to crave. As I step outside, the shadows are long in the bright sunshine, and I hear what sounds like an Eastern European folk song. I follow the tune and spot three old men in the parking lot, one with a fiddle, another on guitar and a bald round guy pounding on a drum with an animal hide stretched across it and a paw dangling from the side. The paw bounces up and down with the beat. I turn away, repulsed. A gnarly guy with a gray mullet and a Hawaiian shirt is circling the musicians with a video camera.

Past the musicians, on the far side of the lot, a huge man in a black and pink striped unitard is lifting what appears to be 300 pounds over his head. Fascinated, I walk over. The dude reminds me of the guy whose picture Grandma kept on her coffee table. The camera-man's assistant is brightening up the scene with a silver board, like the tanning reflector I used to get ready for Philippe's high school prom.

The pain of that memory lingers for a moment and disappears as a second big dude; this one in a sequined purple unitard, lifts a barbell with 320 pounds, then a third steps up with 350 and another and another, and the music gets louder and louder until there are six enormous men in a row with barbells over their heads. Like soldiers they pivot in unison, and I'm thinking "What the fuck?"

The music stops, very suddenly, as if in mid-note, and a bent and wrinkled man in baggy gym clothes walks slowly to a box on the hood of a car. He opens the lid. Inside is an old-fashioned whatchamacallit. A turntable? He mutters an incantation, lifts the arm and drops the needle. There is complete silence except for the heavy breathing of the bodybuilders, who still have the weights over their heads. Then, it begins:

You put your right foot in; you put your right foot out.
    You put your right foot in and you shake it all about.

In complete synchronization, the line of bodybuilders turn their right legs from the hip, quads flexed and toes pointed out. A tableau of poise and concentration. The video guy and his crew are circling like mad.

You do the hokey pokey and your turn yourself around,

No fucking way! Doing a three-sixty and wiggling their asses – while holding up the weight?

That's what it's all about.

They simultaneously fling the barbells down with a thud that I can feel through the soles of my cross trainers. I notice Shearling off to my side in a leopard print jacket, taking a long drag of a cigarette as he watches, tapping the ashes. I am intrigued by his sartorial weirdness.

"You are in a sacred space," he says, motioning to a picnic table laden with antioxidants. Wild blueberries, plums, cranberries, and strawberries. Anti-inflammatories. Chia seeds. Quinoa

"All natural. Grown in an area beyond the government's watch," Shearling says.

"I suppose those Klondike bars in the cooler are a ruse," I say, "to divert suspicion."

Just then a tall, stout nun arrives with a tray of lingonberry jam slathered on apples. Prunes are tossed onto the table. In cut crystal bowls I see sliced candy corn, separated by color, triangles of white, trapezoids in yellow and orange. I hear the whir of a blender and watch as hostesses in tank tops and tight shorts whip up protein shakes and snip wheat grass with rhinestone studded scissors.

One of the men in a unitard, the biggest motherfucker in the lineup, sidles up to me and leans in toward my ear.

"We hear you've got," he whispers, "a secret stash."

I look at him blankly.

"C'mon, baby," he says, "we're talking Special C."

"A new designer supplement?" I ask, trying to act nonchalant.

"Not new... but sacred," he says with a wink.

Next thing I know, a nun is in his face and shoves his thick chest.

"Homeboy, are you messing in my business?" she says.

"Just wanting some of them angel wafers, Sister Mary Benedict. That's all," he says.

She shoots a look my way. I turn from her glare.

"Listen church mouse, you wouldn't be redistributing, would you," she asks me. Is she from the neighborhood? I could swear she was at Grandma's once with a box of counterfeit Lava Lamps. Sans black veil.

"No. Seriously, no," I tell her. "You do the cooking and baking. I'm just using."

"Better keep it that way," she says, "cause the sisters are working on some new recipes. Kale. Wasabi. Bacon flavor! And we are closing in on high-grade acai nectar, too. Just try to find that shit on the market. When we start cutting it with sacramental wine, you'll see everybody who's anybody coming in on Sundays. Weekdays too. You think it's busy now? That's nothing. We'll have to add more Masses to keep up with the demand. The collection plates will be raking in the dough. And in a year's time, I'm outta this line of work. Squirrel a little away and retire to St. Croix."

I'm thinking maybe it's time to get out of here, away from the gym, away from New Jersey. Who knows where this craziness could lead? But then I remember my bod before Steve and his goddamn *Bulgarian Training Manual.* The love handles, the muffin top. I run my hands over my hard abs. I can't stop now. And besides, I got a little more work to do on the inner thighs. I'll wait a little longer, then quit. Go back to, what? Chips? Ice cream? Orange Crush? The thought makes me uneasy, and I reach for mango juice, drop in a few blueberries, and wash down another gluten-free wafer. *In saecula saeculorum. Amen.*

THE THREE LOMBARDIS

———

May your coming year be filled with magic and dreams and good madness. I hope you read some fine books and kiss someone who thinks you're wonderful, and don't forget to make some art – write or draw or build or sing or live as only you can. May your coming year be a wonderful thing in which you dream both dangerously and outrageously.

NEIL GAIMAN, NEW YEAR'S WISH, 2001

———

DOCTOR KILLER

On the street in front of the gym, Joe Fox is idling his old gray Mercedes. In the late afternoon sun, the finish looks like it's been brushed with steel wool. Curious, intoxicated with antioxidants, and eager to get away from the fascist nun, I casually make my way over. He smiles a winsome smile – or is it a smirk? – and opens the passenger door.

"So, Joe," I say, "what's up?"

"It's a surprise," he says. "Are you coming or not?"

I throw my gym bag into the back seat and before I can click the seatbelt, he takes off, synchronizing through all the green lights until he pulls onto the Pulaski Skyway, the bridge that connects Jersey City to the rest of the world. He is wearing his epaulets, so maybe we are headed for Newark Airport. Could this mean a quick jaunt to Miami? Venice Beach? And why now?

I'm guessing Joe has either lost his marbles (unlikely) or he is up to something diabolical (likely) or maybe making drug connections (very likely) or a real estate deal (possibly) or maybe he just misses me because I'm so much fun to be with (dream on).

Drama. Conflict. Tension. My life.

Joe veers off the skyway before the airport and heads north on the New Jersey Turnpike. There's traffic buildup by the Meadowlands for a Giants-Jets preseason game. Joe curses, swerves into the left lane, passes the stadium and exits on Route 46, zipping past used car lots and fast-food joints. If only we were on Route 66 instead of 46, with Bob Dylan and cowboys hanging out on Harleys. The difference one digit can make. Or 20, if you subtract 46 from 66. Add that to the list of places I want to see. Route 66: Check. Cowboys: Check. Cowboys on Harleys: Check. Check. Bob Dylan: Not so much.

Bam! We hit a pothole. Hard. And I slam into the headrest.

"What the fuck!" I yell. "You got passengers you know."

"Yeah, that's the trouble with passengers," he says. "I'm thinking of going to work for FedEx. No passengers. No explanations. Tip over to the side, circle around. Nobody freaking out about turbulence. Or lightning. Or ice on the wing. Well, I would worry about ice on the wing, too, but…"

"Wouldn't that be boring?" I ask, my tailbone starting to hurt.

"Boring, what? FedEx? Aren't you listening? Passengers are boring," he says.

Joe looks in the rearview mirror.

"Slow down," I say, grabbing his arm. "There's lights on this road and…"

Joe hits the breaks, skidding to a stop right before an intersection. A moment later, he makes a hard left. I see a field behind a chain link fence. Lights. Airplane hangars.

"Teterboro!" I hear myself saying.

"So, you can read, Missy," Joe replies as we pass a giant sign that says Teterboro Airport.

I ignore the sarcasm. "Isn't this the airport JFK Junior flew out from, when, you..?"

"Yep," says Joe. "I know the mechanic who worked on that plane. A classic doctor killer setup."

"Doctor?"

"It's just an expression. You see them all over the sky on the week-end. Goddamn amateurs."

"What did he say, your friend, about the, you know…?"

Before I can finish the thought, Joe slows down near a little turbo prop. Real little. Like a carnival ride. Red with yellow decals.

"I'm not getting in that," I say.

"Who invited you, Missy?" he says, getting out of the car.

I follow him to the plane. Cute. On the ground, cute. Joe stands inside the little doorway, reaches out for my hand, and I find myself letting him pull me up. Some guy on the ground shoves my gym bag and a black flight bag inside. Joe shuts the door, and the little bugger starts moving. I put the seat belt on and grip the armrests. I look out the window, which isn't hard to do because the whole fucking windshield is in front of me, and then, all of a sudden, it leaves the ground. It's like I just levitated.

"Please God, don't let us crash," I say under my breath. Higher and higher we go. I imagine for a moment that I am lifted to a heavenly place. A helium balloon to the sky. Away from all my troubles. On my way to instant death. *"Oh God, help me help me help me. I will appreciate every moment of my whole life. I will never be angry or bitchy or sleep late or complain about the crappy food at Schaeffer's Diner ever again."*

I remember to breathe. In. And out. I remember I have no life insurance. Or disability insurance, in case we crash and I am horribly maimed and cannot work or go to the gym or feed myself. I breathe again. In. And out.

"Where are we going?" I ask Joe. He squints into the distance and mumbles something I can't quite make out, pointing toward something I can't see. He turns to me suddenly, very alarmed, like he's forgotten something. I am petrified.

"You got your gym bag?" he asks, pushing aside my legs.

"My gym bag?"

"Do you have it?"

Joe Fox reaches under my seat. He opens the bag, looks inside and zips it back up. I release my death grip on the armrests. "Are you freaking nuts?" I say. "I don't like this. I mean, where the fuck are we going? I will fucking kill you, assuming I ever set foot outside this goddamn fucking plane alive."

"Suit yourself," says Joe. He puts his hand on my knee. "Be patient, kid. This is just a practice run. You got your passport?"

My stomach does a loop-de-loop. I feel like we're falling.

"Passport? Is this some kind of sick joke?"

"Don't worry, you won't need it," he says. "Not on this trip."

Moments later, we touch down at a big airport. JFK? I see a terminal far in the distance. The sunset is a brilliant red and we taxi to a smallish building that looks like the back of a supermarket, with truck bays and guys hanging out. Some geese fly overhead. I picture them getting sucked into an engine.

A Good Humor ice cream truck comes into view, with the bells ringing, and it stops in the middle of the nearly empty tarmac. Joe meets the truck and comes back with vanilla ice cream sandwiches.

"Not on my diet," I say. This is true enough, but mostly I don't think I could put a thing in my stomach now.

"Suit yourself," he says.

"Wait," I say, "do they have *parfaits*? You know, pineapple, chocolate, strawberry, anything?"

"Hey, Missy, I didn't know you could *parlez-vous francais*. Me, I'm just a simple guy. A meatloaf and potatoes kind of guy."

By now, the sunset's gone and it's getting seriously dark. I'm standing outside the little plane and a bunch of headlights are coming our way. The first, a yellow truck, looks familiar. The Taco Truck from Hoboken! Then, behind it, a pickup pulling a float, not the ice cream kind, but the ones they have in a parade, with crepe paper streamers and seats, fake thrones in gold foil. But no one is on board. And then, out of the darkness, I hear a sound like a gallop, and into the headlights comes a horse. The rider is a small woman in a shiny green jockey outfit. She is carrying a whip.

Maybe the little plane did crash. Maybe I've been reincarnated to the circus. A circus family of my own. At Kennedy Airport? Or maybe it's LaGuardia. I might still be in New Jersey for all I know. I should be freaking out, but I'm fascinated.

The horse lady trots over to Joe. I hang back by the plane. The door of the ice cream truck opens, and Big Steve comes out of the cab. He walks toward me holding a cup of some kind. And a long-handled spoon.

Parlez-vous francais?" he says, and shows me a Hawaiian pineapple *parfait*.

"How did you know?" I ask Steve. "Are we going to Paris?"

"Not this time, baby. Come on."

Big Steve takes my hand and walks with me to the float. He places my *parfait* on the ledge and helps me onto the platform. He jumps up, hands me the *parfait* and we both sit on the thrones. Not bad for a guy who used to work at the city dump.

"Hey, Bru," he calls out and the motor starts. I look at Steve, confused. He points to the guy driving the pickup hitched to the float. "My buddy Bruno. From the landfill."

"But where did all this come from?" I ask.

"Left over from the Thanksgiving Day Parade. Bruno's got everything covered."

"Covered?"

Bruno turns around to face me with a manic look in his eyes.

"We are recreating the fascist artist conspiracy experience," he says.

Big Steve stands and throws open his arms. "The antithesis of anarchy and, at the same time, we embrace it." He then strikes a pose at the front of the float, the one where the bodybuilders kind of do a bicep curl with one arm pulled back and the other pointing straight out. Bruno applauds.

"Steve," I whisper as the float moves through the dark lot, "you've changed."

I think of the first time we met, before he became Big Steve, when he was thin and pale Stefano, whose only desire was to save a tree, the tree that helped him breathe. Until, that is, he knelt at the altar of the chiseled gods and became an expert on all things muscle. And now, could this be the ultimate transformation? Where strength and mental toughness are at one with a superior intellectual understanding of life, art, and the universe? The air is balmy, and I feel like everything in life is beautiful and magical.

Steve pulls off his hoodie and underneath is a tight black tank top with the Metallica logo emblazoned on it. His tanned arms and shoulders are huge, oiled, rock solid, glinting in the headlights. He is wearing a gold chain. With charms. I reach over and cradle them in my fingers. Gold crucifix. Barbell. Guitar? I look into his eyes.

"A Rickenbacker," he says. "1968."

"How did this happen?" I ask.

"The manual, baby," he says. "Quit it all. The job. My apartment. My world. But not you, babes. Nope. You and me. I have you alone to thank for all this. We're going places, chicky."

He grabs me by my shoulders.

"Listen carefully," he says. "Think expansively. Whatever our reality is today, whatever you touch and believe in that seems real for you today, is going to be - like the reality of yesterday - an illusion tomorrow."

"What? That's scary. Did you just make that up?"

"No. That's Luigi Pirandello."

"Luigi?" I say. "Is he related to Bruno?"

"Oh baby! We're all related," he says, holding me close. "Interrelated. We are all subatomic particles in an empty and meaningless space, globbed together in an energy that is of unlimited abundance and full of chaos in a beautiful order that brings us together."

I pull back and look at his face, illuminated by the airport lights.

"God, you're amazing," I tell him. "I never, I mean I really, I…" I think I am falling in love.

"I am you and you are me and we are all together," Steve says.

"John Lennon?" I ask.

"You know, baby, could be. But I was thinking more of Freud, Einstein, Moondog."

I'm thinking Steve might be a serial plagiarizer, and then I wonder if you can plagiarize thoughts or if it's illegal only if you write the words down.

"Okay, okay," he says. "Let's just say: The very act of observing another is suspect and changes what is observed."

"Hallelujah!" I tell him. Now I get it. The secret chord. The illusion. What he's talked about so many times. But now I am putting it together. You look in the mirror, stand a certain way, and twist to one side. The poses. The tanning beds. The vascularity, enhanced by dieting and the diuretics. The exploration of the unconscious, the subconscious, the barely conscious. It's in the manual. Chapter 12, Sec. 4.

I hear someone in the darkness say: "The nature of knowledge is questionable."

That voice.

"It is all an illusion. Smoke and mirrors. The myth. The willingness to believe in what we see, and to see what we believe."

There is a spotlight in my eyes in the direction of the voice. A vaguely Baltic accented voice. It's Shearling, walking slowly toward us, blowing smoke rings from his cigarette. He seems to show up at the most unexpected places. As I find myself wondering why, he says in an imperious tone:

"The very act of looking at your image distorts the image, as it does with others observing you and you of them." Raising his voice until he is almost shouting, he adds: "There is no permanence in image, but it is the prevailing reality, which you can seize. And seize you must."

I tell Shearling that what I'd really like to do, at this very moment, reality or no reality, is just spend a little quality time alone with Steve, and we can create our own illusion, which would suit me just fine.

"Baby," Big Steve says. "The man's right. Come with us."

"Us?"

"Come with us to Bulgaria, to restore the Ancient Gym to its place of honor."

"Steve, you been smoking crack? Are you fucking with my head? How about we go to Paris and share *parfaits* on the Champs Elysees?" I notice Bruno has stopped the ride and is leaning against the rim of the float, listening. Ugh. This real estate is losing its appeal. I hop off and wait for Steve to do the same. He puts his arm over my shoulder, which is comforting even if it is some impermanent illusion. I slip my arm around his (trim, six-pack ab) waist.

Joe waves us over and we all get into the back of the Taco Truck, and he shuts the door. Big Steve, Shearling, Joe Fox, and me. Bruno doesn't come with us, and no one seems to notice. I feel the truck moving, but it only goes a short distance and stops. The doors open again, and I step outside. I see the float maybe 300 feet away. I mean, really, it's a nice night. I could have walked. I hear Joe Fox calling us. Behind him is the most ginormous plane I've ever seen in my life.

"Holy fucking shit," I gasp.

"Watch your mouth, Missy," Joe says. I adopt an attitude pose, as in don't-fuck-with-me, and stare him down. He comes closer.

"That there's a Lockheed C-130 Hercules," he says, like he's about to have an orgasm.

"Does it have a first-class lounge with a bar and full recline seats?" I ask.

He looks at me like I just asked an insane question.

"They flew these in Nam," he says.

"It's that old? You sure it can fly?"

"My God. They're workhorses. Beautiful goddamn workhorses, the likes of which you may never see again. A classic." He looks at the others, who are now standing around me, all oohing and aahing. Fucking sycophants.

"Look at that wingspan. One hundred thirty-three feet."

"But does it have full reclining seats?" I ask again.

"No. No first class, no business class. Nothin' like that. No food, no nothing. Just a big wide open space. You can march elephants into that beauty. Couple of Humvees. Maybe a small, armored personnel carrier tucked alongside. And best of all, you can land this girl anywhere. In the middle of a desert. A beach, a farm, maybe a jungle. Don't even need a runway."

"How about Miami International? Or Orly? Can we take this to Paris?" I ask.

Joe looks annoyed.

"How much do one of these go for?" Steve chimes in, patting my butt. I'm thinking maybe we can sit together on the plane.

"You mean to buy it?" Joe says. "Well, jeez. I'd say about $62 million for a new one. Of course, used, depending on the mileage, oh, I don't know. What's the difference? Listen, let's get inside."

"Where are we going?" I ask. "Are you flying? Can I have a window seat?"

I wrap my arms around Steve. "I want the window seat; you can take the aisle. On the other hand, this thing is so big we should be able to have a whole row, no? If it's just us."

Joe walks away and talks to some guy near the plane.

I step inside and look around. All the seats are lined up along the sides, facing the middle. It's like a subway car the size of a Wal-Mart. I feel like we're in a movie. Can't remember which movie. But I definitely know I saw this in a movie, where these soldiers were in seats just like this before jumping out with their parachutes and..."

I suddenly feel my heart beating so fast I can hardly breathe. I look at Joe and yell, "No! No fucking way! I won't do it. I'm not jumping."

Joe tells me there is no reason to jump out of a perfectly functioning aircraft whether on the ground or in the air and that yes, there are parachutes, and yes, he will tell us how to use them, but to not even imagine the possibility, because it freaks him out to think of plane crashes except in the most hypothetical way.

I feel relieved that we see eye to eye on this point until he gets behind the wheel, if that's what you call it. He's actually flying this? A dude in an Air Force uniform enters the cockpit and starts checking instruments. He sits in the seat next to Joe and flicks some switches. My heart returns to normal. I'm glad Joe had the good sense to bring a co-pilot, especially since my guess is he might have had a few Scotches to come up with this crazy idea and who knows what drugs he's been doing. After a couple of minutes, the military guy stretches his arms, looks at Joe and nods. Not a word is exchanged between them as he leaves the plane. The door closes. Joe is sitting at the controls by himself. I'm fucked.

I feel the plane rumble and it gets very, very loud. I close my eyes. I pretend I'm in the little plane again. *Please God please please please..."*

Then the noise subsides. We are still on the ground. The door opens again, and a small woman comes on the plane. She is dressed like a gypsy – wavy hair, bandana, bright red lipstick, thick eyeliner, a big mole on her cheek, hoop earrings – except for her handbag, which looks like those leather doctor bags. She grabs my left hand and studies my palm. She reaches into her bag and places a communion wafer in my open palm. "Eat," she says, "but never on the same day as candy corn. It is ancient Bulgarian way."

"Ancient?" I ask. "This wasn't..." She shushes me and waves her hands. "Not question. You listen me." Her voice grows so quiet I can barely hear. "You parents not you parents. You will know more. Not question."

She turns and walks slowly to the door without another word, just a glance at Shearling.

"Anyone ever tell you that you're the bees knees?" he says to her. A smile crosses her lips. She slaps him in the chest with the back of her hand.

"Hey buster, bank's closed," she says, and lets out a rip roaring laugh, mutters something under her breath, and hobbles out of the plane.

"Ooh, she's a bearcat," Shearling says to no one in particular. Turning to me, he says, "Do you know who that is?"

"Should I?"

"Baba Yaga," he says. "Remember that name. But not her appearance. It, too, is an illusion."

"Baba Yaya?" I say.

"Watch my lips. Baba Yaga. She is fond of chicken, confections of all kinds and," he pauses, *"Dietus Mirabilis."*

Shearling follows her out, and the door closes.

I sit in contemplative silence. Morose.

The engines get louder and louder. The plane is shaking and my teeth start chattering. I squeeze my eyes shut and put my arms around Steve. He holds me close.

"You are what you dream, baby," he whispers, "and you'll never be lonely anymore."

"I'm not lonely," I say. "Are you?"

Steve doesn't answer. Just holds me tighter. I'm happy, but scared, too. He strokes my hair.

"The cross-Jungian anabolic mindset. It's explained for about 15 or 20 pages in the psychology chapter. You are what you dream, baby."

I don't remember seeing that in the psychology chapter. I hear the plane engines whine and feel the plane turning on the tarmac. I flex my biceps and feel Steve's breath on my neck.

"You are what you dream, baby."

THE ART OF THE DEAL

We are still in the C-130 cargo plane, on the runway, waiting for takeoff. My phone rings. It's Larry, the mortgage guy.

"You know that guy who was backing out of your deal?" Larry says.

"My deal?"

"The condo, the one he's buying for his daughter. Well, he's still interested but now we have a little problem. I can get him to qualify with 30 percent down, but he doesn't want to. He has the money, but he says it's 10 percent or nothing."

I start to panic. It's the first time any of my buyers have advanced far enough to talk about financing. Finally, a chance to make a buck and here I am on a plane. I'm about to blow it. I should have stayed home. I take a deep breath, a Sadlyer kind of breath, and stare at my gym bag.

"Tell him he either listens to you or he rents. Those are his only two options. Close the fucking deal." I can't believe I said that.

"What if he doesn't? I mean, he says he won't –"

"Too bad," I say. "I'm busy. I'm done with this crap."

"Listen, he's right here. I mean, I'm at the office, trying to work with him."

"Put him on the phone. What's his name again?" I demand.

"Huh, you don't know? You've been working on this deal for how long?"

"What is his name?"

"Justin."

"Oh yeah, put him on."

I feel energy surging through me.

"Hey *caballero*. You gotta put 30 percent down or walk."

"No no no no," he says. "I'm not doing that. If I gotta do that…"

"If you don't, deal's off. And don't bother calling me again." I hang up. A few minutes later the phone rings again. It's Larry.

"What did you say to this guy?" he asks.

"I just told him to cut the bullshit and do whatever you tell him, and that's about it. Why? What happened?"

"He did the deal. By the time you get back in the office, there should be a check waiting for you."

"A check? How's that possible?" I look at my phone and lean back in my seat. I feel the wheels rumbling down the runway.

PART II
BULGARIA

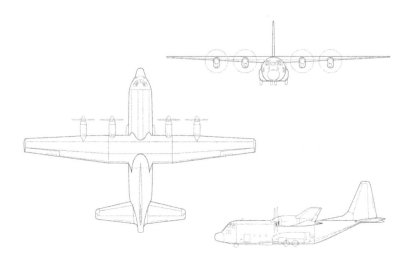

THE PFLAUMEN POLKA

Okay, so we land in the middle of this place – a field, not even an airport - after suffering through hours on a cargo plane with no food, no flight attendants, no movie, not even a can of soda. But plenty of leg room. It's very dark out except for the headlights of a jeep. As soon as we climb in, Big Steve stretches across the back seat and falls asleep. I sit between the driver and Joe. I don't know why the exact seating arrangements are important. But they seem very important to me and despite my fatigue I try ascertaining the significance, to connect the dots. I take in everything, keeping an eye behind my back, in a manner of speaking, to let no detail go unnoticed.

We bounce along a narrow dirt road for what seems like forever. Nothing but trees all around and the moon is obscured by clouds. Steve stays sound asleep until we get to what appears to be a quaint B&B. Joe tells me and Steve to get out, that he will be staying nearby. Steve looks at me with those puppy dog eyes and shrugs. Ugh. I am so bummed that we came all this way to end up in the middle of nowhere, but the B&B seems romantic, like a doll's house, and somehow familiar.

There are white lace curtains on the windows with a warm light coming through, like a Thomas Kincaid painting on a coffee mug. Cozy and creepy. There are also red and white plastic flowers in the pots on the windowsill. The very same fake flowers I saw at The Dollar Store on Central Avenue. Must be the effects of globalization.

Inside, the home is sparsely, but neatly, furnished. There is a huge black kettle in the blazing fireplace, and a polka record playing on an old-fashioned turntable. The proprietors, an old man and woman, seem delighted to see us. She is fat and round, her thin gray hair pulled tightly into a bun. There is a little white doily on her head, attached with bobby pins. She is wearing a housedress, a starched apron, and red spike heels. Could they be Manolos? Or are they fake, too, like the flowers?

The man reminds me of a garden gnome with a cap, a beard and a green wool vest. He is smoking a pipe, and the aroma seems to change with each puff. I am getting a scent of vanilla, followed by chocolate and – Colombian Gold? No doubt. Big Sur Holy Weed? Possibly.

Steve leans in and whispers: "That's good shit. *Thai aus dem Serai.*"

"I knew that," I say.

"No, you didn't," he says. Why does he always have to be right?

The old man takes the pipe from his mouth with his left hand and smooths the vest with his right.

"My ming-ming," he says. "Mama made. Long, long time." He makes the sign of the cross and kisses his fingers and looks heavenward.

"I'm sorry," I hear myself say. "Good knitting." Then I think maybe it is crocheting, not knitting. There is a distinction. This sweet old man might think I am insincere, a shallow pretender, for evaluating the quality of the knitting when it might be crocheting, or vice versa. So, I hedge. Speaking slowly and loudly, so he can understand, I say: "Your mother had talent, talent to make such a nice ming-ming." I touch the vest and smile.

He seems perturbed and shakes his pipe at me.

"No ming-ming. *This* ming-ming." He holds his pipe up.

"Your mother carved that?" I say, trying to be respectful of my host. The man turns to the old lady in the bun, who has not stopped smiling since we arrived – until now. They go into a corner and start talking in some weird language and waving their hands around and then come back. Both are calm and smiling again.

The old lady says, in perfect English, "I am Waltraud, and this is Ewald. Our friends call us Wally and Eddie. We are from the Black

Forest, and we came to Bulgaria after the war to escape persecution from the authorities in Deutschland, where we were unjustly accused of atrocities against children. Here, we lead a simple country life, supplying organically grown cannabis to the locals and manufacturing unique performance-enhancing dietary supplements, which we export."

"Protein powder?" I ask.

The old lady spits on the floor.

"*Dumme Schlampe*," she says.

I look at Steve and shrug.

"She called you a dumb slut," he says. "Sign of affection. Just forget it."

The old man speaks up. This time, his speech takes on a different rural patois. Idaho? Kentucky? The Catskills? I listen intently.

"We are pioneering a three-step method of extracting diosgenin from heirloom yams, extrapolating upon the original recipe by Russell Earl Marker. Yep, farm boy from Maryland, betcha didn't know that, did ya? From hayseed to the Smithsonian. You could do that back in the 30s, you know. Still miss the old man, don't we, Wally?"

I'm amazed at Ewald's transformation, and at the same I'm wondering who the fuck he is talking about and there's no way he's old enough to be hanging with some guy from the 1930s.

"Anyhoo," he continues, "scientists for generations needed eight steps to complete the process, and a few were able to refine it down to six, but most gave up. We are the first to make semi-synthetic anabolic steroids in just three quick steps, all in a cheap motel room on the road to Sofia."

"Why not make it right here?" asks Steve.

"The motel gives us cred," Ewald says, wagging his index finger. "Mind you, it has to be a special kind of motel. Paper-thin walls, semen-stained carpet. Office attendant in a plaid short-sleeved shirt reading *The Racing Form*. And besides, in this place, all the sugar dust in the air would alter the biochemical reaction of the compounds."

That's when I notice the house is covered with peppermint sticks, gingerbread men, candy corn – I immediately think of the gypsy woman's warning on the plane and wonder how long it's been since I swallowed the communion wafer. Is this still the same day? And Shearling's talk of the candy corn at the show. Yellow, orange, and white. Three bites. Everything in threes. Is this where it all started?

"Do you make candy corn here?" I say. I'm trying to make heads or tails out of this, so to speak. "How about Turkish Taffy? Bulgaria is near Turkey, right?"

"*Vielleicht sollten wir sie zum Abendessen essen,*"[1] the wife says, with a slight nod toward the fireplace, "*Mit Kartoffeln und Soße.*"

Steve looks stricken. "*Nicht,*" the husband says. Steve relaxes.

The wife's English accent grows dense and unfamiliar. How do they do that? Maybe they are actors? Linguists? I try not to freak out. I tell myself there is a logical explanation. She smiles, clicks her heels and clasps her hands together.

"Time fur zee bed. Tomorrow, *fraulein,* tomorrow another day. *Ja?*"

"No, no," I say. "You got it wrong. I'm not Ultra Luxe Fraulein. I'm Tina from Jersey. Fraulein works for Lufthansa."

Steve kicks me.

"We are in Bulgaria, aren't we?" I ask him.

"*Ja, ja,* Bulgaria," Ewald says. "*Ja, ja, ja,* little *wunderkind.*"

"Can I take a toke of that ming-ming?" I ask.

The old man and the old lady look at each other. Waltraud shakes her head. "*Achtung!*" she says sternly. Ewald hands his wife the pipe and takes off his wool vest, revealing a white thermal undershirt.

She takes me by the arm to the little sofa in front of the fire and sits. I sit next to her. She plucks a hanky from her pocket and cries softly, dabbing her eyes. I feel sad and put an arm over her shoulders. She adopts yet another accent. In fact, she sounds a lot like Grandma. How the hell are they doing this? What the fuck?

"When I meet moy Eddie back in Deutschland, he wuz a powaliftin' champ," she says. We came here ta escape da cops who was sayin' untrue tings about us. We still got our dream of takin' ova da powaliftin' woild in our hearts, but we know it ain't in the cards. But wit you comin' along, might be da big break we need, ya know? Show dem we ain't gonna be pushed around by dose fucks at da Gangsta Builda Powalifta Gym, huh, Eddie boy?"

"You are what you dream," I sigh. "The cross-Jungian mindset."

She looks sadly at Ewald, who has unlocked a cabinet and is pouring a clear liquor from a crystal carafe.

"He wuz robbed," she added sadly.

Ewald hands a shot to Steve and they clink the glasses.

"What happened to the children?" I ask hesitantly. "You know, the atrocities? Not that you did anything, just wondering how that worked out."

"Hey, we all gotta eat," Ewald says with a chuckle. "Ah, those tender tots."

"Are you telling me? No!"

I feel my heart pounding and my head hurts.

"Never mind!" Waltraud commands. "To bed. Now! *Schlaf gut, fraulein.*"

"What about Steve?"

"*Dumme Schlampe!*" she says, raising her chin in disgust.

"Hey babes," Steve says. "Let it go. Just let it go and get some sleep. I gotta talk to Eddie here. In private."

"*Ja Ja,*" Ewald says. He raises his glass to me. "To your papa! The Austrian Oak!"

I have no idea what he's talking about, and I don't even care. I am so tired and confused by now I can barely keep my eyes open, and no point telling him Rusty G was not Austrian. I climb up a tiny wood ladder to my tiny loft, lay down on a tiny feather bed, with a tiny feather pillow and fall asleep with my clothes on.

[1] "*Maybe we should eat them for dinner*" ... "*with potatoes and gravy.*"

DREAM

I am in the living room of the little house, tied to a chair, a child-sized chair. There is a videographer doing a sound-check. I feel very in the moment, and yet, not.

"Why are you here?" the man asks.

"To find the Ancient Gym," I reply. "But if that's a problem, I'll go home."

Waltraud has calipers and appears to be measuring my body fat. She frowns.

"I think you are losing weight," she says.

"This is good news, no?" I say.

"No," she says.

"What are you guys doing?" I ask.

A black-hooded man with a Kalashnikov strapped across his chest walks up to me and laughs. In his right hand is a Day-Glo orange golf ball, which he is casually tossing and catching.

I feel panicky.

"Not mini-golf!" I say, my chest heaving, my breath short.

The old lady and the videographer look at each other and laugh. I wake up.

THE ESCARGOT COWBOY

Wally and Eddie don't have cable and there's no cell service. I'm already bored after eating my breakfast of whole milk yoghurt with live cultures, organic acai berries, peppermint and a lactose-free protein shake. Maybe my freak-out last night was just fatigue. After all, this place is clean and comfortable, and they did leave a nice probiotic meal for me.

Big Steve is gone and so are the proprietors. I'm thinking of taking a bite out of one of the gingerbread men, but it's not on my diet, and besides the Germans might get mad if they noticed. I take a few communion wafers from my gym bag and head out to the dirt road in front of the cottage. I'm not sure which way to go. A pickup filled with hay pulls up and stops. A handsome farmer leans over and opens the passenger door. I point straight down the road and tell him I would like to go to the nearest town. I am hoping he understands.

"English?" I say. "Speaken zee English?"

"Did I see you in Moscow, in the snow, in the square?" the farmer asks in perfect BBC accented English. I am taken aback.

"I'm from Jersey. I don't think so."

"You look familiar," he says as I climb in.

"Secaucus, at that dive bar?" I suggest. "It was snowing. Yeah, it was you, throwing down shots."

"Jameson Black Barrel?" he asks.

"See. I knew it!"

"No. Never been to Jersey."

"New Jersey to you."

"Same thing," he says.

He slows the truck and stops in the middle of the road, leans his arm over the back of his seat and looks at me. He seems relaxed, friendly. I check to see if the door's locked in case I need to make a quick getaway.

"Are you from Jersey City?" he asks. "The gym in the Heights? I'll bet you live in Hoboken. Tell me about Hoboken. Has it changed? I hear it's hot."

What the fuck? This dude must be fucking with my head. Everybody here is fucking with my head. Are they this fucked up in Paris? Or is it just certain parts of Europe?

"I'll bet you went to cosmetology school," he says. "I have a cousin who went to cosmetology school in Jersey City. She has certifications in airbrushing, extensions, shellac, acrylics, wraps, shrinking, stretching and welding."

"I went to real estate school, thank you. And college. Not a lot of good it did me."

"You are bitter?"

"Who wouldn't be? Can't get a fucking decent job, my deals fall through and my apartment is a hellhole. I am very skilled, however, at folding clothes at the Laundromat. Hey, how come your English is so good?" I ask.

"How come yours isn't?" he says.

I let the insult go. "Now, farming, that's cool," I say. He takes a deep breath and it seems like he is about to say something, but can't quite spit it out.

"Okay. I'll let you in on a little secret. I was trained as an atomic weapons information technology specialist," he says finally. "The farm thing is only temporary. Family business. Until I can get a better gig."

"Hey, it's something. What do you grow, you know, on the farm? Cows? Chickens? Corn?"

I realize that I am alliterating. I blush and hope he doesn't notice.

"Yams," he says casually, as though everybody grows yams. I mean, I guess somebody does because they sell them at the supermarket, but like, if you go for a ride in the country, you'd see cornfields, lettuce, cows. Did you ever see a fucking yam?

"Are they the same as sweet potatoes?" I ask, keeping my more philosophical musings to myself.

He doesn't answer, sinks back in his seat and stares out the window. He seems depressed.

"Any animals?" I ask, determined to avoid awkward silences. "Horses? Goats? You know, my father lives on a ranch in Texas. He raises horses and fixes drains."

He looks at me with intensity. I'm expecting he will ask me about a plumbing problem, maybe unclogging a sewer line, and I imagine how impressed he will be about my expertise in this area, though I'm not going to discuss the sewage incident in my apartment because he could get grossed out. Then again, I don't know anything about horses, and he might doubt that my father is a Texas rancher. On the other hand, he might think my father fixes drains for George W. Bush, and he will be so impressed that he'll smuggle me out of this stupid Eastern Bloc country and its geopolitical drama. The psych major in me says I should keep my mouth shut about politics.

"My family is the prime exporter of grass-fed free-range escargot," he says.

I feel indignant, insulted, irritated and, no, I tell myself I must not think in alliterations, or allow such alliterative feelings to overwhelm me.

"Snails don't eat grass," I say, calmly, while raising my left eyebrow, with a deft Lauren Bacall tilt of the head. "I mean, do I look that stupid?"

"Bingo! You are absolutely right," he says. "We give them arugula, also grown on our farm. Arugula and yams. However, raising arugula-fed escargot is not permitted by the state, and petty *apparatchiks* are everywhere, so please don't tell."

"Okay. I promise. But I must ask you. Are snails considered escargot when they are alive or are escargot merely cooked snails? If the snails are in the barn eating arugula and yams, would it be kosher to say, 'Look at those escargots eating away!' Or would you only refer to them as escargot if you see them on a plate with yams and arugula?"

"Escargots are not kosher," he says, avoiding my question as he takes off down the road.

I sit back and think about arugula, and I imagine it paired with escargots with a drizzle of garlic and lemon on Limoges china. And I wonder when exactly my palette changed. Since when did slugs with bitter lettuce on hoity toity dishes seem like a more desirable alternative to French fries with gravy at the diner? Maybe it's what travelling does to a person. What's the expression, when in Rome do like the Romans do? Being away from home, it's true that you end up doing like the locals do; eating weird shit you wouldn't even taste at home. I notice he is slowing down and, sure enough, we are at the edge of town, literally. The Escargot Cowboy reaches across the cab and flings open the passenger door.

"Next time, we meet at the gym," he says.

"What gym?"

"The one you came to find."

"Who are you? I mean, really, who *are* you?"

"Vladimir Birkenstock."

"Who sent you?"

"Big Steve."

The Escargot Cowboy doesn't seem interested in any more conversation and I let it drop. I don't think Vladimir Birkenstock is his real name. But there is something about this cowboy, something I can't put my finger on. Harrison Ford? I imagine him dressed as Crocodile Dundee.

"Tonight, slip out of the cottage when the clock strikes midnight," he says as I step off the truck. "Come outside to the road, and we will pick you up."

I picture Han Solo piloting the Millennium Falcon for the Rebel Alliance and me in the passenger seat. I'll deal with Steve later.

CATHERINE OF SIENA

I wander through the town after Cowboy drops me off. It's been quite awhile since breakfast, and I feel like getting a bite to eat, something not made of sugar. I don't have any money, local or otherwise, just a debit card in my back pocket. I walk past cute little shops along the narrow cobblestone streets looking for an ATM. I cut through a tiny park where a diminutive woman with a very round face and very pink cheeks is looking after some young children, and I feel like an amazon by comparison. At the other side of the park is a small stone church. The front door is carved with medieval figures, and I'm thinking Bulgaria is adorable. As I'm walking over for a better look, I catch a whiff of an aroma like bread baking. It seems to be coming from inside the church. I try the front door and it's locked, so I slip my ATM card between the door and the jamb like I do back home when I forget my keys (or I try to get into Joe Fox's office when he's not in) but nothing gives.

To the side of the church, I find a large window and peek inside. Light is streaming through stained glass and flowers are on every sill. The strong scent of wheat and lilies makes me lightheaded. I hear a faint sound of music, like a choir of angels, or what I imagine a choir of angels would sound like if there were such a thing. The window frame seems loose enough that I can get it all the way open if I jiggle it. As I start to push, thin pale fingers grab the edge from the inside, and slide it open effortlessly. I jump back and nearly knock some-body over behind me. I turn around and see a woman with long plat-inum hair. Very thin and pale. Like the hand inside.

She is wearing a flowing silky dress, with brocade at the bodice, like something from Romeo and Juliet, which I find freaky weird. Didn't that go out in the Sixties?

"Let's go in," she says in a dreamy voice, a voice that is like, what's the word? Phlegmatic? Phlegmatic, yes, but not quite. She waves her arms, and the front doors open. Inside are more gaunt women in Renaissance gowns, bathed in the radiant beams of the stained glass.

Maybe they're witches. Or maybe I'm interrupting an anorexia support group, which is far more likely. These chicks are bony.

"Hi. I'm Tina," I say, "from Jersey City."

"Catherine," she says. "Catherine of Siena."

The others nod. They are sitting in a circle on the floor and in the middle is a huge gold chalice, the only thing that's big in this godfor-saken little town, which might not be so godforsaken after all.

"You eat communion wafers," I say with an uptick in my voice. Maybe this is the diet chick that they were talking about on Rachel Ray. I wonder if she gets royalties and if business shot up after the show.

One of the chicks plucks a wafer and holds it out to me. I pop it in my mouth without thinking because I'm so fucking hungry that, at this point, I could eat the whole bowl. Since we are in a church, I start to make a sign of the cross, so as not to offend, but this Catherine babe puts her hand on my wrist and stops me. She pulls me close, kisses me on the forehead and then silently walks out the front door.

It occurs to me she might be that woman who drinks the pus of the sick. I go into my backpack and pull out a wet nap and rub my head and then my whole face.

"Do not be afraid," says a black-haired woman sitting in the circle. "We are the #Persecuted #Women's #Collective."

"Don't listen to them," screeches someone outside. I look out the window and it's the little round woman with the abnormally pink cheeks.

"Persecuted, they say," she yells, straining to reach the window. "I'll tell you persecuted. I lost my mother when she was just 36 years old. Heart valve. Same day she went to the doctor and got a clean bill of health. Imagine that! We shoulda sued. Well, what can you do?

Then my father was killed in a hunting accident when I was in third grade, shotgun through the chest. Or so they say. I was stuck in an orphanage run by child molesters, then framed on shoplifting charges. I married to escape my miserable life, only to be abandoned by my husband on our honeymoon in Romania. I was taken in by Gypsies and eventually made my way here. My only sister is 82. She lives in Staten Island, and we don't speak. I'm 94. The thing about living long is that people will all face the same problems 99 percent of the time because we are outliving our generation. So that's my story."

"And you're sticking to it," I add.

"Damn right," she says. "Hah. Talk about persecuted. They don't know from persecuted."

The women in the circle seem bored. One yawns. The round lady keeps talking.

"Me and my ex, we started in the same hospital, that's right, the same nursery together. I was four hours older than him. I was born September third, and my husband right after midnight so his birthday was September fourth. Our mothers were cursed because they were both in the hospital on Labor Day weekend. Very *apropos*, wouldn't you agree?"

I wonder if Catherine will strike the apple-cheeked lady with lightning to shut her up. Instead, Catherine puts her skeletal hand to the window and slams it with such force that it echoes through the church.

"Pay her no mind," she says listlessly.

I hear the round lady's muffled voice screaming outside. "You weirdos! Ya need to get laid, that's what you need." I notice a few of the women have fallen asleep.

"To preserve their energy," says Catherine, "for the battles ahead."

BABA GHANOUSH

I slip out at midnight.

Waltraud and Ewald are busy drinking Dinkelacker and dancing the Pflaumen Polka in front of the fire. Ewald spots me tiptoeing down the stairs and grabs Wally's ass, turning her gently so she doesn't see me leave. I take that as a sign that they want to be alone. I step outside and quietly close the door. A crooked person in a robe is down the driveway. I move closer and see it is an old woman, lurking, where else? In the shadows. She is gnawing on a chicken bone. She pats her belly and offers me a taste. She doesn't actually say anything, just reaches out and extends the half-eaten chicken leg. It is a gesture that I understand in our unspoken language of the moment. I shake my head. She does it again, and again I refuse.

"I am Baba Yaga," she says imperiously.

"I know who you are," I say.

"Do not lie to Baba Yaga. I know you like to eat chicken, eh?"

"Okay, I don't know, well, I like double fried wings but they're fattening but no, really, you're right, I don't know you, Baby Gaga. Never heard of you in my—"

She sticks the chicken leg into her mouth, cracks it in half with her teeth and I am startled by the loud crunching sounds.

"Baba Yaga!" she says with her mouth full. "Show some respect, you bitch slut."

"What did you call me?"

Baba Yaga looks up at the trees and starts to do a little polka, a few steps, stops, and a rapturous smile comes across her wizened face, the lines accentuated by the moonlight. She laughs and then raises her arms to the sky and resumes dancing, faster and faster, greasy strands of gray hair falling over her eyes. Her mouth is open and she seems to have one tooth, a gold one, on the bottom in the front, and I wonder how she could eat chicken with such ferocity. Maybe her gums are super strong.

"I know what you are thinking," she says as she slows her dance.

Fuck it. Does everyone here seem to know what I'm thinking? Am I walking around with a fucking thought bubble over my head?

"Yes," she says. "Your thought bubble, it betrays you."

This is too weird.

"I have molars that have been sharpened to razor edges with spikes, like the incisors of a piranha," she says.

I'm trying to imagine piranha incisors. The things they don't teach you in school. Another reason why I should get my college tuition refunded. I should sue for malpractice.

"You are harboring a negative thought," says Baba Yaga. "You did not read the psychology chapter?"

Oh. My. God. Maybe it's a trap. Or maybe I'm paranoid.

"Chapter?" I ask, trying to be nonchalant. I notice the music has stopped.

Baba Yaga grabs me by the arm and yanks me forcefully, very forcefully.

"Never mind. Get out. Now. The polka has ended."

"Can't. I'm waiting for a ride," I say.

"No time to explain. Come! Now!"

We start to run through the woods, and I am tripping over branches and brush. I glance back a few times and see no sign of a jeep. I'm getting scratched by thorns and starting to wonder why the hell we are running in a forest in the middle of the night – middle, as in after midnight, but I guess that depends on when the beginning of night is. Is it the midpoint between sunset and sunrise? Or midnight on the clock, which would not necessarily be the precise midpoint between dark and light, except maybe when there is a solstice. Is the solstice in the summer or is the solstice in the winter or is the solstice both in the summer and in the winter? I am sure there is a winter solstice, because that's when I am the most depressed, but then I guess the summer solstice is called a solstice too, even though they are different and it's equally depressing knowing that the days are going to get shorter and shorter until I get totally depressed, stricken with seasonal affective disorder appropriately nicknamed SAD after the initials of the diagnosis which is the only diagnosis I can think of where an acronym – would that be an acronym? –is so precisely descriptive.

"Stop!" I yell, putting my hands on my knees and gulping for breath. "I have to know. Tell me."

"You will find out where we are going soon enough," she says sternly.

"No. I don't care. I need to know. I need. Oh God, my lungs are on fire. Tell me, Baba Yaga, tell me why the winter solstice and the summer solstice are both a solstice, which must be, ugh, qualified, ugh, by winter and summer in an adjective-like manner instead of each having its own proud discrete noun. For they are different and yet the same, two parts of the same perfectly antithetical and omigod, where is Vladimir?"

"Is that what he told you? *Vladimir?*" She cackles and rolls up her sleeves, revealing enormous biceps, tanned to a smooth golden brown. "Sunlamp," she says. "Pay no mind." She grabs me by the waist, flings me over her shoulders and begins to run again. I start to cry.

"Steve. I miss Steve."

"You miss his body, you shameful slut. His once scrawny putrid body which is now toned and firm and hard and…"

"No, I miss his beautiful mind," I cry.

"Bullshit. His mind is in the gutter," she says.

"No," I protest, "his mind is pure."

"His mind is filled with pseudo-intellectual bullshit," she says. "The cosmic, communist, quasi-scientific crud that has spawned generations of false prophets, politicians, pagans and prolific perse-cutors of our people."

"Do you realize what you are doing?" I ask.

"I am carrying your lazy ass," she says.

"No, you are SPEAKING IN ALLITERATION!!!" I scream in capital letters. I calm, just a little, to lower case. "Alliteration!!!!!"

She stops and puts me down.

"Are you sure?" she asks quietly.

"Yes," I say, "think about it."

Baba Yaga looks worried. "Do not speak of this to anyone. Promise me." She draws a knife from her skirt pocket and slashes her arm and presses my hand against the cut. Warm blood oozes between my fingers.

"Promise! Cross my heart and hope to die," I say, immediately regretting my choice of cliché.

We look at each other and she leads me to a clearing in the woods.

"I now know for sure that you have the missing chapter," she says. "Even if you don't know it, even if you don't have the book, you have it in your heart and the memory of the ancient wisdom—the pages— are coming to us through you. That is why Waltraud and Ewald wanted to keep you. They thought by devouring you, by making you a *cordon bleu*, they could internalize the secrets of the ancient Bulgarian warlords. They were so wrong."

I turn away from Baba Yaga and lean against a large oak tree. I touch the bark and feel the humid air that has made my hair damp and curly, at once frustrated that I didn't bring a blow dryer and grateful at the same time to be at one with nature.

"Baba Yaga," I say very quietly. "I feel like everything I've ever known, everything I thought I ever was or could be is... I don't know... gone, a lie, a fraud. I mean, *cordon bleu*? My whole identity, my *raison d'etre*, comes down to a high-fat Seventies entrée? Briefly fashionable with the Studio 54 crowd, and now relegated to the gastronomic slush pile?"

"Wrong! *Cordon bleu* is more Sixties than Seventies," she says. "In fact, the earliest *cordon bleu* dates to post-War Switzerland."

"It's not even French?"

"For Chrissake dearie, it's a *Schnitzel!*"

"That's what I am? A *Schnitzel?*" I feel so deflated. I can hear it in my head: a chorus of children wearing drapery, mocking me, singing "with *Schnitzel* and noodles" over and over.

"No. No. No, little munchkin. That's what they thought, Waltraud and Ewald. It is their lack of imagination, not a reflection of your inner worth." Baba Yaga suddenly looks beautiful to me. Her toothless grin bestows a winsome vulnerability, and I now see clearly what I had merely suspected before – that old Wally and Eddy were up to more than sauerbraten and Wagnerian hangovers.

"So, tell me honestly, oh wise Baba Yaga," I say humbly. "When you see me, you don't think: Aha, there goes a chicken *cordon bleu*? Or, just another *Schnitzel?*"

"No. Never!" she says defiantly. "Chicken Kiev. Beef stroganoff. Maybe goulash with noodles. Never *cordon bleu.*"

Why do I still feel like crap? Maybe it's the metaphors getting me down. I plead with her, looking for a crumb of redemption.

"Oh, Baba Yaga, why not veal piccata, blintzes with caviar, moulard fois gras banana bread terrine with crimson rhubarb gelee? Give me something with class."

"Not a chance, kid," Baba Yaga says, touching my arm and brushing the damp hair from my face. "I'm so sorry. If it makes you feel any better, I can assure you that there is a man who has never ever thought of you as a cheesy Seventies dish."

Past her shoulder I see Steve stepping into the clearing, wearing a billowing white poet's shirt and chocolate colored stretch riding pants that show off his muscular quads, glutes and hamstrings. The Lycra jodhpurs taper sleekly over his cut calves to black Converse high-top sneakers. I am astounded.

"Steve," I say hoarsely. "Sneakers? How could you?" I start to sob.

"Shush darling," Steve says, cradling me in his arms. "Baba Yaga has come to help us on our quest, but soon she must go on her way, to drink vodka by the fire in her flying cottage, listening to Mussorgsky in surround sound, reminiscing of the days when together they sucked unhatched chickens from their shells as he composed on the piano."

"Why help us?" I ask Baba Yaga.

"I knew your grandfather," she says. "And his father."

"You from Jersey?"

Baba Yaga starts to laugh with her gold tooth shining in the moonlight.

"Remember what the gypsy told you on the plane?" she says.

I'm thinking I'd like to throw back some shots with Baba Yaga, but I draw the line at sucking unhatched chickens.

"I know what you are thinking," she says. "Don't worry. They are free range, not caged. Never caged."

НАЗДРАВЕ

Baba Yaga leads us to a clearing in the brush. We look over her bent shoulders and see what appears to be an enormous brick building, like an old warehouse or a factory, rising two, or is it three, stories high. There is a faint glow from one of the windows on the first floor. I hear sounds. Thuds. Muffled voices, groans. A slight shaking of the ground, like standing under a highway overpass.

"I know what you are thinking," Baba Yaga says.

Not again. "Synchronicity only goes so far," I tell her. "I was a psych major."

"Do you want to talk about it?" she asks, patting a fallen log. An invitation to sit?

"No, just sayin'."

"You are afraid," she says.

She has a point. There is something about the warehouse.

"There are more than two sides to the universe," she says. "Software has become so advanced that neurotransmitters are running through your brain synapses at this very moment carrying messages hidden in glutamic acid that are barely one neural leap ahead of government intelligence *apparatchiks* and soon the world will be depolarized or hyperpolarized but there can be no in-between. Choices must be made."

Steve presses his body close to mine and says, "She's hot."

What the fuck?

Baba Yaga steps over the log and yanks open a steel door, which leads into a formal vestibule with intricately carved paneling, mosaic patterns on the floor and Victorian chairs with lion's feet. I see a liquor cabinet with leaded glass doors and, in front of it, the back of a man in a black silk robe. "I've been expecting you," he says. The voice is familiar. It's Shearling.

He turns and nods to Baba Yaga. She rocks from side to side in a girlish way, her eyes twinkling like she is remembering something from the past, the far off past. "Listen, do you hear it?" she says, cupping her right hand over her ear.

I do think I hear something. Again. Those faint sounds, dull like distant thunder, the voices.

"The spirits of the strongest among the strong, the poets, the powerlifters, long gone," Baba Yaga says, and then crosses herself.

"At one time, in the ancient lands, all voices were as one," Shearling says, wrapping his arms around Baba Yaga. "Behold. The Ancient Gym."

Steve looks at me. I feel like I can hear my heart beating.

"Built by Alexander the Great. Our proud people, reduced from powerlifters to scribes for invading micro-economies," Shearling says.

"I thought it was invented by the Turks," I say under my breath.

Baba Yaga doesn't miss a thing. "Who told you this?" she demands.

"Big Steve," I say. Steve gives me a signal to shut up.

"How did you get here?" I ask Shearling. Reasonable question since I last saw this dude exiting the plane at JFK.

"I went the way of the ancient masters," he says.

"Cut the crap," I say. "This pretentious affectation of pomposity is getting on my nerves. And, might I add, it is flamboyant and disingenuous."

He looks startled. Good.

Baba Yaga applauds.

"Quite a vocabulary for a part-time real estate agent," he sneers.

"Fuck off, wise ass," I say. "I'm a college graduate. I majored in…"

"Psychology," Baba Yaga and Shearling say at the same time. I feel my cheeks get hot.

"It's working," Baba Yaga says. "The intellectual sapient species of our great leaders walks among us once more, infused with superior yet feminine musculature and *je ne sais quoi* attitude."

"I speak French, you know, so don't go saying anything behind my back," I say. "So what's with the sapient species? Are you calling me a freak?"

Baba Yaga opens the cabinet and raises a carafe filled with blue liquid. She sets it on a silver tray with tiny cut crystal glasses. I turn one over to see if it is Waterford. She smacks my hand and pours the liquid into each glass.

"To the restoration of our glory days!" Shearling says.

This is starting to creep me out. Are chicken embryos next?

"*Steveut!*" he says.

"*Slainte!*" says Baba Yaga.

"*Prost!*" says Big Steve.

"*Skoal!!!*" says Baba Yaga.

"*Nazdravey!!*" they shout in unison.

Wait what? I've heard that before. Recently.

"Bulgarian," Baba Yaga says. "Get used to it, babe. If you know what's good for you." I act nonchalant. It is my personal policy to ignore thinly veiled threats from heavily veiled hags.

"So, hey," I say. "How do you spell it? This *Nazdravey?*"

"Наздраве."

Figures.

"So," I ask, raising my glass and again adopting my reliable tough-movie-broad posture. "Is this going to kill me?"

"No," says Shearling. "And if it does, we'll make you better."

"Ah, attempted Munchausen syndrome by proxy," I tell them, and refrain while they go ahead and knock back the blue aperitif. Not wanting to be a wimp, I hold my breath, swallow it and start to cough.

"Do we know this Munchausen?" Shearling asks, wiping his mouth with his sleeve.

Christ! For a change I know something these knuckleheads don't. I'm starting to feel smart again. Not smart as in "the smart set" of sophisticates or a genius like Jimmy DiNapoli from the neighborhood who played string theory in the school yard. Just smart as in smart-smart. Smart squared, but never a square. To redeem myself, I will tell them about Munchausen. Take charge. Purvey information. Gain authority and, above all, gain respect.

"A clinically proven factitious disorder," I say, with a slight pause for effect. I expect they are waiting with, what's the expression, bated breath? "A disorder where you make somebody sick to make them well, to save, to heal, to restore, and in doing so, look like a hero." I think they are impressed. Why quit now? I seize the moment.

"There was an old lady in my neighborhood who fed the mayor's dog rat poison. It started howling and foaming and the people were horrified. The police were about to put it down when she shows up and shoots a syringe of hydrogen peroxide down the dog's throat to induce vomiting. The antidote worked and her picture was in the paper and she got a medal from the fire department."

They pour another round of the blue shit. I pass.

"In training," I explain.

Everyone gets quiet. Solemn. They knock it back. In unison. And then they all laugh. Even Big Steve. How rude. Whatever is so funny, hahaha, I forgot to laugh. I am totally absolutely fucking confused. I still don't know what's going on here. Maybe we're part of a twisted reality show orchestrated by Joe Fox and Big Steve without my consent. Maybe I'm being watched back home. Right now. At this moment. I glance at my reflection in the leaded glass. Oh my God. I need lipstick, a blow dryer. Who knows what this could lead to when we get home. Maybe a real estate show on HGTV, showing people unusual properties around the world like, well, this place. Or a cooking show. Make some flaming dessert with the blue stuff they're drinking. Make a lot of money. Sign autographs. Show Linda McIntyre from Our Lady of Victories High School that I don't care that Vinnie took her to the prom instead of me, that I've got my own TV show with fans and a makeup artist while those guys are doing the nine-to-five and carpool. If they could see me now.

I fade out of my futuristic fame and fortune fog, forgo my foolish fantasies, forget my childhood hopes of pet farms in Florida. Taz is dead, as in most sincerely dead. Finished. Forever. I walk out of the room and into a hallway, alone with my alliterative thoughts. They don't try to stop me. In fact, I don't even think they notice.

SKULL CRUSHER

While my Bulgarian buds are getting plastered with Big Steve, I meander down the hall and open the door of the next room. I am startled to see a very ordinary office: gray carpeting, drop ceilings, rows of cubicles and people hunched over keyboards, young people, each with a keyboard and three flat screens, their faces spooky in the blue-gray light. They don't seem to notice me as I stand in the doorway.

I am struck by their appearance. A collective sartorial disaster. There's this guy in a wrinkled green polo shirt, Doc Martens, and polyester jeans. And a backwards New York Mets cap. The Mets? Seriously? A mousy chick in orange stretch pants and pink jelly shoes. But then again, this ain't New York. Or even Jersey City. A pale dude with a mohawk haircut and a Pink Floyd t-shirt is typing in the cubicle closest to me. As I approach, he opens his desk drawer a crack and looks at me.

"Got any weed?" I ask him, suppressing the temptation to tell him that mohawks are so passé. Politeness rules. Along with the possibility of copping a bone so I can take a little mental vacay from this badass Baltic edifice. He looks at me blankly, shuts the drawer and grabs his mouse.

"Sorry," I say. "Just askin'. Don't want to get you in trouble or anything."

He puts both hands on the edge of the keyboard and, without looking up, says to me: "I got low-sodium communion wafers. And I can spare some whole wheat, too, if you can handle the gluten."

I lower my voice to a purr.

"I rarely get bloated," I lie.

"There's a missing chapter," Mohawk sighs. "I read the manual 63 times and it doesn't add up. Probably about 150 pages in. There's something that is missing, but within reach. I can feel it, like the cold air left behind by a poltergeist."

"The training manual? You have it too?" I ask. With all the secrecy at my gym, you'd think there was only one copy in the whole world. And this guy looks like he never lifted a weight heavier than a stapler.

"We were a great people once," he says. "Now, outsourced to the West."

I find myself saying: "In your eyes, I see the look. It hasn't disappeared." Steve's words, when he gave me the manual. Could this be the place?

"You have our allegiance and support," he says. "You will save us from generations of consumer servitude to multinational corporations harvesting our information technology skills and adaptable accents cultivated in state schools clandestinely financed by capitalist giants like Amazon, Microsoft, AT&T and Kentucky Fried Chicken, who seek to use us to communicate with customers faking that we are in Boise, Idaho, at the expense, at the… the… the…"

He is panting. I look to see if there is a water fountain, but there is none.

Big Steve appears by the entry, and the Mohawk dweeb straightens up and resumes typing. Steve is still wearing the poet's shirt, but now he has a black bandana on his head. Give me a break. Here's this gym rat from Hoboken with six-pack abs who crawled his way from the city dump. With a tree neurosis and a domineering Sicilian father. Oh, and ginormous biceps. Since when did he morph into some GQ cover with a hyperextended vocabulary and an élan of royalty?

I plop down at an empty desk and lean back in the swivel chair. "Okay, Steve, what's up for tomorrow? *Saturday Night Fever?* What's got into you? You are not the same."

"Neither are you," he says, "but I love you anyway."

"I don't give a flying fuck. Leave me alone."

"I love you," Steve says again. "I love you, not in the carnal sense, but because you let my creative self be real," he says. "With you, I can plunder the ephemeral world and stockpile canned spaghetti or Mallomars or grape soda or whatever I ever want and it's real. I can be a sailor, a king. A real king. A pirate king!"

The Italian Popeye? Which makes me, what, Olive Oyl? My head is throbbing. I decide that I am so over Steve. What did I ever see in him anyway? Maybe it was the glittering lights and the gorgeous meaningless words on the float at the airport, the way he was both needy and aloof, the Italian bedroom eyes, and the chance to make a difference in this world, to rescue him from a life at the city dump. Or, maybe, I was just lonely.

I hear him walk away, and I say, "go fuck yourself" under my breath. I slink down in the chair and close my eyes. It's quiet except for the clicking of keyboards, and my chest is still burning from the shot. I feel someone tap me on the knee. I open my eyes and the Mohawk dude is crouched next to me. He presses something into the palm of my hand, puts his finger to his lips, and then leaves the room. The others stop typing and follow him. Some look at me sadly, but kindly. I am alone among strangers. But I feel at peace. I open my hand and lying in my palm is a whole-wheat communion wafer. My headache is gone and I'm so hungry. I remember the Benedictine Sisters of Perpetual Adoration, and the instructions they included with my order.

For optimal absorption, sublingual administration is the preferred method. Place in contact with the mucous membrane beneath the tongue, where a profusion of capillaries will diffuse the host directly into the blood-stream, thus reducing the risk of degradation by salivary enzymes and the harsh environment of the gastrointestinal tract.

I turn over the wafer and, sure enough, it is stamped "Clyde, Missouri."

I put the wafer under my tongue, and I feel this nervous energy, totally aware, totally pumped, senses heightened. There's a shitload of people I've been hanging with and where are they now, both physically and metaphorically? Baba Yaga, Shearling, Big Steve, Joe Fox, who I haven't seen since we landed, the anorexic chicks, the Escargot Cowboy, Eddie and Wally. I walk down the rows of computers, their screens lighting the way, aware of the sound of my footsteps. I lean in and look at a screen saver, trying to discern some meaning: I watch an image of a barbell disintegrating, crumbling into little dots, and then coming back whole, and each time a little bigger. I'm thinking it's cool, but devoid of meaning. I notice they all have the same screen saver. I hear something again. That faint clanging. For some reason, I'm no longer freaked out. There it goes again. Like a déjà vu. But it feels like someone else's déjà vu, if that's even possible. Can you vicariously experience déjà vu? I vow to look it up when I get home.

I leave the room and follow the sounds down the hall. I stop before one of the doors, a wood door, handmade from thick boards. I hold my breath and listen. There is the rumble of something dropped, something bouncing off the floor. I see a keyhole. An old-fashioned keyhole. I scrunch down and peek. Two red gym benches with torn padding. A few rusted dumbbells and rebar. Some pale guy with a gut is straining to do a skull crusher with a measly 35 pounds. This is too much. I turn the knob and push open the door and before me is an enormous room. Like a decrepit high school gymnasium. Super high ceilings. Exposed brick walls with vines growing through empty mortar joints. Wrought iron windows that rise almost to the ceiling, wire mesh glass coated with yellow grime. I like it. The kind of space people are dying to rent back in Hoboken. Or Brooklyn. I know people who would pay good money for this.

Inside are about a half dozen ordinary looking guys and two chicks, one with a limp ponytail and greasy bangs and the other has short dark frizzy hair, like it was fried from a bad perm. I remember these people. They were typing on the computers a few minutes ago. The frizz girl has bad posture, shoulders slouched, chewing gum. She is watching the ponytail girl do a barbell curl. Well, attempt a barbell curl. Instead of keeping her core tight, arms into the waist and lifting from the elbows, she is swinging the freakin rebar like it's a cowbell. That's not going to get her anything but maybe a bad back. Then again, it's only 25 pounds, so no harm, I guess. Just a waste of time. I take in the scene quietly and step out into the room. When they see me, they stop cold, almost in mid-motion. Why? Is mascara smeared over my face? We are still staring at each other when Mohawk steps forward and points to the side of his hip. I slip my right hand into the pocket of my hoodie and feel another whole-wheat wafer. A Clyde original. Or, perhaps, a counterfeit? I could swear he only gave me one, but who knows? I put it in my mouth, and make a quick sign of the cross. I take off my hoodie and drape it over a barbell. I pull my t-shirt over my head and reveal my racer-back tank top. I look around and notice there is an entire mirrored wall over on the left side. The mirrors are stained with spots and look moldy. Some are cracked.

I don't know what to do or say, but I remember Steve's words when we were standing by the mirrors in Jersey City and he was first teaching me how to pose. I had zero interest at the time—in posing, that is. My interest was in watching him pose, and I just went along and put up with his lectures about my pear shape and fast-food diet.

"It's all an illusion," he would tell me. "You work and get big and diet and get ripped but, in the end, on the stage, it's an illusion that you create for yourself. The way you stand, the foot, the flexing, the tilt of the head. The tanning. The oil. You must project everything you want them to see, but only what you want them to see." I hadn't thought of this since before we left, when we were on the float. And before that, just after the flood, when I sat in the sun in my backyard, waiting for my apartment to dry out. I was sitting on the grass with the manual and, having nothing better to do, I flipped randomly to certain chapters. But was it random? Is anything random? I am filled with amorphous thoughts I cannot name or even repeat and they bathe me with pheromones until I feel like I've just swallowed ecstasy, not an ordinary communion wafer from the Midwest. I stand tall, throw my shoulders back and face the cracked mirror.

It is all an illusion... There is no permanence in image, but it is the prevailing reality, which you can seize. And seize you must... The great gyms of the past have vanished.

I make a fist with my right hand and slowly lift my elbow and then, squeezing as hard as I can, I pull into a bicep curl. I am astonished to see the peak on my bicep: a chiseled, perfect Mount Rainier of a bicep.

A weight drops and echoes and I snap my head around. All the dweebs applaud. Mohawk rushes toward me and bows deeply.

"It is you," he says.

Yeah, well. Hello?

They gather around me. Gym rats or drowned rats? I try not to be cynical. We make the usual introductions, and of course they have Bulgarian names, and I don't speak Bulgarian. They tell me not to worry, that they all have American aliases, too. I always thought the alias thing was a Korean manicurist device – but they explain it is necessary because of the outsourcing. They need to pretend they're

Monica from Des Moines or Bill from Arkansas, however here every single guy's name is Mike, and the two girls are both Jenny. Ok, easy enough but how will I know who is talking about who, or is that whom? Never could get that straight, the who and the whose and whom and of whom and for whom. If I get mixed up, I'll look like a dumb slut. Maybe that's what I did when I was talking to Wally. Maybe that's why she threw the *Dumme Schlampe* bomb at me. Not that I care, I mean, I don't give a rat's ass what that old Nazi bitch thinks of me anyway. She can take her *Dumme Schlampe* and shove it where the sun don't shine. I'll settle for my own made-up names.

All these thoughts are going through my head as more of a feeling than a bunch of words, compressed into a split second, which really isn't a split second, is it, because a half a second would be too short to even think, like a nanosecond, or perhaps more accurately, a demi-second, like a demitasse, which is like a half a cup of coffee, assuming you started with a small cup of coffee and not a big mug.

I ask Mohawk how come his English is so good and why he sounds like he's from back home, not Jersey, but maybe someplace in upstate New York, like Syracuse. He tells me all the dweebs have American accents, even the ones who speak lousy English, and that some have multiple accents. Mohawk tells me one of the guys can do 17 American regional accents, his best being Dallas, Minneapolis, and Buffalo.

"How about Hoboken?" I ask. "Or Jersey City?" The girl with greasy hair blushes and shakes her head.

"You can teach us," Mohawk says.

"How?" I ask.

"Just talk to us. We have a program that will synthesize your speech patterns into a full series of language learning modules. It is then incorporated with pictures and fun learning games. No boring repeat-after-me tapes. This is the wave of the future, and we have the technology. We take a series of the base dialogues, the scripts we need to talk to customers about our client's products, and create any dialect we need, and we do it effectively, as long as the customer does not force us to go off script. If they do, it blows our minds, and we keep repeating the same thing over and over. The system does have a few bugs."

Mohawk looks at the others and they shrug and nod, like it's no big deal.

"But this is not why you came here, to this ancient gym," he says, "to join us on hallowed ground."

At that, the others bow their heads.

I notice the wood floor creaks like crazy and the boards feel thin and soft.

"You drop a weight and it'll probably go right through to the basement," I tell them, stamping my foot on a particularly sagging section. "They should just tear it out and put in a new one."

"They?" Mohawk says. "There is no *they*. It is only us—and you—and these are the floorboards trodden by my ancestors. And yours."

I am startled by this reference to my ancestors, and I think he just is being polite. If he only knew about Grandma chugging Bud on the old sofa, her thin strands of hair, her skinny legs covered in bruises. Better to keep this to myself.

"I guarantee you none of my ancestors hung out here," I tell him.

How they can work out in this dump? My gym at home was no Equinox, but this looks like it hasn't been upgraded in a thousand years.

The dweebs glance at one another like they want to say something but keep it to themselves. I used to be shy, so I get it. I like these guys, despite the bad clothes, bad hair, bad skin, bad posture and all. There's something about them. Maybe I'm a dweeb at heart. That is a scary thought. Then again, nobody from back home will ever know I've been hanging with these losers, provided I don't pick up any bad habits or, worse, bad hair.

"You know, it's going to be a helluva a lot of work to get this place into decent shape," I tell Mohawk. "Why not just turn it into a museum of the olden days, sell tickets, bring in revenue and then go work out someplace else? I mean, this can't possibly be the only gym in Bulgaria."

Mohawk hesitates and looks away, moving his gaze up the tall windows.

"Yes, there are other gyms," he says softly, "clean, well-equipped, climate-controlled. But they are all clandestine enterprises under the control of, well, maybe I have said too much."

"Too much? Are you kidding me? Look, I'm a long way from home and we really need to level with each other. What do you mean clandestine? Is everything a secret here?"

He looks at me. "You know then?"

"I don't know shit." Mohawk winces and I am suddenly embarrassed at my crudeness. I have to remember that I am a tourist, and like Grandma always said, when in Rome do like the Romans do, and I guess that goes for the Bulgarians too. Except, I have very little idea of what they do.

"Okay," Mohawk says with an exaggerated sigh. "The Gangsta Builda Powerlifta Gym has wrestled control, pardon my pun, of all the independent gyms in our land. This syndicate has forced them to pay dearly for security and has stamped out their right to free artistic expression."

"I get it. A classic shake down," I say. "Maybe Jimmy Hoffa is buried here."

"Be careful," Mohawk warns, not even cracking a smile at my lame attempt to add levity.

"Sorry, but you have to admit, that is a ridiculous name for a gym. Gangsta Builda?"

"Do not underestimate their thirst for dominance and cultural appropriation," Mohawk says. "Their mentor was a physicist exiled to a Siberian camp in the 1960s," he says. "He worked on his physique in order to pass the time and trained his guards in order to curry favors. He was a great fan of American arts and letters, and took upon himself the *nom de plume* of Dr. No. On his deathbed, he managed to smuggle out a manifesto. He said it would come to pass that the American television would spawn prophets that would help them take down Western civilization. His followers model themselves on cultural icons. Fresh Prince of Bel-Air. Cake Boss. Snooki."

"I don't know," I say, "the gangsta thing is a little passé, ya think? What's their gym like?"

"Massive," he says, "and well funded. The door of each gym is marked with a symbol, the Higgs Boson particle, etched in gold."

It's a nice story, but back to the here and now. The guy who was doing the lame skull crusher steps forward and motions toward his bench.

"Please," he says.

I take it as an invitation. He hands me the 35-pound preacher bar. I brace my feet, bang out 12 reps, get up and stretch. They all smile and give each other high fives. I tell one of the girls to get on the bench. I would've started with the Mohawk dude, but I don't want to emasculate him right off the bat.

She lies down and wiggles her head because her scrunchie is in the way. I motion for her to sit up and pull it off her head and throw it on the floor. She lies back down, and I show her how to wrap her hands around the bent bar but funny thing is, what is so natural to me is a mystery when I have to explain it to someone else. Do I open my palms to the inside or the outside? I go through the motion in the air. Yes. Outside. But how then do I slide my hands in place? The upper part of the bar or the lower? I tell her to get off and figure a picture is worth a thousand words or, more accurately, a live action picture of me just doing the damn thing in slow mo.

"Elbows in at the side," I tell them as I raise the bar slowly. They move in closer, cramping my space, but not too much.

"Look. Wrists stay in a straight line to the elbow. No wigglies. Strong. Think strong. Bar moves with your forearm from the waist until it's straight. See? Like this. Drive up, then down slow, very slow. Feel the negative."

I get off the bench and the chick lies down, grabs the bar just like I showed her and pushes it straight up and then, before I have a chance to stop her, she lets it drop down with lightning speed, finishing maybe a half inch from her forehead.

"We call this French press," she says.

"Back where I come from, they call this a skull crusher. For a reason. Take it slow, chicky. You don't want to go busting your head open, do you?"

I hate rhetorical questions, but I have to make my point.

She shakes her head and repeats the exercise, this time very slowly and super controlled. She gets up, takes a bow, flings her hair over her head and back, and throws out her arms. Like a gymnast at the Olympics. Like – Nadia! Her friends give her high fives. Don't take much to get these people excited, I tell you.

I check out the equipment. Not too many machines, pretty outdated: a beat-up treadmill and a few old gray Nautiluses covered with graffiti. I look closer at the lat pull-down and on the side of the base, scratched into the paint, I see:

Борис любит Инну

The girl from the bench is twisting her scrunchie back on. She smiles shyly and her whole face starts to get red. Mohawk winks.

"It says, "Boris loves Inna," she says.

"Is that you?" I ask her. "Are you Inna?"

"No," Mohawk says. "It is long story. Right?" She makes a little circle on the floor with her foot. "In Bulgarian, we call her Little Beast." I am taken aback and do not know if this is a term of endearment, some ironic putdown, or if she is a force to be reckoned with. There was a tourist boat at South Street Seaport called The Beast. Could there be a connection?

"So what is *your* name?" I ask Mohawk. "I mean, not the Mike name, your real name."

"Vanya," he says.

"You mean *she's* Vanya?"

They laugh and the ponytail girl, a.k.a. The Beast, says. "No. Here is men's name."

The Mohawk kid says, "Ivan Petrovich Voynitsky! Friends call me Vanya."

"I'm Cristina Acqualina Bontempi and my friends call me Tina," I say.

I tell him his name sounds familiar, reminds me of a book I read in school. Still, I prefer to think of him as Mohawk.

The Beast hands me another communion wafer and I pop it in my mouth. I hear music in my head and the tune starts to come into focus, a movie hit from back in the day. My grandmother used to listen to it. From *Dr. Zhivago*. She'd get all teary eyed.

"My name Tereza." It's the frizz girl, who until now has not said a word. "But Jenny is ok. Welcome to Ancient Gym and our beautiful country," she says. "We were told to expect you. We are all, what you call it?"

"Atrophying?" I say. "No offense."

"You like gym?" she says.

"Gym blows man, sorry to say. But it could be awesome."

Seems like forever since I've been to the gym and I'm feeling this craving, like it's 110 in the shade and I'm staring at an ice-cold orange soda. That kind of craving. The I-have-to-have-it-now kind of craving. It's only been, what, a few days since we landed? Or is it weeks? They say you lose track of time when you're on vacation. Either way, I'm making friends and I feel like these dweeby people need me. I am moved by pity, a shared destiny, a sense of complete boredom that I have to shake. I look at the brick walls, the ceiling, the beat-up floor. I stretch and an adrenaline rush surges through me.

I step up on a bench with my hands on my hips and stare down this rag-tag crew. "Hey guys! You want to make this place rock?" They nod.

"Then move your sorry-ass butts. Start by painting the floors, cleaning the windows, and over there, come up with a row of new mirrors, eight feet high. And when you're done, maybe some rubber mats."

Mohawk says there's no money for mirrors. The girl with the ponytail smacks him across the face. I step back, freaked out because I don't want to start a brawl or have this guy hate me.

"Thank you, comrade," he says to her, straightening his shoulders. He pivots to me and says, "At the expense of the bodies that were once the envy of the world, a gene pool that responded with exceptional perfection to the rigors of a training routine and diet that had been ours alone, a regimen of mental, physical and spiritual guidance that could be found only in…"

He pauses, looks me in the eye, and I say, "*The Bulgarian Training Manual?*"

"Precisely! And we, our eyes weakened by hours in front of cathode ray tubes and laptops, our souls subservient to…"

"Look," I say, "cut the crap and get to the point."

"You," he says, "you alone have the missing chapter. You and Big Steve. And for this, we pledge our lives to you."

Uh, yeah.

THE THREE LOMBARDIS

———

Since the days of ancient Rome at least, men of extraordinary dimensions have been displayed in the arena, on the track and in the ring, but until quite recently they were regarded as Freaks.

I remember, for instance, the heavyweight boxer Primo Carnera... the crowds cheered for his smaller, more human opponents to bring him down. I saw him in the flesh... with my son, then only five or six, who cheered with the rest when the Giant was finally pinned, but wept when we encountered him in the corridors afterward, battered and bleeding and blind—drunk—but somehow all the huger, like Polyphemus himself.

LESLIE FIEDLER, *FREAKS, MYTHS & IMAGES OF THE SECRET SELF* (1978)

———

IRON LADIES (AND THE MEN WHO LOVED THEM)

I'm still wrapping my mind around this guy's amazing vocabulary for some backwoods foreigner in some backwoods part of a backwoods country, when Mohawk turns to the pathetic little group and, pumping his fist, yells: "Shout out to the one we have been waiting for, who will reverse the curse that has been our fate, the one who will restore our birthright. She is come forth from the diaspora, the ghosts of her great lineage shall at last have peace in their cold anguished graves."

Mohawk kneels at my feet, bows his head and says: "It shall come to pass. The writings of our prophets will return unto us in our hearts, our bodies, and our souls. Behold the only living descendant, who shall lead us from the tyranny of the weakened shells of ourselves."

I'm getting creeped out by this mumbo jumbo, which is way more whacked than anything the nuns said at Our Lady of Victories.

"Uh, listen dude," I hear myself saying, "I think maybe you think I'm somebody else. I told you I'm from New Jersey." I look around to see if there's smoke or soldiers or lightning or some other crazy shit because this has been one fucking weird day. "I am not your descendant. I am not Bulgarian. I'm Italian. My dad, he's – "

"Rusty G! Hahahahahahahaha."

It is the old lady from the plane, the gypsy lady. I remember she too called herself Baba Yaga, same as the hag with the giant tooth. Are there two Baba Yagas? Or did she have a makeover? Twice. You know, I never did see them in the same room. I try to recall what I ate today. That communion wafer Mohawk gave me. Was it laced with some bad shit?

"You parents not you parents!" she declares, and the others genuflect before me.

Wait, what?

She pulls from her doctor bag a long clear bottle with herbs in it, yanks the cork out with her teeth, raises it into the air and proclaims:

"Long live Georg Karl Julius Hackenschmidt!"

Georg? Grandma's secret crush? The dude in the Speedo and black knee socks? Whose signed photo she would place on her sagging bosoms as she sprawled on the couch, one leg draped over the side, while flailing a can of Brewski, shouting at the wrestlers on her black-and-white TV: "Dere ya go, fuckin' hamma' da joik, ya pussy!"

"Excuse me," I say. "Grandma told me Georg was from Estonia, and in any case what does that have to do with me? And you? Here in Bulgaria?"

The frizzy haired girl pushes her way from the back of the group, lugging a thick black book, maybe two feet wide, with thin strips of leather worn off the binding.

"This is book," she says.

"Yeah. It's a – book. And?"

The girl places the book at my feet. She carefully opens the cover and – holy fucking shit! Right there on Page One. It's Grandma's photo. Or, at least, a reasonable facsimile. I am amazed to see old Georg's mug. The girl starts twirling her hair with her finger and she looks upset.

"This book. He's book. Book life."

Mohawk steps in and apologizes and explains that her English is terrible. Uh, tell me something I didn't know, please. Really. He is about to continue when the girl waves her hands and says "NO! NO! I feeeniish." I think she is about to cry, so I indicate that she should hurry up and finish. "Yes, FINISH," I shout, extra loud so she can understand me better. Where was she when they were giving out those language modules?

"Georg live many years in Estonia," she says, "but not of Estonia.

From other country. Germania. Russia. Hollywood. He travel and he strong man, most strong man who ever live. And wise. He write many book."

"He was a philosopher," adds Mohawk, who's busting a gut to get this out. "Known as The Russian Lion, born in 1877 in the ancient land of Livonia. Hackenschmidt was an enlightened man, the one Aristotle envisioned so presciently. He is our incarnation of the philosopher king, inventor of the Hack squat and the professional wrestling version of the bear hug, all the while maintaining a strict regimen of weight training and an impeccable diet, drinking 22 pints of milk per day, with a willpower of steel so mighty he could on demand direct his kidneys to function in an alternating fashion so as to have periods of rest for each one, and thus prolong their optimal life span."

I try to imagine the alternating kidneys, but I already feel psychosomatically bloated from the 22 pints of milk.

"The great one gathered together his own theories and those of the other masters. Great men, all. Look." He starts turning the pages, and each one has a black and white photograph in the center, held to the paper with white scrapbook corners. Some pictures are crinkled up and brown on the edges, and the yellowed pages are very thin. Under each picture is a name and a description in Bulgarian, written with what looks like a quill pen with lots of fancy curves. Mohawk translates.

PIERRE GASNIER - 1862-1923. The French Hercules, Barnum and Bailey Circus.

The dude has a bushy mustache and the weirdest fucking dumbbell ever. I mean, the ends aren't plates like you normally use, but big round cast iron balls the size of, well, like the globes you see in a classroom. I tell Mohawk he looks a little puny.

"Yes, Pierre was a small man, just 5-foot-3, but his success was partly due to an optical illusion. You see." Mohawk pauses, like he is groping for the right words. "He had a very big head – and big hands, too, which made the rest of his body look even smaller, and made his strength appear to be more impressive. Hoisting his enormous dumbbell, the audiences went crazy for him. Women lined up after the show just to caress it."

EUGEN SANDOW - Father of Modern Bodybuilding. Born Friedrich Wilhelm Muller, 1867 Prussia. Died 1925 England. Inventor of the spring-

grip dumbbell. His Institutes of Physical Culture was the prototype of the modern gym; organized the world's first bodybuilding competition at London's Royal Albert Hall, an event that could be considered the pre-cursor of Mr. Olympia. The statuette awarded at Mr. Olympia is modeled on Sandow, who modeled himself on the Roman statues he discovered as a youth fleeing military conscription in Prussia.

"Sandow is the real deal," says Mohawk. "Although he was said to be very, very strong, he was maybe the first guy to focus more on the aesthetics of muscle development than brute strength. The ladies loved him but not so much his wife Blanche. She refused to mark his grave when he died, and it was left that way until some bodybuilding fan erected a stone. They say he died of a brain hemorrhage caused by lifting his car out of a ditch, but rumor has it that it was an aortic aneurysm brought on by syphilis."

JOHN HOLTUM - Born 1845 Denmark. Died 1919 England. Known as Cannonball King, he was undeterred after losing three fingers on his first attempt to catch a 50-pound red-hot cannonball at 100 mph.

"Moderation in everything," Mohawk says with a wink.

I grab the book to get a better look at what appears to be a small painted poster with *Folies Bergere* in big letters and, slightly smaller, *Tous les Soirs*. This guy in a red leotard is sticking his chest out as a cannonball is flying toward him. Underneath, it says *L'Homme aux Boulets de Canon. L'homme* is the dude, that I know from high school French. But I'm not sure about the *boulets. Bou... bou... Boulets. Bouill-abaisse?* No. Button. No, that would be *bouton*. Don't ask me how I remember that one. *Boulets.* Bullets? *Boulets de canon?* Bullets de cannon? I get it. Cannonball. Amazing how the brain is stuffed with useless knowledge. Like French, which makes me think of Philippe, and as far as he is concerned, I don't give a flying fuck, as opposed to a flying cannonball, which obviously was very important to this guy's career.

I hear Mohawk say, "Let's move on. Really. Holtum is not too important."

Embarrassed, I turn the page, where I see this guy with smoky eyes and black wavy hair wearing a gladiator outfit, helmet, and toga. Like a silent movie star. Very hot.

"Looks Italian," I say to Mohawk.

"Look again," he says.

SIEGMUND BREITBART - זיגמונד ברייטברט *Known as Zishe. Born 1893 Poland. Died 1925 Berlin. American Vaudeville.*

"Hebrew," Mohawk says.

"Ya' think?" I say. "I'm not exactly from Podunk."

"Where is Podunk?" he asks.

"Just an expression. So, what's the deal with this dude?"

"Werner Herzog made a film about him, *Invincible.* You saw it, maybe?"

I shake my head and make a mental note to add it to my long list of movies to check out on Netflix when I get home.

"His parents were blacksmiths, *shtetl* people. Cut his teeth biting through iron chains. Broke horseshoes in half by the time he was 12."

"If he was so strong, how come he was dead by 32?" I ask. Mohawk shakes his head slowly and sighs. Such a fucking drama queen.

"On stage, Zishe had this act where he drove spikes through wood with his bare hands. One went too fast. Rusty nail into his thigh. Leg was amputated in Berlin. But a pretty face, strength and glory were no match for the Angel of Darkness. It was Fate that called him."

"Fate, my ass," I say. "Grandma told me that back in the day, they used moldy bread for penicillin. No wonder he dropped dead." I'm wondering if they fed Zishe green bread before chopping off his leg. Maybe it's not kosher. Grape jelly's not kosher. Oreos used to not be kosher when I was little but now, they are. The things you learn growing up in Jersey City. But green mold? I couldn't say.

Mohawk turns the page to a lady in a fancy beaded dress from the early 1900s, with a humongous white feather in her hat.

KATIE SANDWINA - *Born Katharina Brumbach. Born 1884 Vienna. Died 1952 New York City. The Great Sandwina, Woman of Steel. Ringling Bros. and Barnum & Bailey Circus.*

"Katie's signature act was lifting her husband above her head with one arm while drinking a glass of champagne in the other," Mohawk says. "Women cheered and men masturbated at the sight of her bare arms and ankle boots, the titillating illusion of female inebriation and muscle, the elegant dominatrix."

"She was born into a travelling circus," Mohawk says, "and became known as Sandwina after beating Sandow in a weightlifting contest. Katie hoisted 300 pounds over her head, and Sandow only made it up to his chest. Or so the story goes."

I'm impressed and wondering if there are any other women when Mohawk turns the page.

LOUIS CYR - 1863-1912 Quebec. Lifted 500 pounds with one finger.

"Aaaahhhh Loooieee," says Mohawk, falling backward. "Louis, the Canadian Samson and pastry chef extraordinaire. This man tied fifty-pound weights into his hair and went twirling around just to get the audiences warmed up. He was lifting live bulls right off the ground until one of them kicked him in the balls. But did that stop him? No! Instead, he tethers himself to horses, arms outstretched. Guys whip the horses into a frenzy. They pull in either direction with all their might and still, they cannot not break free from the master's iron grasp. He might have been the world's strongest man ever, stronger than Hackenschmidt. But – he had a fatal flaw. Can you guess what it was?"

Mohawk looks at me and I feel this kind of *déjà vu* coming on.

"Wait, wait, don't tell me," I say. "His diet."

"Correct!" he says. "He's the guy who invented the precursor to the Twinkie – which can infuse a helluva martini but I digress - and they say that he ate upwards of 50 of them a day, and it is documented that he often consumed six pounds of meat in one meal," says Mohawk.

"And that's where he lost his way." I chime in. "You cannot digest massive quantities of Twinkies within 24 hours after having a side of beef. He must have developed chronic nephritis. And that's, uh, what the hell, just my theory."

"Yes!" he says. "I knew it. You got it! You *are* the real thing."

"The real what?" I ask. He looks at me stony faced and doesn't answer.

I see on the opposite page pictures of a little girl with long wavy hair, a flared dress down to her knees and button up shoes. Maybe 10 years old. She has big, sad eyes and she is holding a small dumbbell in the air.

"This dumbbell was made specially for her," says Mohawk. He gazes at it with a far-off look.

"What's with this kid?" I ask Mohawk. I lift the book for a closer look at another picture of what seems to be the same girl, only younger, maybe four or five. She is wearing a sleeveless sailor top and a pleated skirt. One hand is on her waist and her other is in a fist, like she is doing a one-arm dumbbell curl.

"Is this fucking photo-shopped?" I say, "I mean, what little girl has biceps like that? Look at that peak! You can even see the muscle in her forearm. Sculpted. Massive. Totally ripped. Even her tiny fingers look strong."

"No trick," says Mohawk.

I am amazed even more by the dark eyes. Fierce. Piercing. I can't turn away. I mean, this kid is spitting fire through those black eyes.

"Who is this?"

"She appears in photos with numerous strongmen of this period," he says. "Many children would go onstage and assist – usually with their fathers, you know, a family act," Mohawk says. "This one, she is not with any particular family. She is everywhere." He flips through some pages to find other pictures of her. In one, she is doing a one-armed handstand on the shoulders of a huge muscle man, and in another, she is holding a Shetland pony on her shoulders while licking an ice cream cone. Mohawk points to a small inscription, sideways along the photo.

The Mighty Orphan. Active ages 3–14.

"Little is known about her origins," Mohawk says quietly. "Almost nothing. But we have our suspicions. And someday the truth will be told."

I touch the picture and feel a pull to this wunderkind.

"Look familiar?" he asks me.

Yes and no, these children with distant, delicate, stern faces.

"I feel we are on the verge of knowing more, much more, about this child of steel," he says. "Here, take a look at this one."

It's a poster, and the same girl is standing next to an enormous muscular woman, under a sign that says: *Bijou Theater, Hoboken.*

"Hoboken!" I am weirded out by this. "No way!"

Mohawk puts his finger to my lips and says, "Listen. Hear what the great strongmen and the iron ladies have to tell you. And observe. What do you see?"

That look. Those eyes. Like Nadia. I remember Steve's words:

That look in her eyes. That's it. You can spot it. Like that! Immediately. And after reading this, you'll be able to spot it anywhere. Trust me.

That's it. Just like he said. She's got it. But why? How?

Goddammit, Tina, you'll get all this when you read the manual. It's the mental training. The Bulgarians developed special mental exercises with the lifting.

Mohawk puts the big scrapbook on his lap and slips his fingers further into the book, to a section separated by a string. He points to a picture of this girl, older now, a teenager, with Georg Hackenschmidt himself. This little dudette got around, so it figures she would end up crossing paths with Grandma's Big Man.

"Listen, what else do you know about Hackenschmidt?" I say. "Did he have some secret potion or something, because it seems like he outlived a lot of these guys."

"Georg was ahead of his time," Mohawk says, "A man among men, timeless and of his time."

Oh. My. God. I want to smack some life into this dweeb. "And?" I say, with as much sarcasm as I can without pissing him off, but let's get to the point already.

"As I started to tell you before, Georg used his mighty willpower to control the very organs involved in digestion, not just the kidneys, but the liver, the pancreas and the gall bladder. Complete domination. He drank no alcohol except for absinthe. It is not proven, but we believe that to be true. And he made sure the absinthe was not taken too soon after the milk."

"What is absinthe?" I ask.

"The blue shit you all were drinking," he says. "So, anyway, one night Georg stuffs his notes – pages and pages of writing – into three burlap sacks, with some hay purposely sticking out of the top of the bags and disguises himself as a peasant farmer. He goes to a monastery in Bulgaria, where the kindly monks are drinking grog and the nuns are sitting on their laps telling knock-knock jokes and stroking their bald spots. The sight repulses Georg, but he does not waver in the quest to preserve his life's work. He convinces the monks to replicate this for the sake of civilization and their eternal souls. So they hid in their root cellar, copying the pages painstakingly while fending off marauding ex-Bolsheviks, the secret police, syphilitic prostitutes, and internecine strife among various monastic orders.

"And, not to digress, but you may be wondering why the monks agreed to this arduous task," he says, looking at me like he expects some kind of response.

"Well, I'll tell you," he says, lowering his voice in a pretentiously conspiratorial tone. "It is because their order was founded by surviving members of the paramilitary monastics known as the

Livonian Brothers of the Sword – Livonia, as you may remember, being Georg's birthplace. These warrior monks were defeated by the Samogitians and the Semigallians in the Battle of Saule in 1236 and a fragment fled and founded the monastery of which I speak."

"Excuse me," I say. "Did you say Samogitians? I had a Tamagotchi once. I didn't clean its poop and it died."

Mohawk frowns and says sternly: "Do not ever speak of the T word again, do you hear?" And he goes on with his story.

"The great Hackenschmidt dreamed of disseminating his work to the great populace as a gesture of divine reconciliation for the world. Sure enough, the monks sold a simplified version to the Reader's Digest Condensed Books in the 1950s to fund their sorely depleted pensions. This is the origin of what common gym rats call *The Bulgarian Training Manual*, but described among the cognoscenti as *The Secrets of the Bulgarians*.

"Wait. Are you telling me a Swedish-German guy in Estonia wrote the manual? Mass produced for mid-century Americans eating TV dinners?" I ask. "And what's this Russian Lion crap?" Wally's words *Dumme Schlampe* again come to mind, and I decide to end this line of questioning.

"Please. Much information for brain," says the frizzy babe, who I'm now thinking knows more English than she's letting on, and I'm sensing a little attitude, too. "Georg. Kind. Wise. Strong." She wipes her eyes with the back of her hand.

I hear faint sounds of music. *Kumbaya?*

Mohawk continues. "I did not say he *wrote* it, because such a book can't be authored in the normal sense. Rather, he brought it forth into the world, the inspired words of a great man, built on the sweat of sages and given manifestation today by a select few who carry The Truth.

"Hackenschmidt dared to put his training and his diet and his sexual proclivities onto the world's stage, so to speak, all the while fearing his book would be lost amid the onslaught of sexy new titles from Dale Carnegie, Napoleon Hill and Norman Vincent Peale, that they would quickly be remaindered back to his publisher, all of which could have played a part in his quest for a broader marketing platform, and..." Mohawk stops. "I lost my train of thought," he says.

"Something about being a multi-culti kind of guy," I say. "And sexual something or other."

"Yes," he says. "There you have it."

"That's it? And this has to do with me, how?"

Mohawk and the others look stricken, like I asked some kind of weird question. I mean, I'm thinking it's perfectly reasonable.

"Are you telling me that for Grandma, Georg was more than a long-distance fantasy, a coffee table fetish?"

Mohawk nods and closes the book. Now I'm sure these guys are taking me for a ride. I glance around for the Exit signs. There are none.

"Well, of course," Mohawk says, "It's obvious. You are his only direct descendant."

"Listen, dude," I say. "Grandma was born in Jersey City."

Mohawk lowers his voice and says, "The sad little girl, the one in the sailor shirt, taken from town to town? For many years, we did not know what became of her. Until now."

There is silence. Baba Yaga, now back as an old hag, a change I no longer find astonishing, clears her throat, a phlegmy growl, and spits the glob onto the floor.

I ignore this, and gaze into the early morning sun streaming through the windows. The light seems to wash over me, and I feel a great calm. I take a step back and look at the minions before me who have lost their way. I feel like they so want to be in this game. Baba Yaga nodding her head with a decrepit smile. I look her in the eye, and I feel myself standing straighter, taller.

I take in the tall brick walls, the peeling paint on ceiling, benches with torn vinyl, rusting rebar, a lat pull-down with a bungee cord holding the plates together. And beyond the doors, in the antechamber, the glowing computer screens, electrical cords hanging from the ceiling, rows and rows of shiny identical metal desks with their identical screen savers, the barbells disintegrating and then reappearing. I see a vending machine in the far corner of the gym, humming loudly, stacked with communion wafers in a dazzling array of flavors: honey-nut, cilantro-lime, salty sweat mocha. I imagine the gym back home, Julio at the desk, waiting to be enlightened. The dozens, the millions, the billions of overweight, underweight, cholesterol laden human beings with torn rotator cuffs from poor musculature and bad technique.

In my head, the barbell screen savers break up and re-emerge and

I sense a voice filling my soul, Dr. Sadlyer, speaking to me through the warm lights of the Hypno-Tan bed:

Remember the image of the little you looking up? Now, imagine you have the big you, looking down.

Just when it feels like this is all too much for my once puny, now firm, shoulders to bear, I feel a jolt from out of the blue, as they say. Can it be? Yes! It's Grandma, whacking me on the head with her loving words: "What da hell is wrong with you? Move yer ass."

I feel a tingling energy rising within me. I stretch and my right knee starts jiggling. I feel like I can stare down a gang of thugs, crack tree branches in my teeth, lift Grandma over my head with ease as the Olympic judges slam down 5 - 5 - 5 - 5 - 5 – all 5's. I can see it now. Perfect form, perfectly executed. The cheering crowds. The flag, the anthem. And Grandma, cheering me on. "Atta girl. Do what da hell ya want!"

A huge adrenaline rush surges through me. Gotta move. Gotta move! I clap my hands together and jump onto a bench.

"Listen up!" I shout. "You want that Ancient Gym, right? Yeah, you goddamn whiny motherfuckers! Let's rip this place apart!"

I hear booming rock music and this time, I'm not trying to figure out where it's coming from; this time, I am not connecting the dots. I am totally in the moment. My body is pulsating and Mohawk and the girls and the dweebs are sprinting in all directions, giving high fives.

Mohawk ascends a scaffold at the far end of the gym with a cordless microphone in his teeth. When he gets to the top, he pushes his shoulders back and lifts the microphone and his voice booms.

"Comrades! We are at the cusp of a great victory over oppression. Over corruption. Over weakness. Over fear. Over the forces that would keep us subjected to multinational plutocratic servitude and government-sanctioned organized crime and genetically engineered diet soda."

"Unfurl the banners," he orders, "in honor of our American heroine."

I glance around to make sure they're not talking about somebody else, but no, they are most certainly, absofuckinglutely, looking at me.

"Listen up," I yell, "behold the words of Conan the Republican, the great Terminator, the one and the only Pumping Iron hero of the planet: "Start wide, expand further *and never look back!*"

Then I hear a voice. That accent, that oh so familiar... oh... my...

god... Arnold? Is he here? Where? Is this a recording? A black and white image of a young Arnold doing a bicep curl with his muscles bulging out in all directions is projected onto the brick wall. Everyone gets totally quiet, and I catch my breath as I hear him say:

What we face may look insurmountable. But I learned something from all times when I didn't think I could lift another ounce. What I learned is we are always stronger than we know!!!

I remember reading that quote in one of the bodybuilding magazines. Is he plagiarizing himself? Is that even possible?

The resistance you fight in the gym is the resistance you fight in life!

Ok, but I happen to know that Arnold also has said, "My body is like breakfast, lunch and dinner. I don't think about it. I just have it." I know that quote because Big Steve had it silk-screened onto his gym shorts. In fact, a lot of guys liked that one. Once when I came in, Jose at the desk leaned over and, looking down my tank top in a way he shouldn't, said, "My body is like breakfast, lunch and dinner." I slammed down my bag and told him I'm a diet.

The Arnold voice stops, and a guy drags a huge ladder across the floor. The two girls are lifting benches and weights and carrying them to the middle of the gym. The littlest girl has a forty-pound dumbbell in her right hand and is resting it over her shoulder as she walks to the growing pile and I'm thinking how can that scrawny chick do that? Now, if these guys can just unglue their eyes from these fucking computers once and for all, they can just maybe be awesome.

The kid with the Mets cap on backwards - what I assume to be a pathetic attempt to look cool - carries in two five-gallon paint buckets and I'm wondering how they can possibly get stuff in here so fast.

One of the dweebs opens a plank in the floor and pulls out some vertical banners and starts handing them out to guys adjusting ladders along the walls next to the giant iron windows. One after another they are fastened and unfurled.

Georg Hackenschmidt. Louis Cyr.

I am thinking this would be so cool to do in the gym at home instead of just pictures torn from bodybuilding magazines taped on the walls. They got some good shit here.

Sandwina. Arnold Schwarzenegger. Big Steve.

Wait. What?

I look around the room and there he is, in the back corner, looking smug, his arms across his chest. Steve points to the front of the room and I turn back around and there on the next banner is a gigantic picture of me, yeah, me, and my face feels hot and tingly. Where the hell did they get that and why didn't anyone tell me? My hair looks amazing, flowing thick and wavy, falling over one eye. I'm pretty sure this is one of the pictures Steve took when he was teaching me how to pose. But that bod! How? There I am wearing those dorky striped Lycra shorts that I always thought made my ass look too big, but in this picture, this banner, it follows the curve of every muscle. Hell, that's not a soft cellulite ass; they're glutes, cut and firm in the way that says power and strength and, yes, say it – Beauty! Form! Discipline!

I look in the mirror and hit the same pose and notice that my arms are bigger, my waist is smaller.

I pull off my t-shirt and fling it to the floor, standing in my sports bra and shorts and sneakers and then I stretch my arms out wide, the way I practiced in the locker room when nobody was around.

I curl my fingers into fists and pull my forearms in from the elbows, lifting the elbows higher as I squeeze, and two peaks rise on my biceps. I twist my upper body from one side to the other. Legs firm and strong. The music is getting louder, and the dweebs are screaming and cheering like they've just seen a rock star.

I am.

I am!

I am - what?

I hear Big Steve murmur, "Just go with the flow." He is standing next to me now.

I grab the microphone and look out over my people and shout, "Breakfast! Lunch! Dinner! I get your pain. I know what it's like to go from mac and cheese to *cordon bleu* and back. But no more! Think strong. Think… Think…! No! No! Don't think. Just do it! Do. It. *Now!*"

THE THREE LOMBARDIS

————

The fairy tale, the myth, and the divine comedies of redemption. These, in the ancient world, were regarded as of a higher rank than tragedy, of a deeper truth, of a more difficult realization, of a sounder structure, and of a revelation more complete.

The happy ending of the fairy tale, the myth, and the divine comedy of the soul is to be read... as a transcendence of the universal tragedy of man. The objective world remains what it was, but, because of a shift of emphasis within the subject, is beheld as though transformed... as indifferent to the accidents of time as water boiling in a pot is to the destiny of the bubble."

JOSEPH CAMPBELL *A HERO WITH A THOUSAND FACES*
(1949)

————

A SONG TO REMEMBER

It's been a week since what I like to think of as "the big day," and I've been training like crazy in the ancient gym – without air conditioning, I might add. And on some days, without electricity. Two hours at a time, three times a day, following *The Bulgarian Training Manual* as closely as I can.

Back in Jersey, the very idea of this would seem impossible for anyone except a fanatic with no life and a gullible, addictive personality, someone who needed step-by-step instructions on how to live each waking moment. Someone like – Big Steve?

Now, I have a different conclusion.

Even with all the convoluted charts, graphs, lists, recipes, and workout routines, there's something I can't put my finger on that isn't spelled out on the page. I don't mean a missing chapter. More like some unfinished business. Of which there seems to be a lot in my life, but let's not go there.

That picture of Hackenschmidt, the way he looked at the camera. He knew. I don't know what he knew, but he knew. Baba Yaga knows, too, but she ain't telling. Grandma would know, but she's not here to tell.

I have so many questions.

·Why am I not totally bat-shit crazy by now and exhausted from lifting?

·Why am I not puking my guts out after scarfing down black-bean brownies sprinkled with crushed communion wafers or banana-wheatgrass shakes with chopped quail embryos?

·Hackenschmidt drank great quantities of milk, yet I am lactose intolerant. What does this mean?

·Back home, just having the freaking manual in my gym bag made me feel stronger, even on days when I sat on my ass and ate donuts. Is this a coincidence? Or was it psychosomatic? Or could it be biosemiotic, a fucking awesome paradigmatic shift in the mind-body realm, where the synthesis of donuts is blocked by more profound forces?

·I have learned that Big Steve has memorized all the lines from *Viva Las Vegas.* How is this possible?

·Why *Viva Las Vegas?* Does he have bad taste in movies?

·If so, why not *Love, Actually?*

·Is it something about Ann-Margret?

·Mohawk's favorite movie is *Bye, Bye Birdie.* Could there be a cosmic connection?

·Why did he reveal this to me?

I've been staring at Georg's picture at night, searching for answers.

I took it from the scrapbook. I convinced Mohawk to let me have it in exchange for a cut on whatever drugs Joe Fox brings back, assuming he ever comes back, because I haven't seen that fuckin' dude since we arrived. At this point, I don't care if he is *shtupping* the Fraulein all over Bulgaria, as long as he eventually comes back and takes us home. But not yet. There's more to do. And things are looking up.

I'm still staying with the Germans, but they've stopped talking about me as an ingredient in their noodle pudding and they leave me alone. In fact, Waltraud seems goddamn deferential, and she has put a framed photo of Schwarzenegger on the mantel next to the candy canes. She points to it when I come and go, which I manage to do as quickly as possible. Eddie's been giving me a lift into town. I sense Wally doesn't approve, but that's her problem.

Oh, and I hooked Steve up with the little apple-cheeked lady, who rented him a little bed in a little room in her little house on her little street, instead of the roach motel Joe Fox put him in.

TALK, TALK, TALK

I am goddamned fucking famous.

Yes, I am.

Famous.

At least famous here, which is better than not being famous at all.

I was on TV twice last week and I'm scheduled for another TV show tomorrow morning, and now, like right now, in a few minutes, a radio station wants to talk to me, my third radio interview of the day. And it's only 9 o'clock in the morning. Everyone has heard about me and Steve and the gym and whatnot. The next one is in what, 15 minutes? Yup. 9:15 AM. Then 10 AM, then 11:30 AM, then 4 PM, or 1600 whatever, because in Bulgaria they do military time, left over from when they were dominated by the Ruskies, and I have to check my schedule to see what other times. It's so cool. Way, way cool to be famous.

I'm standing up and pacing the floor with the phone. They say people sound better standing. Charlene back at the office had these Tony Robbins CDs which she made a big deal of because she traded in her cassettes in for CDs because even she knows nobody has cassette tapes. "Hey, how about mp3s?" I asked her, and she got mad, and I think I might have hurt her feelings but what the hell. I mean, I have no patience for people like that. Anyway, she let us sign out the CDs like signing out the keys. Such a production. But the point is, I remember Tony saying posture counts in public speaking and in life in general, which is what Big Steve always says, about life, not public speaking. He's very quiet.

So, anyway, the deal here is people call in to the radio and I talk in English and some guy translates back and forth in Bulgarian or whatever. They all want to know about the gym. Sort of. Sometimes they ask questions that have nothing to do with the gym or training. Sometimes it gets a little too personal. But that's the price of fame.

Maybe when I get home I'll get my own reality show. Better yet, a TV talk show. I would like that. I'll be the host. Something like, I don't know, The View, or whatever, where you get a bunch of chicks talking about whatever. Or better yet, forget the morning, I'm talking prime time. I'll be the next Letterman. No, Johnny Carson. Something classy.

Omigod. The phone. It's the host.

CALLER: Tina?

ME: That's me.

CALLER: What is your favorite color?

ME: I like all colors, and I respect every person's choice of color, but I think blue would be my personal favorite if it is like a royal blue, as opposed to a sky blue, or robin's egg blue or gray blue or navy blue. Why do you ask?

CALLER: I like green.

ME: That's your problem.

HOST: Let's try another call.

CALLER: How do you feel about the privatization of gyms, the corruption at government sports federations and what would you do to reform it if you could?

ME: Can you repeat the question?

HOST: Next caller is Ludwig from Latvia.

CALLER: Thanks for taking my call.

ME: Hi Ludwig. Is it a coincidence that your country and your name both start with L?

CALLER: Please don't tell anyone.

ME: Promise. You have a question?

CALLER: My question is in two parts. One, how can wheatgrass be gluten free? And two, do you recommend it as a supplement? And three, is it better in powdered or liquid form?

ME: Yeah, can you believe it? Wheatgrass is gluten-free. I remember an episode on the food channel where a chef added it to hamburger. It contains chlorophyll, vitamins and enzymes.

CALLER: So does my lawn. What's the difference?

ME: Photosynthesis. The ancient Egyptians loved wheatgrass, and they lived in the desert. Go figure.

HOST: Olga is on the line. She wants to talk about Hoboken.

ME: No shit! Hoboken! That's a subject I know a lot about. Am I allowed to say the word "shit" on the radio here? Do you bleep words out?

HOST: Doesn't matter. Most of our listeners don't speak English. We translate as we see fit.

ME: Cool.

HOST: Cold?

ME: No, just cool. So, Olga, what do you want to know about Hoboken?

CALLER: First, I speak English. I come from ancient city of Plovidiv. My mamma very old lady and she tell me story of strongman and acrobat who perform at Theater Bijou in Hoboken. This is true, da?

ME: Yes, there was a theater in Hoboken, the Bijou, with circus acts and feats of strength. Back in the day. But I don't know much else about it.

CALLER: Mamma here with me, listening to radio. She not speak English. She say she think you know something. What? No. *Mamochka*, no. Cannot interrupt lady. Mamma, ok. No. Uh, so sorry. Mamma want to get on the phone. She not hear good. This is ok?

ME: Okay.

CALLER: Mamma not speak English. No. Mamma stop. I explain. She say she old, but she in circus, travel to America, and she remember child of strongman and strongwoman. They give her to acrobats. Girl feed elephants. You know this girl?

ME: No.

CALLER: Okay. Thank you very much. Mamma please. Leave lady alone. Mamma! Thank you.

HOST: That's all we have time for this morning folks.

CALLER: Excuse me. Mamma want to talk. Mamma say you know this girl. She is friend to elephant and other circus animal. Girl very strong. Marry carpet installer. They have nice carpet in New Jersey. She keep picture. Wall to wall. You know this?

ME: What?

CALLER'S MOTHER: *Kakvo se sluchi s instalatora na kilim? Toi beshe mnogo krasiv. Momiche e prostitutka!!*

CALLER: She ask you. Hoboken. Is still good place? Nice carpet? Good place to retire? You see Ringling Brothers? Mamma, no more. Please. We have nice carpet, too. No need to move to New Jersey. We stop bothering the lady.

YOU PARENTS NOT YOU PARENTS

Here at the ancient gym, soft, skinny arms are showing signs of development, and the dweebs are standing taller. The Beast seems to be shampooing her hair because now her ponytail has bounce and sheen, and her oily T is no more. Shearling keeps coming around for no discernable purpose. Today, he seems fixated on the formerly greasy-haired ponytail girl, who is sitting on a pile of mats reading a book. Yeah, reading. These guys don't hang out and shoot the shit between sets like they do in Jersey.

"Can you tell what she has? Goethe, maybe?" he asks me while my knees are bent on the squat rack. I grit my teeth, push through my heels until my knees lock and take a deep breath.

"No. Maya Angelou," I tell him. "She's been translating it."

"Ah, yes, the caged bird," he says. "We are all caged by our histories, by our collective consciousness, the grave of dreams."

"Don't kid yourself," I say, racking the bar. "She found it at the flea market. In a trash bin." I wipe my face with the towel. It's stifling in here today, not even a warm breeze from the windows and doors, which are all wide open. But I am determined to fight through it.

I move to the bench press, feeling juiced and thinking maybe today I will top my personal best, which is now an amazing 115 pounds, up from 65 just a few weeks ago. Just one rep at 125, that's all I'm looking for right now, and any more will be icing on the cake, to use a hugely overused cliché, which nonetheless seems right for the moment.

It is said that in weight training, the quickest gains come in the beginning, the first few weeks, if you train with intensity. Then you plateau and feel like the walking dead. That's where the mental toughness comes in. Plowing ahead when it ain't easy. Big Steve used to tell me this back home and I never took it seriously. Thought he made this stuff up. He didn't. He just stole it from the Bulgarians.

I secure the plates on the rebar. I lie down, tighten my abs and dig in my feet. One. Two. Three, push. Maybe, just maybe. As I strain to lift the crushing weight on the bar - steady, steady - I glimpse a face in the window on the far wall. It's there. And gone. Breaks my concentration completely. I rack the bar on a low rung and sit up. There it is. Again. It's that Catherine chick from the church, and she is motioning for me to come outside. I don't want to because I'm in the zone and freaked out by the fact that she is here.

I drop my towel on the bench, grab my water bottle and head out the back door. I squint in the hot sun and find her standing primly in the middle of the parking lot with purple and pink flowers in her hair, like an emaciated fairy princess.

"What's up?" I say. "You want a guest pass?" I figure she probably feels the urge to spend a few hours on a StairMaster, you know, burn more calories. Except we don't have a StairMaster. Just a broken-down treadmill. Fuck it. She can use the jump rope.

"You must kill him," she tells me.

Uh, wait, what?

"He lured me from my home and took advantage of my circumstances," she says.

"Who the fuck are you talking about?" I say.

"Don't use foul language!"

I look around. Nobody but us.

"Did you ever see your mother?" she asks me.

"She died when I was a baby," I say.

"Oh yeah?" she says haughtily. "Where is the grave?"

I can't imagine where this is leading, so I play along. "There is no grave," I say. "That's what Grandma told me."

"That's what the old bag told you, eh?" she says with extreme sarcasm.

In the sunshine, without the candles in the church, her skin looks pasty, even crepey, with lines around the eyes and neck. I cross my arms over my chest, the old don't-fuck-with-me pose, a.k.a. the don't-let-anyone-see-you're-freaked-out pose. I lean on a red Fiat parked in the handicapped spot. The metal feels hot against my ass, but I don't let on.

"Look, I'm from Jersey," I say. "You can't bullshit the bullshitter. So cut the crap and tell me what you're after."

I stand firm as she moves closer, crowding my space. She bends delicately and peers into the driver's side mirror of the Fiat. What's up with this? I scan the parking lot for accomplices, but I see no one.

She inspects her forehead, squeezes a pimple and then licks her fingers. I tell myself not to get too grossed out. That this must be some kind of mind game. Toughness rules even under extreme grossness. An image comes to mind. Rachel Ray, perky, smiling, overweight. Didn't she say St. Catherine drank the pus of the sick?

And how could she possibly know Grandma? I conclude that this is an attempt at character assassination meant to rattle me. The old take-out! For what reason, I have no idea. But I will not, under any circumstances, be rattled. Unless she tries to eat a green booger. Please God, don't let her do that.

She straightens up and looks at me with hatred in her liquid blue eyes. "Stop calling your immediate progenitor by the ridiculous moniker of 'Grandma.' That battle-ax squandered her share on elite hyaluronic acid, Retinol-A and hydrating serums smuggled from Uma Thurman's facialist in a fruitless attempt to counter the effects of booze."

This is cutting a little close to home, home being more than Jersey City, but that place in my gut, the stale smell of beer, our front stoop, the purple bruises on Grandma's arms. I try to remember what 'progenitor' means. It's on the edge of my brain. Catherine looks at me blankly. The word "vacuous" comes to mind. So does "vapid." And "legerdemain." I do not know why SAT words are popping into my head. And why 'progenitor' eludes me. Why am I thinking in hoity toity prose instead of my favorite clichés, which, after all, wouldn't have become clichés in the first place if they weren't useful. Maybe it's the clean European air. Maybe it's the company I am keeping. Maybe it's something I read. The manual?

I turn my attention back to this waif of wickedness. She raises her right eyebrow, independent of the left, a trait that I happen to share, and flares her nostrils. I wonder if we share any other genetically transmitted traits. I seriously hope she is not a relative. I'm thinking maybe she's bluffing. Yes! A naked play! I test my theory: "So, if you're such an expert on Grandma, tell me: Why Budweiser instead of Heineken or Corona or Yuengling or some exotic Belgian suds brewed by Trappist monks like Chimay Bleue?"

"How the hell should I know?" she says. "Maybe it was the price. Maybe because it was made in America. She couldn't stand the krauts, you know, or the Belgians. She called them Waffle Turds."

Waffle Turds? I never heard Grandma utter those words. As a point of fact, there are no Belgian people in Jersey City, at least not in my neighborhood. This bitch has to be a total fraud.

"So, assuming this is true," I tell her, "that Grandma despised Belgians for no discernable reason, that she directed a peculiar ethno-political bile toward the dim-witted inventors of the waffle, a Belgianophobia manifested in a spurning of their ale, what else do you know?"

"You were an ugly baby," she says.

It occurs to me that I have never seen a picture of myself as a baby. Was I so hideous that the offensive images were destroyed to protect me? She pulls a picture from her bodice. It is a photo of a little girl with a round face, sparkling eyes, and dimples.

"I was beautiful!!!" I exclaim, with multiple extraneous exclamation points to add emphasis and drama.

"Not you" she says abruptly. "Me."

Ouch.

"So, tell me this," I ask her. "Did you ever meet my father? Is he really a plumbing tycoon in Texas?"

"Rich, yes. Plumber, no. And no, he is not in Texas and never was, you ugly, stupid wench. Your father is a misogynistic plutocrat living off the smoldering ashes of his narcissistic past as the sun sets on Muscle Beach."

Maybe I should just punch her lights out.

"He speaks with a pretentious Viennese accent, if you know what I mean. And your so-called Vladimir, his main man, is using you," she says, "to strengthen his connections to a déclassé coterie of West Coast politicians, East Coast financiers, red-carpet liberals and red-necked bikers." She raises her dress and points to a small dimple in her thigh.

"Do you think this is cellulite?" she asks.

"I don't know," I say. "Could be."

Catherine's eyes redden and she bursts into tears, flinging herself over the hood of the Fiat. She is sobbing and coughing. Omigod, how high maintenance. I feign empathy.

"Look, maybe it's not cellulite," I reassure her. "Maybe it's just a, well, a dimple, like you have on your face, only it's migrated to your thigh. A dimple is nothing. An irregular dominant trait controlled by a single gene. No biggie." She straightens herself up and tries to hug me. I back away. My preservation instinct tells me that homicide may be an immediate concern.

"So, what's your gripe with Vladimir?" I ask.

"He dumped me when he found you, and I do not react well to rejection," she says.

"And that's why you want to kill him?"

"No!" she says. "I want *you* to kill him. It will be infinitely more humane. Otherwise, I will be compelled to stick a letter opener through his ear and carve out his brain. I will gather the girls to break our fast and eat his entrails."

Too much information. I want to suggest anger management therapy or maybe Dr. Sadlyer. A little Hypno-Tan chill. My knee is jiggling involuntarily, and I feel a migraine coming on. Maybe it's the letter opener. I close my eyes and drink more water. I suddenly figure out the meaning of *immediate progenitor*.

"Are you suggesting my grandmother is my mother?" I ask, "and that Rusty G was a hoax? That the miserable asshole I thought of as Grandpa was an imposter, a violent fuckwit shacking up with Grandma, who was really my own mother, while my actual, real, honest to goodness biological father was enjoying steak tartare with the Kennedys?"

She smiles and nods.

I am thinking this bitch is full of shit. I grab her bony shoulders. "If Grandma ain't Grandma, then who is Grandma?" I demand.

"The Mighty Orphan," I hear a man say. I turn and I see the Escargot Cowboy himself, sitting on the hood of his jeep in the parking lot. When did he get here? And how? I didn't hear anyone pull into the lot. Beyond him, where the parking lot meets the forest, I catch a glimpse of Baba Yaga, this time in her robe and cane. She laughs, waves and scoots behind a dumpster.

"You remember The Mighty Orphan," he says, "from the scrapbook?"

Yes, in fact, I do. The girl with the dark eyes.

"Let's cut to the chase," I tell Cowboy. "How do you guys know all this about me? What's up with you and the crazy ho? You two are fucking with my head, and I swear to God, I will find out why."

At the mention of "God," Catherine gasps. Cowboy hops off the jeep and walks toward me, in a slow, sexy gait. He tips his hat to shade his eyes.

"Your mother, that is to say the woman who you've been calling Grandma," Cowboy says, "met up with us when you were a self-absorbed teenager paying little attention to the events outside your bedroom. Through our shared Bulgarian-Teutonic-Hoboken connections, which I'm not getting into now, we cooked up a scheme to dominate the resurgent Lava Lamp trade. Eastern European villagers had a head start making high-quality lamps, getting hard currency for them on the black market. Bulgaria. Romania. Yes, even Estonia and Latvia. But they had few raw materials and rival gangs were smashing production lines in petty feuds.

"We were put in touch with quote-unquote Grandma by a mutual connection, and quote-unquote Grandma found a bunch of people from the hood to manufacture them for us in great numbers and colors. Orange and red, of course, because they were the most popular. But we also had chartreuse, tickle-me-pink, indigo, and burnt sienna.

"Finally, the day came to deliver the lamps to Port Newark, to a container that would be sent to Istanbul and transferred to a network of smugglers utilizing what was left of the heroin trail through Turkey. It was perfect. At the appointed time, Catherine and I flew to America to pick up the stash and get it on board. We stood to make a killing on this, with mammoth distribution and licensing deals in place."

"So, how come we aren't all very rich?" I ask. A reasonable question.

"The delivery date to Port Newark coincided with the Mr. Universe pageant which, in a bizarre confluence of events, was being held at the same time as the World Wrestling Federation championship and the New Jersey Golden Gloves final. A strongman trifecta! Your quote-unquote Grandma had stockpiled enough beef jerky and beer for the whole block, and the whole block did turn up and stayed until she'd passed out cold and slept it off for two days.

"When Catherine and I showed up at Port Newark, the place was crawling with KGB, Darzhavna Sigurnost, FEMA, and Interpol, and your quote-unquote Grandma was nowhere to be found. We assumed she skipped town, and we headed back empty-handed."

I can't take anymore.

"I wasn't an ugly baby!" I say defiantly.

Catherine gets in my face. "You're even uglier than your quote-unquote Grandma! Your arms, my God—those arms! Cover them up!"

"You mean this?" I ask, flexing my biceps.

"Disgusting," she says, averting her eyes.

"No," I say. "It's pure muscle. I will make Hackenschmidt proud."

"He's dead, girl," she says.

"No! He lives. He lives in the gym, every time a Hack squat is performed. He lives in the psyche of anyone who has seen those innocent eyes, pure in thought and deed. The great Hackenschmidt lives."

"Stop!" she screams. "Just stop. Do not ever utter that name again. Ever."

"What? Hackenschmidt?"

She puts her hands over her ears and starts singing, perfectly in tune:

Don't it feel like the wind is always howlin'?
Don't it seem like there's never any light?

"Wait! Wait! Don't tell me. 'The Hard Knock Life,'" I say, pleased with my superior ability to name a tune.

She looks at me in shock. And her face, at first just ghostly, turns a whiter shade of pale. Never understood that song until now. Funny how things connect in the most unexpected ways.

"Hackenschmidt!" I repeat, a little louder: "Hackenschmidt! Hackenschmidt!"

Next thing I know, she's running through the parking lot, hangs a sharp right around a bunch of shrubs and she's gone. Vanished. Jeez. I think I need to go home. Or at least back inside the gym, because at this point, home is relative. I feel shaky, but I am determined to keep my cool. My mind wanders to the manual, Page 437:

We are masters of our fate, captains of our soul. A mantra repeated eight times per day in the holy tradition of the lauds and vespers of the mother church. Words marketed blasphemously as motivational self-talk, words attributed to Zig Zigler who, in fact, knew it to be wisdom passed down from generations, before the Ancient Gym had arisen in the land, and then, incorporated in Bulgaria as part of the mind-strengthening regimen for the most elite athletes of the 20th century.

I am not sure how I thought of this particular excerpt at this particular moment, but I know for sure that, until today, I never saw a Lava Lamp in my past, present or future.

We are masters of our fate, captains of our soul.

I feel like something about all this is making sense, but I can't figure out how A is to B which is to C which is to B and, fuck it.

"What's with you and this Catherine chick?" I say.

"Nothing," he says. "It's all nothing. Bad breakup."

I sit on the curb and put my head in my hands. A picture comes to mind. Estonia in the winter, even though I have never been there. Those photos of Hackenschmidt. The little girl with dark eyes. Proud men with waxed mustaches and Amazon women in corsets, freaks peering into the future, only to grow old and die. To fade. Maybe I'm just overly stressed. But why? Am I rationalizing? Yes, I am rationalizing, a self-protective psychological reaction to external stresses of things unknown or not easily explained, having encountered once again, moments ago, a person channeling St. Catherine of Siena who has by the power of persuasion or otherwise, found kindred spirits who have taken up residence in a church in Bulgaria, desecrated my childhood memories, and attempted to de-stabilize my fragile ego by shattering the myths I have clung to and in doing so, to brain-wash me into thinking I was a homely child. No, I will not be reduced to rationalizing. I will not be co-dependent on myself. I am strong. I am powerful. I am coolness beyond measure. And these people who don't mean anything to me, they just might mean everything. Might. Mean. Everything. I inhale deeply, and exhale and look up.

The Escargot Cowboy is leaning against the pickup, chewing on a sprig of arugula and staring at me.

"Trauma can result from stress that exceeds one's ability to cope or integrate the emotions involved with that experience," he says gently.

"Everyone is vulnerable to this condition," I say, "but elite Bulgarian athletes have trained themselves to deflect it rapidly. Effective methods include primal screams while swinging kettle bells or ingesting communion wafers sublingually while focusing on the image of a cerulean sky."

Indeed, the sunshine feels warm and tingly on my face.

"The missing chapter, the chapters yet to be written," he says. "The way it all connects with the whole. It is your inheritance. It is in your DNA. There was a powerful mantra used by Jim Morrison, who discovered its curative powers from a Bulgarian roadie: 'You cannot petition the Lord with prayer.' Unfortunately, he wasted this wise saying on a provocative song and ended up in Pere Lachaise. *C'est la vie.*"

"*La vie en rose,*" I say.

"Yes, and *carpe diem,* too. It is the wisdom of the ages speaking to us, through you. I'll bet you never saw pictures of your quote-unquote Grandma when she was young, or her mother's mother," he says. The man has a point. "And those muscle magazines she kept under the coffee table all those years, can you recognize a common theme? Think about it."

"Omigod. All of them had Arnold on the cover," I tell him.

My breath comes rapidly, and I struggle to stand. I am in a full-blown existential crisis. The gypsy lady on the plane told me: "*You parents not you parents.*" I am trying hard to connect the dots, but they are ricocheting in my mind like a pinball machine. I focus my concentration on what's before me, here, right here, in the sweltering parking lot of the Ancient Gym, on the outskirts of some two-bit town in Bulgaria, where some protean locals are playing mind games. I stare hard at Cowboy.

"I asked Grandma about Arnold once, when I was a kid. Her words were: 'He's a bum. On da juice. Eh. Not like da old days. Dem days is gone.' I said to her, 'But Grandma, he is a cybernetic organism.' And you know what she told me? She said, 'Kid, dese is da woids to live by: Anger is more useful than despair.' In my cluelessness, I did not realize, until now, that she was quoting from *Terminator 3: Rise of the Machines,* and in a totally personalized context."

I'm now thinking in overdrive. How about Hackenschmidt?

Where does he fit into the picture? If not Grandma's crush, then what? I remember Mohawk's words: *"Well, of course. It's obvious. You are his only direct descendant."*

Direct descendant. Okay – he died before I was born so that rules out me being his kid. But, if we go up, say, one generation? Could it be the man in the Speedo who quote-unquote-Grandma pined for all her life was really her very own father? My grandfather? Who travelled the world and barely gave her the time of day? An Oedipal pattern she repeated with Arnold? Was my mother, like her mother before her, tethered to narcissistic, unavailable, over-achieving men with spectacular bodies? Come to think of it, am I? Or is none of this the least bit true? Is lust for pulchritudinous men an inherited trait, like the ability to raise one eyebrow? Is it sheer coincidence that Catherine does this, too? Is the insertion of pretentious words like pulchritudinous into my thought process the result of the antediluvian masters inhabiting this Ancient Gym, speaking to me through the manual, or are they guiding the hand of chapters unwritten? Am I destined to fulfill my dream of having my own reality TV show? Or a Laundromat with mounds of quarters so high I'll need to take a backhoe to the bank? A condo of my own with floor to ceiling windows and a swimming pool and a doorman? And from my balcony, will I wave to my adoring fans like Mussolini, or shock the world like Yukio Mishima while paparazzi jostle for position? The choice is mine. I take a deep breath and another swig of water. And another, and then pour the whole fucking bottle over my head.

"Tina," Cowboy says. "The Great Sandwina. She was in Hoboken. At the Bijou. From the shadows to the spotlight. The strongmen. The iron ladies. Migrating from Bulgaria, Germany, Estonia, to America and back, through a century of repressed collective memories. It's not just Hackenschmidt. You know this, don't you?"

The metaphorical post-modern collective consciousness, unfolding, unfading, from black, white and brown to Technicolor, Dorothy stepping into Oz and Alice eating the cake that made her ginormous. I feel a rush like downing Dexedrine, ephedrine and a triple espresso all at once. My right knee is jiggling uncontrollably. I run back inside the gym and adjust my eyes to the darkness. I see nothing but the bench with my towel, exactly as I left it in what seems like a lifetime ago. I pull a 45-pound plate off the rack and shove it on the rusted bar. And then another. Quarters. Tens. Fives. I feel a rage that won't go away. I lie down and curl my fingers around the cold black rebar. I press my lower back into the vinyl padding and hoist the bar off the rack. It's heavy, crushingly heavy and my arms are trembling. I can barely breathe. I unlock my elbows. Slowly, very slowly, I bring it down, down, down within two inches of my chest. I squeeze my eyes closed, set my jaw, inhale and push with everything I've got. *Control the rep. Control the rep.* For a moment I feel a twinge of panic, and then I regain my resolve. *Control the rep.* I will not fail. I cannot fail. *Keep going. Keep going.* I imagine again the scene in my head from the Olympics. The 5's. The judges. The cards popping up. *Keep going. You got it.* Four, three, two, one and my elbows are locked straight again. My arms start to quiver, and I clench my teeth so hard it hurts. In the nick of time, I feel someone lifting the bar and setting it back on the rack. I hear clapping. I open my eyes and see Big Steve.

"Two hundred thirty-five pounds." Steve says. "More than twice your body weight. How the hell did you do that?" He smiles.

I look at him and shake my head.

"I don't know," I whisper.

"Muscles have memory," he says. "Wait till next time."

AABBA

"Your modesty is a disguise for your prescient soul."

It's Shearling. I'm still on the bench and he's standing a little too close. Steve has gone back to the "office" with Mohawk, and I sense that they're watching us.

Shearling very dramatically cups his right hand over his ear and says: "Listen! The groans of the dead poets have stopped. It is a new era in our land. The prophecies have come to pass."

Ok, so the dude stopped hearing voices. Sometimes, quiet is just, well, quiet. But I don't tell him that. Wouldn't want to bust his fantasy. Instead, with a feigned naiveté, I respond, "Why do you say that?" and wipe my face and neck with a towel.

"When I was a boy, my grandfather took me to the bazaar after Ramadan. There were lanterns and figs and stalls selling Tamagotchis. Grandfather was wearing a red fez, and when he lifted me into his arms, I grabbed the black tassel and thought someday I too will have one."

"Same kind you're wearing?" I ask, hoping to find some crumb of significance.

"No, mine is gray. Just gray."

Do I denote sadness?

"Your grandfather," I ask, "did he write poetry?"

Shearling looks startled.

"You may have heard people say that he was a master of the limerick. There are even those who say he was an ardent fan of the pun. These vicious rumors caused me great humiliation."

My mind flashes back to Our Ladies of Victories. I struggled but could never master the AABBA rhyme scheme under pressure. It was only at home, at night, with the white noise of wrestling on the TV that I could muster anything at all, liberating a mind tormented by "Waterloo" and "Dancing Queen."

Shearling grabs my wrist. He's usually so cool and suave like, I don't know, an enigma. Yes, an enigma. But now, it looks like he's busting a gut.

"My grandfather escaped his literary enemies with the help of an extraordinary dark-haired girl – they say she was The Mighty Orphan – who led him to this very village, where he cultivated the artistic expression of a cadre of avant-garde warriors with immense physical prowess. They aestheticized violence to bring down the emerging capitalist state and replace it with anarchic artisanal creativity. When they were pressured into subjugation by the Soviet state, he took off for Sofia to redirect them with a post-modernist sensibility long before it became fashionable. And that was the last anyone saw of him, except for this."

He pulls a Wrigley's Spearmint Gum wrapper from his pocket.

"I felt his presence the moment I found this on the window ledge of a Kentucky Fried Chicken in Kazakhstan. You see, I had just walked over to a window seat with my extra crispy chicken tenders, which I would not have ordered if I hadn't encountered a hawker giving away discount coupons three blocks away. Of more than 21,000 KFCs worldwide, why the one in Kazakhstan? That was six years ago, and I knew I was destined to carry on his dream."

"There is synchronicity in the universe," I tell him. "Everything happens for a reason. You were meant to receive that coupon at the exact moment when you had cravings for something hot, salty, and crisp. And then, the sunshine by the window drew you over, where you sat by the ledge with the wrapper. I'm telling you. This is how movements are made, how the world can be changed."

He presses the wrapper into the palm of my hand. I open it and I see gibberish scribbled in blue ink.

"It means, *'Don't worry. Be happy,'*" Shearling says. "Words from an Indian mystic, preserved by my grandfather. And now, I pass them on to you."

THE THREE LOMBARDIS

———

When he flexes, he expands like a rippled blowfish. The front of his thighs are something a balloon artist with too many balloons might create. His arms look like gnarled oak. His relatively narrow shoulders, once a drawback, are broad knots of deltoids and trapeziuses. His back is a relief map...

People sometimes walk up and touch him, as if unsure if he is a man or a machine. What they do not realize is that beneath the stony exterior and self-assuredness is a squishy sense of anxiety and vulnerability. Heath gets nervous every time he strips to his posing trunks. He is rarely satisfied with what he sees in the mirror. He is persistently worried about imperfections others might find, too.

FROM PROFILE OF PHIL HEATH, SIX-TIME MR. OLYMPIA, BY JOHN BRANCH, *NEW YORK TIMES*, OCT 28, 2016

———

THE PRICE OF FABULOUSNESS

Steve motions for me to come inside the "office." He has sheet-rocked over a decrepit corner, painted it white, and dragged in a desk and a computer that no one uses. He appointed the dweebs "trainers in training" and gave them T-shirts to prove it. Steve says a real gym needs an office and a staff. Without this, he says, a gym is just a warehouse with weights.

"It's the look," Steve says, "the impression of something important." I have to agree on that point. If it doesn't look important, is it important?

Anyway, I go into the office and there's Mohawk eating acai berries with Steve. It smells like tuna fish, and I notice they've left empty cans in the wastebasket. Mohawk offers me some and I pass.

"I never mix fruit and fish," I tell him.

Mohawk seems nonplussed. This is, by the way, one of my favorite French words, spelled *nonplussed* but pronounced non-ploo-say. You would think the French would spell it *nonplussait*, like parfait. More elegant that way. But hey, some things are out of my control.

"Don't give me any non-ploo-say attitude," I tell him. If I'm royalty here, I may as well talk the part. Mohawk seems unfazed.

"As they say in the old country," he says, raising his palms, "Then, if for my love, thou my love receivest. I cannot blame thee, for my love thou usest."

He winks at Big Steve.

I stare, pokerfaced, at the two of them smiling at each other. I am not sure what to say, except that I know a good *plussait* when I hear one. But I'm not about to let on. I'm still on a high from my big lift.

Mohawk takes my hand, which I find a little presumptuous, especially since his hands are sticky from eating berries. I pull away.

"There is something about me you must know," he says earnestly. Too earnestly.

"I am the co-founder of the National Federation for the Prevention of Plagiarism and Corporal Corruption, also known as the NFPPCC." He bites his lip and looks at Steve. I give him my "what the fuck" attitude. If there's one thing I've figured out here, it's this: there's an attitude for everything. It will keep you safe, command respect, and get you where you want to go. Sometimes.

"NFP what? Is that like NLP? Because if it is, that's nothing new."

"Never mind the acronym," Mohawk says. "There is more, but this is not the time. Brussels has criticized our country for failing to prosecute those who will use copyrighted material, disseminate puerile poetry, and cheat with banned substances that enhance creativity and physical prowess. But we are intent on creating a new world model. Our domination of sport and art will be unsurpassed. And you will be part of this."

"He wants to be your spokesman," Steve explains. "Your agent, your PR guy, your branding executive."

"You heard me on the radio," I say. "They love me. I don't need an agent."

"Listen up, we could take this so much further," Steve says. "Intellectual heft. Physical prowess. Agility. Grace. Beauty. Your pedigree. God, Tina, just look in the mirror. We could leverage you."

"What's in it for me?" I ask. "And what's his cut? And yours?"

The price of fame. Everybody wants to talk business. Even my friends.

"Think about it," I tell them. "Meanwhile, I got work to do, like the song says."

"Song?" asks Mohawk, confused.

"AWB," I say. "Average White Band. Look it up." Ugh. He is so Eastern European.

I take my gym bag and head into the locker room, locker being a euphemism because there are no lockers here. Just a room with a bunch of hooks and a filthy toilet.

If it were up to me, I'd put in a eucalyptus steam room. I'd stock kumquat shampoo, Egyptian cotton towels and Waterford crystal bowls filled with M&Ms to grab while passing from the shower to the sauna. I asked Steve about finding a blender to make banana-acai smoothies for a little potassium and antioxidants on ice, and maybe a few vanilla-scented candles. He takes the position that there's no place for any of it in a gym promising hard-core results. I disagree. I think one can be chic, *soignee*, *elegante*, and yet *de brute, sauvage*, and, well, you know, a badass motherfucker. They are not, in my opinion, incompatible.

"You should be snorting ammonia before facing down a stack of iron," Steve told me. "Not getting some fuzzy head from eucalyptus. You're liable to kill yourself sniffing eucalyptus before executing a clean and jerk."

I'm not letting their negative attitude and crass exploitation get me down. I stand in front the mirror and do a bicep curl. Nice. Very nice. I take the manual from my bag and pick out a routine to follow for the week.

But which one? It's probably the only thing I can't stand about the manual. Vertical Split routines? Heavy days, low reps? Light weights, high reps? Same exact exercise four days on and one day off? Or something different every set, three days on, two days off? Ugh. I can't decide. All I know for sure is: It starts with the set.

The set. Master the set. Light, lots of reps. Alternate weeks or days with shorter sets, heavy weights. Three sets per exercise. Three exercises per large muscle group. Two for small muscle groups. I'm thinking maybe instead of working out, I'll just walk into town. It's cool and sunny with bright blue skies. My mind wanders to other places with bright blue skies, places I've never been. Muscle Beach. Venice Beach. The Big Sur. The Pacific Ocean. The golden age of bodybuilding. I picture Arnold and his buds, meeting for breakfast before hitting the gym, hanging out at the beach in the afternoon, then back for a split set at night. Basking in the glow.

I want to go back in time. Be in that space. Just for a few days. I think of the black and white pictures in the scrapbook. The dark eyes looking at me from the past. The little girl with eyes like Nadia that seemed to look into my soul, seeking to tell me something, but what? A little girl with superhuman strength who grew and grew until she was over six feet tall, and they called her Sandwina, the strongest woman on earth. And I, cosmically connected. The knowing. It's there. A knowing of something I don't know. Like we are part of the chain of life. The circle of life. Simba?

Being fabulous isn't easy.

TAKING CARE OF BUSINESS

I'm walking down the main street of town, and as I pass the church, the front door opens and it's Catherine. She is all in black, with a crown of thorns instead of flowers. Behind her, I see the other pale skinny women gathered just inside the vestibule. They, too, are in black.

"I'm sorry," she says, "for saying mean things to you."

"It's okay," I lie. "I just need to be alone."

"Here," she says. "Take these. My gift to you. A peace offering. Peace be with you." She presses two communion wafers into my hand. "I would just like one thing. Just a small request, and we promise to leave you alone," she says. Catherine gazes at her flunkies who are staring back at her with spacey eyes.

"I'm not killing Vladimir or anybody else, so don't bother asking again," I say.

"No, no, nothing like that. We just want to borrow your book, the one you call a training manual. We want to, well, we would like to, you know, get stronger. Get more energy. Get muscles." One of the women in the doorway opens her mouth and starts shaking her head, like she just heard something scary. Did someone just kick her? They are moving slowly, like they're in a trance.

"You could start by eating French fries and gravy," I tell her. I am in no mood for negotiations.

"Please help me," she says. "My father, unlike yours, was an impoverished second-string clown who swept elephant dung in a travelling circus; an idiot savant who could juggle 27 balls at once. Gradually, he expanded his repertoire to plates, knives, diabolos, tennis racquets and even small rodents. His rivals, intimidated by his brilliance, were determined to drive him away. Whenever my father would step into the costume wagon, they would cruelly taunt him by singing 'Send in the Clowns,' knowing how my father detested Sondheim. Sadists! In desperation, he branched out to flaming torches in hopes of being recognized. Sadly, his clown costume was highly flammable. And so was known posthumously as The Torchman."

I am trying to follow this tale of patrimony and pyrrhic arts. "And this relates to me, how?" I ask.

"When dad went up in flames, my mother found a new flame, Arnold, who was preening his over-juiced musculature in Berlin. She followed him throughout Europe, selling me off to a bunch of local yokels in Bulgaria. An adorable blonde child, worth big bucks and a load off their hands. But she got her comeuppance when she found herself on the verge of menopause with an ugly baby. That, by the way, would be you."

"How do you know this?" I ask.

"You're not getting it, are you?" Catherine says raising her eyebrow.

Omigod, could what I suspected once for a split second be true? That this weirdo could be my sister? Half sister? Do these people think I'm that gullible? I need to think about this, put two and two together. We share the raised eyebrow trait and, dare I think it? An aversion to Sondheim? Yet, I refuse to accept that musical taste is imbedded in the double helix. I think it's more like whether you prefer Colgate, Crest or Tom's of Maine.

I stick my hands into the pockets of my jeans and I feel something hard, like a little stone. I take it out and it's a snail. What the fuck?

Catherine jumps back and one of the women in the doorway screams.

"Time is short," Catherine warns, backing up toward the church door. "You must not speak of this meeting."

A snail hits my clothes, and another goes right by my face into the church. The girls flee further inside, leaving Catherine at the

doorway with her gold chalice of communion wafers. I turn around
and see the little apple-cheeked lady waving at me.

"Go home. Now!" she orders. "Stay away from these ditzy broads."

Broads? Didn't Humphrey Bogart use that colloquialism in *The
Petrified Forest* to freak out Leslie Howard? Or did he say "dame?"
Why can't I remember these things? My pondering is cut short by a
loud noise, like a car skidding. Catherine's eyes narrow into evil slits.
It's the Escargot Cowboy, again, and his jeep stops between me and
Catherine. Maybe this really is a movie set because the apple-cheeked
lady leaps into a martial arts stance, like Ken Miyagi in *The Karate Kid*.

"Get in, kid," Cowboy yells. I climb into the jeep as Catherine
hurls the gold chalice at him. He catches it in his left hand while grip-
ping the steering wheel with the right. Communion wafers scatter all
over the ground. He backs up, turns around and speeds away. I see
Baba Yaga standing where the apple-cheeked lady was moments
before. She is laughing hysterically, and her gold tooth is glinting in
the sunlight. I slink down to the floor and hold on to the seat,
screaming as loud as I can. Not that screaming does anything, but it
makes me feel in control.

The cowboy yells: "I vowed to protect you, and I intend to keep
that vow." I close my eyes and keep screaming until we are out of
town.

Eventually, the jeep slows down, and I scramble onto the seat. I
am amazed to see snow-capped mountains and fields of wildflowers.
It looks like, I don't know, *The Sound of Music*. Good thing I watched a
lot of movies growing up. Otherwise, I'd have no frame of reference
for anything.

He stops by a lake with weeping willows all around. The water
reflects the mountains, the trees and the crisp blue sky. It even smells
clean. I get out of the jeep, and I stretch out under a tree. Cowboy
does the same.

"Listen, Tina," he says. "I want you to know that it's not true, what
Catherine said. I didn't dump her for you. It wasn't like that."

"Tell me something I don't already know," I say. I feel relaxed and
at peace.

"I'm your brother."

Fuck.

"Only kidding," he says. Yeah, so funny I forgot to laugh. Or so I
would say when I was a kid, but now, the juvenile thought pops into

my head and I'm embarrassed. I never liked people fucking with my head, and that hasn't changed. He opens his shoulder bag and offers me a bottle of mineral water. I twist off the cap and suck down half the bottle. I start feeling a little more grounded, clear-headed. "Actually, half-brother," he adds with a wink. I ignore this. "Only kidding," he says. "You have enough whacked out relatives."

"What do you know?" I ask him. "Tell me."

"Where should I start?"

"Grandma. My parents. Everything. I mean, the whys and wherefores of it all. What else do you know? I'm so confused."

Cowboy leans his head back and swats something from his face. Then he smirks like he is seeing something funny. For a change I don't want to smack him on the head. I just wait. He reaches into his back pocket and takes out a white cocktail napkin and a pen, leans it against his knee and begins to write.

"Remember the pictures in the scrapbook? The *wunderkind*? The child with the dark eyes, the sailor shirt, known for her enormous strength and powers of concentration? She was a big deal in the ring and at freak shows, where people would pay good money to see this little girl lift grown men and huge barbells and so on."

"Yeah? What about?"

"She grew up to be the 6-foot-1 phenomenon known as the great Sandwina. The world today knows little about these people. What you read and hear, it's mostly wrong. Sometimes by design to keep their secrets, but usually misinformation carelessly changing hands.

"But this much I know for sure. Sandwina was the child of travelling circus people," Cowboy says, "and she was your grandmother. So, imagine this kid –"

"I've already figured all that out," I say.

"Let me finish," he insists, "she's this kid, performing with a family here, a family there, a little girl with ferocious intensity and strength. People were fascinated. But terrified, too, because when that child looked at you, it was like she was looking right through you. A freak. She was borrowed, you might say, passed around by various strongmen of the era. Or so they say, 'they' being the stories passed down."

"By the time your mother came along, Sandwina would have been getting on in years, but then, this was a tough cookie who was still performing feats of strength well into her 60s. Ringling Brothers was her claim to fame, and she travelled the world with The Greatest Show on Earth.

"There are a few who would hypothesize that your grandmother was the long-lost daughter of Louise Leers. Luisita, as she was known on stage. Unlike the amazons of her day, Luisita was winsome, wholesome, with arms of steel. Trained by her stepfather to be a star. A baby would have spoiled everything. There is talk that her family shushed the whole thing up. Just a theory, and a good one. But really, I've got my money on Sandwina."

Luisita? I pick at the grass. "I don't remember pictures of her," I tell him.

"You must have only looked through part of the scrapbook," he says. "Most of the women and children are in the last pages. You know, it's just the way it was."

"Wait, this is too crazy," I tell him" It's impossible." He hands me the napkin.

Tina
|
Arnold+Angela (Grandma)
|
Hackenschmidt+The Mighty Orphan (Sandwina)
||
G. Heinrich Hackenschmidt +Ida Johansson Philippe

Philippe? Is this a joke? Grandma, who used to yell *ah fangul* at the TV, was what? Austrian, Estonian, Bulgarian, German, Swedish. French?

"You've got it wrong," I say. "Maybe some of it is right, but not all."

How does he know these things about me? Why am I here? Is any of this true? Can this Arnold stuff be for real? I mean, is somebody putting me on? I can just hear millions of people laughing the minute I buy into this. I imagine being in fifth grade with all the kids in the schoolyard at Our Lady of Little Victories surrounding me, pointing at me, falling down hysterical. Ah, but then Arnold shows up and they tremble at the sight. I stand tall and proud and they back off. Arnold disappears and they kneel in my presence.

I hear Cowboy say, "Tina, are you listening? I'm not boring you, am I?" I apologize. I want him to finish his story.

"When the child known as The Mighty Orphan was a teenager," he says, "she caught the eye of the great Hackenschmidt, and he took her under his wing. Remember, he was a huge success at the time. Debonair, refined and built like a brick. And she was a hot little number herself. Little, that is, compared to the big man.

"So fast forward. Despite the great difference in age, she and Hack travel throughout Europe and together they promote their seminal book *The Way to Live* at physical culture conferences, which delves into mind-body-nutrition-spiritual issues way ahead of its time. Of course, the book is credited solely to Hackenschmidt, due to his marketable name, good looks and, well, you know, testosterone.

"One morning, they wake up in a boutique hotel in Lichtenstein and, over a bowl of muesli, The Mighty Orphan, who will eventually become The Great Sandwina, tells Hack that she had a dream in which a spirit tells her this thin book can be much, much bigger, that there is more to be made manifest, that they can reveal the lost wisdom of their ancestries, the collective knowledge of the great and strong among them. It is to become the ultimate training manual, the way to develop an ordinary human being into a physical and intellectual powerhouse unlike any other.

"She even had a fully formed marketing slogan: *You don't have to be great to start, but you have to start to be great.* These brilliant *bon mots* are today attributed to Nightingale-Conant motivational author Zig Ziglar, but we know where it originated.

"Anyway, Hack's not buying it. He suspects she is trying to rope him into a long-term commitment and by this point, his life is getting complicated, if you know what I mean.

"Hack tells The Mighty Orphan that Las Vegas is the wave of the future and offers to set her up with a singing career and a makeover – wardrobe, hair, elocution lessons, the works. He promises to write and send royalties when he can.

"Well, the gig didn't turn out quite as planned, which is the way life is, isn't it? She, who was once The Mighty Orphan, ends up the laughingstock of Vegas when she appears in low-cut sequined gowns with her enormous muscles. She gets some offers, mostly tired burlesque acts. Vaudeville is dead, so she heads back to the circus, where she resumes her career, making a big comeback on her own turf, working her way to top billing at Barnum & Bailey. There are pictures of her in a skimpy corset and boots, hoisting grown men over her head. Hercules and Venus all in one person. But we all get older, even the great ones, and eventually she marries her sidekick and opens a tavern in New York City called Sandwina's. Her name is still a big draw, and cops, longshoremen and numbers runners hang out at the joint. They do okay."

This is all well and good, but I still don't see the connection to *me* and I tell him so. "Jesus, get to the point! How do I fit into this?"

"Are you taking the Lord's name in vain?" he asks me.

"Are you religious?" I reply.

"No. Just saying," he says. "Look, I'll cut to the chase. For years, Hack sends ardent letters, which Sandwina hides from her husband. They are loaded with erotica like his yearning to lick pungent sweat dripping from her hairy armpits and his desire to be intertwined with her while executing 600 pushups in an audacious act of extreme carnal endurance. After years of titillation, in 1946, he is in New York to headline a charity banquet sponsored by the Fraternal Order of Estonian Machinists. Sandwina arranges a rendezvous at Coney Island, and that very night, Hackenschmidt fulfills his pledge to 'do it' one more time, and they do, on the Cyclone. They were the original Mile High Club.

"Now get this, they are both in their 60s and when he leaves, she finds herself with child. You'd think that would be impossible right? But these two had the secrets of the ages embedded, like Abraham and Sarah and Rebekah and Elizabeth before them. And because of this, Sandwina doubles down working on their manuscript from the old days, while sending her pliant husband out to satisfy her exotic food cravings: borscht, Cheerios, kimchi, prosciutto bread, Sugar Babies.

"The night she goes into labor, she writes the penultimate chapter between contractions. As the midwife implores her to push, with the baby's head crowning, she screams: "Georg! It is done!" Sandwina names their masterpiece *The Estonian Training Manual* and christens the baby Angela. She has every intention of ditching the husband and reuniting with Hackenschmidt in the belief that, together, they will complete the final chapter and change the world.

"But Hack still has zero interest in a new book. He's too busy globetrotting to lucrative celeb appearances, negotiating a picture deal with Paramount, going to Hollywood parties and sniffing up Lana Turner's butt like a dog in heat. Sandwina tries to publish the manuscript "as is," but without Hackenschmidt's star power, the publishing houses aren't interested. Disillusioned, she sells it for chump change to a Bulgarian gangster who is a regular at her tavern.

"Flash forward to the 1980s. Grandma, a.k.a. Angela Hackenschmidt, is working the beer concession at the newly opened Meadowlands Arena in New Jersey when a security guard, "Fast Al" Bontempi, promises her a backstage pass to meet Bruce Springsteen in exchange for sexual favors. Fast Al is a known scumbag. In and out of the big house. But Angie feels she has nothing to lose. She has already tried the travelling circus bit in Europe, using her mother's connections, shacking up with lion tamers, aerial artists, and cotton candy vendors. She hooks up with Fast Al, they get married and move to a cold-water flat in Jersey City. By this time, bodybuilding has captured the public imagination. *Pumping Iron* has achieved cult status and Arnold is a superstar. One day, Arnold calls on Angie to pay homage to Sandwina and Hackenschmidt, who are both dead by now. They have a fling, and just like her father did with her mother, he knocks her up and jets back to the glitterati. So, Angie spends her days duking it out with Fast Al and sitting with the homeboys on her stoop. To spare her child – that would be you - the disgrace of this low-life squalor, she pretends she is your grandmother."

"And you're telling me all this because?" I ask.

"Because I like you," he says.

"I grew up on that stoop." I tell him "Don't bullshit me. Nobody does nothing for nothing. What's your angle?"

"I can franchise you," he says. "I have zeroed in on a spot in Southern California where the climate is perfect for growing arugula and snails. We can replicate my family's anabolic steroid operation and get efficient distribution over the entire nation. Big Steve knows people who know people. We start with reps in every Gold's Gym and grow until we reach the summit: executive gyms, where men in new Mercedes S600s will pay good money to achieve that Marlboro man look in no time with very little effort. We think it will be an opportunity for you."

"What do you take me for, a mac and cheese?" I ask. "Do you have any backers? You know, money people."

"*You* do."

"I do?"

"Let me spell it out. D.A.D. And I'm not talking Rusty G."

"Are you telling me that my father really is Arnold Schwarzenegger?"

A sepia image floats through my consciousness, a distant, hazy shadow, like an ectopic spot floating across my eyes. A tall woman with a white feather in her wavy brown hair. She has a kind smile and 17-inch biceps. I don't know who she is, but she feels connected to me. Men on a beach, tanned and oiled, preening before the cameras, while women in bouffant hairdos caress them. My mind is racing. Image is everything. What you see. How you project. The illusion. The sepia woman steps toward me in a sequined corset with a veil undulating behind her. She bends her knee to reveal a perfectly cut calf. I feel like I have an understanding of something far away, that I can't quite make out.

He shows me the napkin again.

"How many times do you have to be told?" he says.

I am putting two and two together, and I look into Cowboy's eyes.

"You sure I'm not Italian?"

MOOSE AND SQUIRREL

I'm leaning on the cement windowsill, looking out at the gym parking lot, and my stomach is doing flip-flops.

People are all over, rushing around with papers, hooking up cords to a truck with a big-ass antenna on top, and in the center is a huge yellow van with blackened windows. Inside the gym, a guy with a shaved head is setting up laptops on folding tables while a cameraman is testing video equipment.

I'm wearing my black Spandex capris and a hot pink t-shirt. I ripped the sleeves off and cut it shorter, like a midriff, to look cool and show off my biceps and abs. Steve is next to me with his arms crossed, rocking side-to-side, defensive posture squared. We're waiting while the anchor lady gets her hair and makeup done in the van. My insides start making gurgling sounds and I'm praying it won't get picked up on the live mic.

"Got any gum?" Steve asks, staring out the window.

"No. Wish I did," I say. "Are you nervous?"

"No. Hey, get a load – you see that?"

The van is open, and I see a chick sitting inside wearing a low-cut purple silk blouse, a tight purple skirt and pink bunny slippers. Roadie types roll red stairs to the door, and she stands imperiously, with cascading black hair and unnaturally arched eyebrows. She takes a drag from a cigarette holder and flicks the ashes. I wonder if she knows we are watching.

"Bulgarian. National. Television." I say the words slowly as I stare out the window.

"Don't be nervous," Steve says. "I mean, it's Bulgaria. Who's going to see us, right?"

"You never know," I tell him. "Maybe important people. Maybe they syndicate the show to, I don't know, Romania?"

"That's my point," Steve says. I think he is trying to reassure himself.

"Okay, so it's not ESPN," I tell him. "But this show is big here. And you gotta walk before you can run. Or crawl before you walk. Whatever. My point is this could lead to something big. Mohawk says this anchor lady is the Oprah Winfrey of Bulgaria."

"Oprah never looked that foxy," Steve says, his eyes glued to the action outside.

I watch one of the roadies kneel on the pavement in front of the red stairs. He is helping foxy mama slip on black patent leather stilettos. She adjusts her blouse to reveal more cleavage, tosses her hair and pouts her crimson lips. A cameraman gives her a thumbs up and she steps down the stairs. She is very tall with long legs.

I grab Steve's arm. "I think she's ready." I reach into the pocket of my gym bag and pull out my lipstick. I quickly put some on and then realize I didn't look in the mirror. Oh my god, what if I look like those old ladies with a smear across their faces? I run over to the mirror by the free weights for a look. Perfect. Just perfect. I remind myself to stand up straight, and I pretend a string is pulling my head up. I adopt the gym swagger, arching my back and folding my arms over my chest like Steve. He nods and makes a fake smile. Oh, yeah, right. I smile, too, as the camera guys and the anchor lady walk into the gym.

The anchor lady stops in front of the row of free weights and lifts a 5-pound dumbbell. The cameraman moves in real close and points the lens at the dumbbell in her hand. The guy with the laptops starts typing like mad. I take a few steps back to see what's up with the laptops. One laptop seems to show whatever the camera guy is shooting, and another is just flashing pictures and the third one is doing fancy stuff with combining video and pictures and commercials and subtitles. I look at what I think they're showing on TV:

(Rack of dumbbells from muscle magazine. Pink, green, blue Bulgarian currency.)

The anchor lady is talking to the camera in Bulgarian. Her voice is deep and husky. I ask one of the tech guys what she is saying and he says: "Welcome to Bulgarian National TV. World of Sport." She walks over to us, stands right between me and Steve and tosses her hair again. In heavily accented English, she says:

"Vee haf 204 nation in Olympics. Seventy-three haf no medal. Not even von medal. Many year and never, never a medal. Bulgaria, my friends, ees *not* one of dese nation."

Another man, short and round in a dark suit with greased black hair and a cigar, steps in front of Steve with a microphone. His English is excellent and he talks very fast. In fact, he sounds a little like Groucho Marx. Maybe it's the cigar. Says his name is Boris.

"With 220 medals, folks, Bulgaria ranks in the top 20 of all time Olympic medalists. Bulgaria's medals come primarily from two sports: wrestling – that would be 68 of 'em – and weightlifting, 36. If bodybuilding were an Olympic sport, there would be many more, my friends, I am sure. And you can believe we are working on that one, too. Meanwhile, in the turbulence following the fall of the Communist regime, between 1989 and 1990, institutional support for the Bulgarian Olympians waned, and by the 2012 London Olympics, Bulgaria was no longer even among the top 50 in medals of any kind. It was a disaster."

(Travel poster of London, superimposed with Bulgaria Air Embraer E-190 aircraft and photo of Joe Fox in pilot uniform)

"Total mess!" the anchor lady says, shaking her head.

"But now, my dear Natasha," he continues, "As we stand here on the site of the legendary Ancient Gym, our proud heritage is before our eyes and within our grasp. Look around at our youth. Without the aid or the blessing of the authorities. Right here. Rising. Risking all, to make our great nation number one again."

This Boris dude walks over to the dweebs, who are standing in a row behind the bench press. He signals with his cigar, and they lift the ponytail girl like a plank over their heads. The cameraman runs in for a close-up. Boris sticks his mic in her face and asks her to say a few words to the Bulgarian TV audience.

"Please ask state to make repair to *Krasno Selo* traffic signal. Is near Tsar Boris III Boulevard. Maybe you see this, no? This very bad. Oh, please find me rich and handsome husband. Maybe American, yes?"

(Cut to Pizza don Vito, 80 Tsar Boris III Boulevard.)

The girl then leaps off, and they quickly form a pyramid. A guy gives her a pom-pom and she scrambles to the top of their shoulders.

"Rah, rah, sis, boom bah!" they shout in unison. "America, America, friend to Bulgaria!"

Boris nods to the anchor lady. The camera swings around to us. Boris keeps talking into the mic at a rapid clip.

"And now, here we have the leaders of this brave effort. Big Steve from America. A good man who found our lost Bulgarian daughter in Hoboken, New Joisy, and brought her back to us."

(Carlo's Bakery, Hoboken, NJ, studio shot of smiling Cake Boss)

I look at Steve and raise my eyebrows. Did he actually say *"Joisy?"* I'm thinking Steve would at least chuckle, but he doesn't. I guess he wants to maintain his on-camera face.

"Wait!" a familiar voice shouts.

It's Mohawk. He grabs the mic and walks in front of the camera.

"To our citizenry, listen to me. We must stop those who denigrate and commercialize our sport. These are the same who promote derivative, saccharine poetry to the detriment of innovation and new artistic frontiers."

The guy at the keyboard is typing furiously.

(Open-air book market Sleveykov Square. Flash images: Selected Poems of Li Po. Leaves of Grass. Dallas Cowboys cheerleaders)

The camera is on Mohawk yakking away.

"We must merge the disciplines of rigorous verse and the physical arts. We must beat back technocrats, corporate raiders and politically appointed poet laureates, and especially visual artists going for bourgeois cheap sentiment."

(Thomas Kinkade's Graceland Christmas, superimposed over customer call center number and MasterCard symbol)

"They are all part of the same banal, supersized, anti-intellectual disease, which has weakened our people. The domination of sport and art as one must be raised up once again."

Boris wrestles the microphone out of Mohawk's hand and they have a heated exchange in Bulgarian. I listen but I can't make out a word. I guess Mohawk was harshin' his mellow. Or the other way around.

The cameraman runs over to the anchor lady and me. It's about time. She opens another button on her blouse, turns slightly and gives a half-turn nod to the camera.

"Let us geeve varm velcome to Tina from America," she says, staring straight ahead.

Boris steps next to me and puts his arm around my waist. His breath smells like liverwurst and onion.

"Comrades! The great Tina, who you see here, is descended from the great Hackenschmidt, and a cousin twice removed from the great Bulgarian wonder woman Ivana Sofia Amazonas, whose fashionable gowns at state dinners were slit to the waist to show off her cut calves and quads, a body that was the object of desire by men throughout the world and coveted within the Politburo."

At the mention of Politburo, the anchor lady spits on the floor. The camera swings back and she says:

"And she come from ze great Ahnold Schvarzenegger. Man of taste. Man who appreciate beauty of Bulgarian vooman."

The dweebs cheer and the cameraman wipes away a tear. Boris sticks the microphone in front of my face.

"Tell us, Tina. Can we call you Tina? Or do you prefer Valentina? Tell us. What is it like to be a child of celebrities dating back more than one hundred years?"

I don't know where he is going with this, and after my talk with Cowboy and some locals I am sure there is no Ivana Amazonas. Just a crass parochial bid to snag a local angle out of this. But I'll wing it. Did he say Arnold? I look into the camera and smile. I do not toss my hair.

"The Terminator movies were great, right?" I jump into a military stance for the camera, simulating a warrior aiming a semi-automatic weapon.

(Dove deodorant. Andre's Military Surplus Supply. Flash ammo, Kalashnikov, shoulder-held rocket launcher. Rhinestone hair accessories.)

I straighten up and point to the camera. "Take it from me. Linda Hamilton, she had the total look. Right down to the aviator sunglasses."

(Ray-Bans)

"Now, my friend Big Steve, he likes the chicks in the fitness divisions, you know, the big hair, the nail extensions, the boob jobs."

(Hospital St. Lazarus, Sofia. Flash: Breast Implants, Laser Vaginal Rejuvenation, Facelift with Thread)

The anchor lady and Boris look at each other. They seem confused.

"Tell about *Ahnold*," the anchor lady says. "Sexy, like in movies, no?"

"I guess. It's not like I ever met him or anything. Can I do a pose for the camera? Maybe a double bicep curl?"

There is an awkward silence. The cameraman fidgets, and Boris comes to the rescue.

"Bodybuilders with their perfect Hellenic physiques, the enormity of discipline that was once a pariah, an irritation, an illegitimate cousin to our proud wrestling champions, our strongmen, our powerlifters with their astounding technique, executing a flawless snatch in one breathtaking sweep. Until now. Until the great Arnold – former Mr. Universe, seven-time Mr. Olympia and Mr. Stud of America – who recognized the beauty of our strong Bulgarian women, of the preciousness of noble ancestry not to be denied. And now, our greatest progeny: Tina, who has come all the way from America with the blood of a great people."

The anchor lady says under her breath: "Zay somesing, and not somesing stoopeed."

She's right, here's my chance, so why blow it? Maybe I'll get a reality show out of this. A little cash, maybe a lot of cash, go to Paris, tell Philippe to fuck off, have a parfait.

"What you can tell Bulgarian television about Ahnold?" she asks.

Omigod, Arnold, again? I think fast. What can I say? I got it. The quotes!

"At my gym, back home in Jersey, there's posters of him all over the walls," I say. "Him and Lou Ferrigno, Lee Haney, Ronnie Coleman. But what's different about Arnold is the way he integrates food and life to a higher meaning, and no, I don't mean that famous one about breakfast, lunch, and dinner. That's so passé. The one I'm thinking of is, well, there's this saying he has about being continuously hungry, but you can't take that out of context because the beautiful thing about Arnold is he is a man of metaphor, a man of simile, and of similar things. Like the hungry quote, if taken out of context, just sounds like he wants to eat all the time, and while I am sure he eats a lot, you gotta know the whole quote to understand, and I can quote the quote in its entirety: 'For me, life is continuously being hungry. The meaning of life is not simply to exist, to survive, but to move ahead, to go up, to achieve, to conquer.' Now aren't those beautiful words? Tell me, people, are those not beautiful words? Say yes. Come on! Say yes!"

(*Cut to Kentucky Fried Chicken - KFC Garibaldi, 2, Angel Kanchev str. Sofia*)

Boris and anchor lady seem pleased. Standing next to each other, they also appear familiar, you know, the old déjà vu thing. Like it's on the edge of my brain.

"It is hard to be hero in America. Better to be hero in Bulgaria," she says to the camera. Huh? Did she just...? I don't care. I lean into the mic. I'm beginning to get the hang of this.

"Out of suffering have emerged the strongest souls," I say. "The most massive characters are seared with scars."

Then, I look into the camera and wink. "Thank you, Arnold!"

Boris looks pissed. He frowns, and I think I know who these guys remind me of. Maybe it's the accent. Maybe it's the cleavage.

"Cut!" he shouts. "That was *not* Arnold."

Wait. What? Not Arnold? What is this dude, a Schwarzenegger fanatic?

"No? Well, it kind of fits, doesn't it? I mean, does it even matter? Arnold did lift some heavy-ass weight."

The anchor lady shouts. *"Nyet. Nyet. Nyet.* That Khalil Gibran, son of Ottoman Empire."

I need a comeback. Save face. Think fast. Push back against these post-pinko pseudo-cognoscenti. Fuck the alliteration, or is it still alliterative if it is pronounced with an S? No time to lose by over-thinking.

"You're right – and he inspired Arnold who inspired Rocky," I say with false cheeriness to shift the momentum. "Remember? Of course you do!"

"Sylvester Stallone?" the TV guy pipes in, his face brightening up.

"Could be," I say, "but I was thinking more in terms of moose and squirrel. Catch my drift?"

He clears his throat and signals to turn the camera back on. He is clearly out of his element now, and I'm psyched. The anchor lady fakes a smile and Boris points the mic at my face again.

"In closing, what best practices can you share with the Bulgarian Television Network?" Boris asks me with a hint of hostility. "Words to inspire youth. *Bulgarian* youth."

Woohoo. I look into the camera.

"Listen up," I say, "I'm giving you words to live by. No, not Arnold's words. That's so Seventies. New words. Words to shout every morning to the face in the mirror. Yeah, that would be you. I train like a beast, and you should, too. If you can put one quote over your bed and look at it every goddamn morning when you wake up, your one overriding thought of the day, it should be this."

I take a deep breath, shift my hips and point to the camera with both hands.

"To anyone... that ever... tells you that you can't do something... tell them to go fuck themselves!"

Steve applauds. I take a bow and wave. I hear the anchor lady ask Boris off camera: "You know who is this moose and squirrel?"

THE GAUNTLET

This dude with thick gold chains and a crucifix enters the gym while Steve and Mohawk are spotting each other on the squat rack. He's got a lavender calico bandana around his head and his pecs are busting out of a wife-beater. This guy's quads are so big, the seams of the track pants are pulling apart. In his left ear is a skull in diamond chips and tattooed on his right arm is a full-color image of the Higgs boson, the *raison d'etre* of matter obtaining mass. It is also the mark of the Gangsta Builda Powerlifta Gym, where massiveness rules.

"Yo' trailer trash," he shouts, looking straight at me. "Get down, shut down, sit down, face off, jerk off, get off, go back to where you once belonged, ho'."

"Listen Rat Bastard," I yell back, my voice echoing in the almost empty gym. "Trailer? You got no geo-graph-y. Jersey City is the place I be. And don't go appropriating my cultural terr-it-tor-y."

"Two gyms diverged, in a nearby hood," he says in a menacing tone. I see where he is going with this, and I ratchet it up a notch:

And sorry we cannot pump iron in both
And be as one, long have I waited
To look down at you, dirtwad, in-sati-ated.

To my surprise, he takes the bait and says:

And both this morning equally lay
In muscle no fist had trodden back

Oh, I keep this fist for another day!
Yet knowing how way leads on to way, yo!
I interrupt:
I doubt you motherfucker shall ever come back.
And I will tell you this with a sigh
Somewhere ages and ages from now
Two gyms will collide in this hood, and I –
I will take the juice less u-til-ized
And that, rat bastard, makes all the difference.
"Easy does it, Sweet Loretta," the dude says, backing away.
I throw down my towel and make a fist.

"You and your ass-wipe friends. You and Muscle Beach. You and Cripple Creek, Rock City, Bitter End Bullshit, Whit-man, Every-man, Plath-baiting Frost; You He-man, She-man, Buk-owski, Maya Angie-Lou."

"What are you getting at, sister?" he growls. "A poetry slam?"

Am I? Inspiration smacks me in the head.

"Poetry *body* slam!" I say defiantly. "Week from Saturday. Bring a photo ID. Be prepared to pee in a cup. Main event at sunset. In the Ancient Gym. Face down your peers at the world's first International Poetry Body Slam. We will see where greatness lies."

Steve and Mohawk look at me with an expression that says, "What the fuck?"

"Deal!" the dude snarls, and then heads for the door.

"*Da nada,*" I say. I can do this. We can do this. For Grandma and for every goddamn soul whose Lava Lamp dreams have been dimmed but not exploded.

"Hey, Freak," I call out. He turns around. "You tell your boss, I've seen people like you, but I had to pay admission." He flips me the bird and walks out.

"Poetry Body Slam?" Steve asks.

THE THREE LOMBARDIS

Luigi has recommended, against the advice of Pietro and Frankie, that we should include here that the marriage of intellect and muscle dates to the ancient Greeks and Romans, with their perfectly proportioned gods and goddesses, and, more recently, to the West's greatest literary genius (in Luigi's opinion), James Joyce, even though he was Irish. The editors concur with Luigi.

The popularity of Sandow and the system for bodybuilding that he designed is clear when James Joyce's Bloom in *Ulysses* (1922) thinks he must begin again those Sandow exercises in "Calypso" and "Circe." When Bloom arranges Sandow's famous book *Strength and How to Obtain It* next to Shakespeare's *Works* in "Ithaca," he juxtaposes "low" popular performance and "high" drama.

CARRIE J. PRESTON *MODERNISM'S MYTHIC POSE: GENDER, GENRE, SOLO PERFORMANCE* (2011)

SEIZE WE MUST: A CARPE AND AN IDEUM TO GO

It's only 10 o'clock in the morning, but me and Big Steve, we've been in the gym for five hours already, wiping down the benches, pushing heavy equipment to the side, stacking mats and setting up chairs. The microphone stand is in place and we're ready, very ready, for what we are calling the world premiere of the First Annual International Poetry Body Slam. Right here in the so-called Ancient Gym. How cool is that?

People are coming from all over the world, or so we hope. We've had a ton of publicity – radio, TV, the works – and our gym membership roster is skyrocketing – paid members, not just us. People just keep showing up. A lot of flabby, pale guys and mousy girls, nerdtypes. A few big guys too, but usually not too well proportioned - wide lats and shriveled quads.

One big man knelt and kissed the threshold. Before stepping through, he mumbled something in Bulgarian, then covered his face and wept. Mohawk says it's the realization that the Ancient Gym, so long silenced, has been restored to glory. I'd say my great marketing angles had something to do with that. But, hey. We have had so many people signing up for personal training with Big Steve he might have to raise his rates.

Joe Fox is even trying to muscle in on the act, so to speak, calling

Big Steve from some remote place with loud salsa music in the background, saying he heard about us and is there franchising potential? Said he could make some deals. Maybe get Arnold in as a partner and open up in Malibu, Manhattan, Vienna. Even buy out our old gym in Jersey City. Got Steve all jacked up, telling him he could call that one Big Steve's Original Ancient Gym. When I got wind of this, I told Steve no way I'd let him exploit The Ancient Gym. That would be so wrong. It has to be Big Steve and Tina's Ancient Gym. Or better yet, Tina and Big Steve's World Famous Original Ancient Gym: capitalize on a proven pizza formula and give me top billing. At first, he questioned the "world famous" claim, but I explained the obvious: If we are famous in Bulgaria, which we are, then we're world famous by definition because we are famous in two different parts of the world. I told him nobody is famous in the whole entire world, like you don't have to be famous in Rome, Hong Kong, and Secaucus all at the same time.

Cowboy wants to dovetail with us, take the escargot and arugula operation public, and could I help him find an IPO lawyer in the U.S.? I tell him maybe, but we should see about the nuns in Missoula because their holistic communion wafers are natural tie-in with the organic supplements and health food market. Maybe put a nun in our logo. Like Steve always says, it's all about perception. The image. The pose. The illusion.

Personally, I'm thinking I'd like my own reality show, now that I have some TV experience. I can be my own backer with the cash I'll make from our product ventures. I picture a cocktail party, with jumbo shrimp and ice sculptures and celebrities. I imagine myself in a studio being interviewed by Ellen DeGeneres. I think of my apartment back in Hoboken, and I wonder if it is full of mold or if I even have an apartment because I am months and months behind on the rent and what happened to my stuff and did my real estate license lapse and, if it did, would it matter? Can we really do any of this? Or are we totally fucked by some cosmic bungee cord?

No, I tell myself. My days of *parfaits* and *Veuve Clicquot* are yet to come. I feel the synchronicity of it all, of all the yesterdays, todays, and tomorrows, colliding and morphing into something new. I think of what Shearling told me on the tarmac just before we came here, when I was on the float with Steve. "The very act of looking at your image distorts the image, as it does with others observing you and you them. There is no permanence in image, but it is the prevailing reality, which you can seize. And seize you must."

The Beast has a new hot pink scrunchie in her ponytail and a stack of registration forms at a folding table near the main entrance and we're expecting competitors to start arriving any minute for pre-judging, weigh-in, and, of course, the pee-in-a-cup ritual, which will be left to Shearling and his buddies who run a lab. But make no mistake. The rules are strict. Every applicant is given a 42-page rule book during pre-judging: No blatant commercialization, no props, three-minute time limit, points deleted for every second over, and only pre-recorded music. All poems must be originals and recited either in English, Bulgarian or Esperanto (Mohawk's idea, to make it truly international and politically correct). We don't actually expect anyone to follow the rules or even read them, of course, but having rules gives us cred. Steve and Mohawk agree on this and came up with the lists, while the dweebs did all the typing, printing, collating, and stapling. It's a beautiful thing to be in charge.

Since this is a poetry slam, in order to weed out plagiarizers and other cheaters, after the urine testing and before the actual competition, the contestants are to be quizzed via Zoom by a panel of bold-faced names in the literary arts. People like best-selling romance writer **Nora Roberts** (author of 209 novels in 35 years, or about one every other month!); jingle writer **Barry Manilow** (author of "You Deserve a Break Today" and "Like a Good Neighbor, State Farm is There" and no, he didn't write the songs that made the whole world sing, he wrote the jingles that made the whole world buy – and we like that); poet **Billy Collins** (invited because he was a poet laureate of the USA and, like me, can't stand it when kids play Marco Polo in the pool and he, unlike me, wrote a poem about it); poet **Nikki Giovanni** (not really a bold-faced name, but Steve insisted we needed diversity and Tupac is dead and Jay Z declined. I personally don't see how inviting an Italian solves the problem); literary agent **Amanda "Binky" Urban** (invited because she nails seven-figure book deals and you never know what she can do with *The Bulgarian Training Manual*, a.k.a. *The Secrets of the Bulgarians*, newly revised and edited by yours truly) and that fabulously wealthy patron of the arts, **Joaquin "El Chapo" Guzman** (who, according to press reports, was reading Cervantes' *Don Quixote* to curb his post-incarceration depression).

After these formalities, it's on to the main event. We notified all the TV and radio people we could find. And I really talked a good talk in the pre-event interviews. The media wanted to know why we are doing this, why we're going through all this trouble to stage a Poetry Body Slam, which right now has zero precedence in Bulgaria or anywhere else in the world, and why I'm not entering the Ladies' Division of the Bulgarian International Everlast Body Building and Powerlifting Strongman Championship instead, which is being held on the very same day in Bucharest.

Luckily, I didn't miss a beat.

"Good question," I replied, then immediately veered off topic. Truthfully, I have no answer except:

1. I'm not all that muscular, preferring a highly toned but exceptionally strong physique to excessively roided bulk.

2. I only found out about the Bulgarian International Everlast Body Building and Powerlifting Strongman Championship a few weeks ago and it was too late to enter without paying excessive bribes.

3. Since I'm famous now, I might as well capitalize on it.

4. I can't back down from a dare.

5. It's our baby, and we're running with it. Could be the break we need. Our go-out-on-a-high moment. You see, "we" as in "me" figure it this way. Align with the buzz surrounding the Strongman Championship, be the smart alternative event, pull in the intelligentsia and capture the market: Those who think, those who do, those who think about doing. It's a no brainer.

One can see, if one is astute, that it is all about excess and perception. The ultimate in competition and art. Which is what we told reporters gathered for the big announcement. In that instance, "we" being me, Steve, and Shearling. We didn't want Mohawk getting into any of his crazy political rants. Leave the official statements to Shearling, who is now our communications attaché. As Shearling said to the press corps:

"Harold Bloom has called the Poetry Slam the – quote unquote – Death of Art. We respectfully disagree. We believe that, packaged correctly and paired with the liberating forces of muscle, physical beauty, and brute strength, we can rocket humanity to the zenith of the art-body connection. In other words, we're gonna rock their world."

THE THREE LOMBARDIS

It is the mythic monsters – those who, before they were exhibited at fairs and the courts of kings, already existed in fable and legend because they projected infantile or adolescent traumas — who most deeply move spectators to this very day. I recently made a pilgrimage to the Circus World Museum in Baraboo, Wisconsin... And there, in the midst of old circus wagons... I found the side show tent, where, fixed on a platform forever, stood the plaster images of representative Freaks. The statues were dressed, appropriately enough, in Victorian garb. But I was not surprised to discover that the choice of figures to occupy that limited space responded to our basic insecurities, the sort of primordial fears... about scale, sexuality, our status as more than beasts, and our tenuous individuality... so that the distinction between audience and exhibit, we and them, normal and Freak, is revealed as an illusion, desperately, perhaps even necessarily, defended, but untenable in the end.

LESLIE FIEDLER *FREAKS, MYTHS & IMAGES OF THE SECRET SELF* (1978)

THE MAIN EVENT

The big night is here, and I am on a stepladder hanging the last crepe paper streamers across the gym with The Beast. It is hot and humid, and of course, there is no air conditioning. Behind a velvet curtain, tanned and oiled contestants in string bikinis and Speedos are already lining up to the side of a makeshift stage. One muscle man is cradling an impeccably groomed bichon frise, which is becoming streaked with orange residue from his spray tan.

We've got at least 300 rented folding chairs facing the stage, and the hum of the crowd is growing louder. We had so many people waiting to get in that we opened the doors early. Spectators in the rear are tossing a beach ball to one another, and I detect the scent of cannabis. Queen's "We are the Champions" booms from dozens of tiny speakers that Steve bought from the apple-cheeked lady and the competitors walk onto center stage. The crowd erupts in cheers. They strike a pose of their choice, and then all but one move to the side of the platform. Two volunteers, male and female, dressed in black jeans, dark glasses, white t-shirts and Doc Martens, are standing at each side of the platform. They will read the poems aloud while the poets perform their bodybuilding routines to music.

A bell rings, signaling the first competitor, former Olympic powerlifting qualifier Aleksandar "Mr. Groovy" Zivkov. I get off the ladder, step to the side and watch. It's a "people's choice" format, where the audience gets to choose the winner.

Mr. Groovy announces his poem "Think One Thought and then No More" and strikes his first pose as his chosen background music, the final movement of Tchaikovsky's *Violin Concerto in D Major, Op 35,* begins a slow crescendo. A woman in the first row with a Higgs boson cascading down her left arm faints and no one notices as the audience stares at Mr. Groovy's poses, nodding their heads to his every word:

Think less, lift more.
      Think one thought and train some more.
      Stimulation, visualization, specialization, periodization
      Vascularity, viscerality, vodkatonic, vesicate and venerate
      Diuretic dilettante. Shrink-wrap fascia. In your face, grunt like a
brother.
      Dead lift, hammer curl. Barbell.
      Feel like shit, but squat like a motherfucker.
      Ephedrine, cytomel, methylhexaneamine.
      H. G. H.
      Clean and jerk, snatch like a dream.
      ADD training at its core.
      Think one thought and train some more.

As Mr. Groovy exits the stage to enthusiastic applause, three teenage girls teeter onto center stage in gold stiletto heels, black track pants and black t-shirts with the words Gangsta Builda Powerlifta Gym stenciled in white block letters. The girl in the middle steps to the microphone and addresses the crowd. I get an uneasy feeling about this, but decide maybe I'm overreacting to my encounter with that thug.

"Hello comrade. Monika, Olga, me, we work from school computer lab as claim administrator for Aetna, United Health and Geico. We like American music video. LA you rock! Our poem name 'Ode to the Set.' It graduation project and we, how you say? Proud. We thank coach, teacher, and yes, sponsor, many sponsor: Verizon,

Pfizer, Oskar Tanning Salon, Sofia Walk-in Breast Implant Clinic, Ivan's Kabob Shop and WFAN Sport Radio."

At the first thundering beats of 'Gonna Make You Sweat (Everybody Dance Now)', the girls peel off their t-shirts and yank the snaps of their track pants to reveal fluorescent orange and yellow bikinis. They flex tanned and sculpted muscles, then flip around, revealing Higgs boson tramp stamps. In unison, they snap into double bicep curls. The crowd whistles and hollers. A burly man in the fourth row stands and yells "Drill, baby, drill!" Others try to pull him back to his seat. The girls pivot to face the audience and Olga grabs the microphone from the poet reader:

Shake my ass and lift with sass.
> See some skank with my man.
> Swing my rebar, let it fly.
> Take my verse, sonnet and cinquain. *(other girls echo cinquain in a* drawl)
> I'd give ghazal, but I know no Urdu.
> And my girls say, no! Only haiku.
> Find new boyfriend with haiku?
> No!
> Naked, yes, I reveal
> My iiiiii-ambic pent-ameter
> He curses me as just blank verse. I say
> We don't waste time on mindless rhyme.

They walk off with raised fists, and I watch in awe as a massively shredded man with a thick white mane and a leopard loincloth moves to center stage. The announcer says it is Ankar Gustavson from Sweden, fitness model and successor to Fabio in the romance book industry. His music is the 1960s instrumental "Love is Blue." His poem is titled "Elizabethan Interlude."

Shall I compare thee to a summer's day?
> Yes. Let me count the ways.

Alas, summer's lease hath all too short a date.
So no more time to count the ways.

I hear women wailing as he struts off. Then applause, at first tepid, rises like a wave, and I watch a bunch of girls in tight midriffs stand on their chairs stomping their feet and chanting: "An-kar! An-kar!" He blows kisses, flashes a boyish smile, and gives an extra bicep flex before exiting.

Next, a pale thin man in baggy gym shorts steps nervously to the mic.

"Ladies. Gentlemen. I am Marco Stojanov. I study American poet Edgar A. Poe, especially, how you say, across-the-stick poem. This homage to poet Edgar and great Bulgarian coach Ivan Abadjiev and great Bulgaria, too. I call poem "Samson and Delilah.""

He then lets the assigned poet read as he poses to his chosen music, the mournful Bulgaro-Macedonian folk song, "Zaidi, zaidi, yasno slunce."

Feel heart beat in big chest
    Under big shoulders
    Call me Samson. You will be my Delilah?
    Killer couple we would be.

And so it goes for the next two hours, one homeboy after another, reaching for a chance to grasp the stars. Tough girls with boyfriends trailing them. A nun from Albania who trains in the catacombs of her abbey. A humongous, ripped man who passes out from dehydration. A Mr. Rogers look-alike disqualified because he would not remove his cardigan. Gangsta Gym members showing plenty of skin and attitude. And, finally, Mohawk, Mr. Dialectical himself, who we have saved for last because we don't want to start a riot.

Mohawk steps to the stage in a black metallic Speedo with a skull bandana around his forehead. He is wearing mirrored aviator sunglasses, like a cop. I notice for the first time that he has a tattoo on his chest. It appears to be the sun surrounded by the planets. Under Pluto is etched "au revoir mon ami." He is more muscular than I'd imagined, probably because he works out in oversized t-shirts and sweatpants, "work out" being generous since he never seems to break a sweat and doesn't lift heavy weight. But he pops communion wafers like some people chain smoke. *Dietus mirabilis.* He poses to a Gregorian chant.

It is said there is a moment
    In the very beginning,
    When you have to jump across
    A precipice.
    You have written I shall never jump again, Jean-Paul.
    But jump I must
    From the loins of Hackenschmidt
    To the Terminator of Time.
    Nevermore The Apprentice, but Master of Malibu.
    Come join us Freaks. Come with the
    Queen of the Heights, Heroine of Hoboken,
    Cast off the false gods of Cliff Notes and Red Bull, of Netflix and
taco chips.
    And let my people rise once again!

There is a long, stunned silence. Mohawk stands with his head bowed and eyes closed. He then looks up, and raises his arms, palms open. The Beast is weeping, wiping her eyes with her ponytail. Dozens of people stand in unison, then more, jumping up onto the folding chairs, cheering, screaming until the windows rattle. The cheering continues for a full seven minutes, then seven and a half, almost eight. This is significant to me because it beats the seven-minute applause by 50,000 fans at Yankee Stadium on July 29, 1978, when Bob Sheppard announced that Billy Martin would return as manager, less than a week after George Steinbrenner fired him. It is that kind of moment.

Disgruntled Gangsta followers are making their way out of the crowd, and they exit the emergency door, setting off the alarm. Streamers fall from the ceiling and men carry Mohawk on their shoulders as hundreds wave and shout in a sea of adulation. I am flabbergasted. As I watch from the back of the room, Mr. Groovy himself breaks through the crowd in my direction. Is he looking for the restroom? No, he is coming straight at me. Before I can figure out what the hell is going on, he lifts me to his shoulders and takes me to the front of the stage. I high-five Mohawk and the crowd roars. I see Big Steve, in his quiet way, giving me a thumbs up. If only Charlene and Deno could see me now.

NO TIME FOR LONG GOODBYES

It's been a long night. Mohawk and the other winners are signing autographs, and I'm looking forward to the after party. While I'm paying the caterers, Joe Fox sneaks up on me from behind. He says that it's time to go. Time to leave Bulgaria, to go back home. Now? In our moment of glory? Is he nuts? And where, exactly, has he been all this time? I hadn't seen him since shortly after the competition started, standing quietly at the side of the room in his epaulets and pilot's cap. And before that?

I tell him we are on a roll and can't turn back now. He says it's nothing compared to what we can do in the States and, besides, the plane leaves in an hour and the ride's free. He says Shearling is staying behind with the locals, and we should get going. He seems in a hurry, no mood for small talk. Says he will see us at the airstrip and walks out. An hour?

I notice Baba Yaga in the corner of the gym, waving at me to come over. I shake my head. Cowboy is next to her and I wonder what's up. Steve sees them, too, and gives a little flick of the head that means 'check it out.'

"Time to go," Yaga says. "Now!"

"Were you talking to Joe?" I ask. She shushes me, and takes us all into a side hallway, up some stairs and over by a ladder to the roof hatch. Cowboy climbs up and opens it. I'm not liking this. First, because I'm afraid of heights, and secondly, because there's an awesome party about to start downstairs.

Peeking over the roof, we see black Lincoln Town Cars and big men in tracksuits from the Gangsta Builda gym. A bunch are entering the back door while others are hanging out in the parking lot, probably the lookouts. There's a skinhead in a sleeveless hoodie cradling an AR-15 in the rear, the telltale Higgs boson tattoo on his arm. That Catherine whack job is on the hood of one of the cars making out with one of the Gangsta guys, and he makes his way down her flowing skirt and sticks his head under it. I look away.

"The buzz is that you've got the manual, Coach Ivan Abadjiev's personal handwritten manual, the most complete version of the Bulgarian training method in existence, with annotations going back hundreds of years. They say it deciphers the hidden meaning in Bulgaria's ancient secrets of strength and power, and that you not only have his one and only original copy, you alone have the missing chapter, too." Cowboy says.

"Everybody has the manual," I say. "What's the big deal? I mean, even Jose at my gym has it."

"Fakes!" Baba Yaga chimes in, and then bites her knuckles.

"There are plenty of knock-offs," Cowboy agrees, "by celebrity doctors, coaches, shrinks, and sycophants of every kind. Some of Coach Ivan's closest protégés have tried to distill the training into their own words, but they never had the complete picture. Coach Ivan himself was pursued by spies who infiltrated his gym in Sofia, mobsters who tempted him with riches and even sent prostitutes with scopolamine smeared on their breasts to his gym in an attempt to get their hands on his training manual. And now, since his passing, we know there exists only one true version. And Ivan didn't have it."

"Who has it?"

"You," he says.

"What? Where? That's impossible," I say as I frantically try to remember where I left it. Back at the cottage, where Wally and Eddie might at this moment be selling it on the black market? In my gym bag downstairs? And if it's so rare, how did Steve get it? And mine isn't handwritten."

"Don't panic, kid. What you think of as the manual," he says calmly, "those pages Steve gave you are a good imitation, a great approximation, a brilliant fraud. It's close, but not the real thing. The actual manual – the genuine, definitive, unadulterated article – it's in your head, or, more accurately, in your DNA."

For once I keep my mouth shut as I think over what he is telling me. Does he really think I'm that stupid? That gullible?

"It's in your mind. In your pores. In your nasal cavities. In your fingers. In your supercharged waveforms of the electromagnetic energy that connects you with your past, of past lives and of ancestors born of suffering and strength. You did major in psychology, didn't you?"

Ouch. One more reminder that I should have taken up something else. My useless college degree.

"Oh, that," I say, feigning boredom. "I assume you mean Carl Jung's concept of the collective unconscious? It's all in the cerebral cortex, you know, and mine came fully loaded."

He looks impressed. "Yes! I knew it. You can spot these links immediately."

"Like Nadia's eyes?" I ask, recalling the moment Steve gave me the manual.

"You know more than you know you know," he says.

Baba Yaga laughs and claps her hands.

"So," I say, "You are telling me I could just sit in a café, order up a cappuccino, write down everything I know and it would be, what?"

"The definitive manual," he says.

"Like Ivan's?" I ask.

"Better than Ivan's. He doesn't share your lineage. There are passages, chapters, in his that are somehow incomplete. You, Tina, are the only one who perfectly synthesizes superhuman strength with intellectual heft, philosophical perspective, and, above all, superior artistic sensibility."

If that's true, then why until recently was I making no money selling real estate in Hoboken? I'm so confused. All I know for sure is that I am missing a fabulous party downstairs, with media, celebs, and booze, while I'm making small talk on a roof.

"Let's go back inside," I say. "There are TV people downstairs. They want to interview me. I can't keep them waiting."

Cowboy grabs me and looks into my eyes. "You and you alone embody the unconscious and subconscious collective consciousness that is reflected in the brick-and-mortar physicality of this ancient and mystical edifice. The ghosts of this building's past are manifested in you. See those goons in the track suits?" he asks, pointing to the parking lot. He slides a finger across his throat and grimaces. I get the picture.

We creep back down the ladder. A metal door slams. The Gangstas have rushed the gym and Cowboy grabs my arm and runs straight through the crowd, which is heavily partying and unaware of the alarming turn of events. A girl gets in my face and starts quoting from *Ulysses*. Cowboy pushes her away and keeps running, knocking over the folding chairs as we make our way across the gym floor. I don't see Big Steve or Baba Yaga, but there's no time to look around. The Gangstas are following us. We jump over a workout bench and make it outside while the dweebs led by Mohawk rush the enemy and, with their newly honed mental and physical strength, push them back against the brick wall. Cowboy and I leap into his jeep and take off. We catch up with Baba Yaga about a mile up the road, at the edge of the woods. Big Steve is next to her. I wonder how they got there so fast, but no time to ask questions. We slow down, and Steve hops in.

Baba Yaga hands me a small bucket of candy corn, Thin Mints, and M&Ms. "Eat a handful every half hour. Wash down with Gatorade. Ivan's orders." She waves goodbye.

I get it. Digestion of candy can take anywhere from 15 to 45 minutes before it is absorbed by the circulatory system and stored as glycogen. Then, energy kicks in.

We get to the airstrip and there's no plane. No Joe. Nothing. Maybe we're in the wrong place. But where is the right place? And where would somebody hide a C-130 military cargo jet?

A plain looking woman in a Lufthansa uniform and sensible shoes walks up to the jeep and hands us a note from Joe. His connection turned bad and he couldn't wait. Not to worry.

Connection? What the fuck?

"Who are you?" I ask the airline chick.

"I," she says, "I am the Fraulein."

The Fraulein? She is so plain. Thick waist, no makeup. Not even blonde. Does she know I was fucking with her instant messages to Joe? The Fraulein hands us first-class tickets to Newark Airport and jumps behind the wheel of the jeep. She drives us to the airport in Sofia and, bypassing security, escorts us to the tarmac, where the stairs are being rolled to a Boeing 787. Before saying goodbye, the Fraulein salutes and gives us goodie bags of Bulgarian souvenirs, including a DVD of the poetry slam and a locally produced Lava Lamp. She blows kisses as we board the aircraft.

From inside the plane, I see a woman on the tarmac struggling with a large suitcase. It pops open and her clothes spill out. I rush down the stairs and in seconds I am expertly folding her clothes into such precise and small bundles that it closes easily when I repack it. The woman wants to know if I learned my skill from Japanese tidying guru Marie Kondo, but I tell her no, just Clean Machine Laundromat in Jersey City, that everything in life counts and never to underestimate the value of blue-collar dreams. She thanks me profusely, hands me a Sharpie and asks me to autograph her bra.

As I step back into the plane, I make my way to the empty seat next to Big Steve, who already has his headphones on and has propped a pillow under his head.

"It's a new world, baby," he says. "You have the secrets of the Bulgarians. And with those secrets comes the responsibility to reconcile and restore humanity's physical and intellectual and artistic sensibilities to a level unsurpassed since the ancient Greeks."

"Fuck you and the horse you rode in on." The day is catching up to me and I'm feeling irritable. "I was thinking more in terms of the old, 'if it ain't broke, don't fix it,'" I yawn, reclining back in my seat. "And if it *is* broke, it's none of my business, baby. I've got my own Lava Lamp dreams."

"Did I tell you how much I love you, Kitty Cat?" he says.

"Like hell you do," I mumble.

I lean against his arm and try to calm my anxiety.

"Sleep is when your muscles grow," he whispers.

I watch as Baba Yaga and the trees and the grass and the terminal and houses all fall away to the gray mist and clouds and then to blue sky. I wonder what has become of Mohawk and if he escaped the angry mob. A flight attendant comes by with a hot, moist washcloth. Another follows right behind with a tray.

Steve is asleep.

"*Veuve Clicquot?*" she offers. "And a blueberry *parfait?*"

I take one of each.

Hasta la vista, New Jersey.

THE THREE LOMBARDIS

The choreographer and the dancer must remember that they reach the audience through the eye. It's the illusion created which convinces the audience, much as it is with the work of a magician.

GEORGE BALANCHINE (UNDATED)

PART III

BACK IN THE U.S.A.

COURTYARD BY MARRIOTT
OAKBROOK TERRACE, ILLINOIS

I would like to thank the members of the American Coin Laundry Association for honoring me tonight in beautiful Oakbrook Terrace. I especially thank your mayor, Tony "Red Panda" Ragucci, who thinks he is Italian, just like I used to think I was Italian.

I have to tell you, this is almost as exciting as opening my first fitness franchise, which was, in fact, eclipsed only by my Nobel Prize in Literature. Why? Because folks, this honor is totally out of the blue. When I won the Nobel, we had a good idea of the odds. My business manager had some connections, if you know what I mean. He's Turkish and so was this writer who got the Nobel a few years before. So, he gets this dude to help us behind the scenes in exchange for me promoting all things Turkish, which is why we sell Turkish Taffy at our Laundromats and we have free samples today in the back of the room. Oh, we ran out of banana.

Jeez, I can't read my own handwriting with all the cross-outs. What are these notes along the side? Well, I'll wing it. This is a good crowd.

Not to get sidetracked, but who knew they had a Nobel Prize for books? I mean, when you think of the Nobel Prize, isn't it always like Mother Teresa or Gandhi, who, by the way, didn't get the prize? Sucks, but that's the breaks. Can you imagine? I mean, Gandhi? Peace? Hello? And then there's Nobel Prizes for, you know, scientists like Enrico Fermi, the Italian guy who invented nukes. Did you know he is buried less than an hour from here? Oak Woods Cemetery. That's right. Illinois. And if you don't believe me, download the app. It's called Find-a-Grave. Great for travelling. Anyway, point is, there are a lot of Nobels, and they give out good money with them, too.

I have copies of my Nobel speech available for sale, and if we have time, I might read a few excerpts because if it was good enough for the Swedes, it's good enough for you. Actually, that didn't come out the way I meant it, but you get the picture.

OMG total silence. Tina, don't blow it. You were on a roll during the cocktail hour. You want these people to buy your book, invest in a franchise.

The lady who introduced me at the podium described my gym-laundry-nutrition trifecta as quote-unquote an example of thinking out of the box, and I appreciate that. Who wants to think or even live inside a box? Not me. Not while I'm breathing.

Good. They laughed. Tina, don't worry, these guys love you.

I was asked during the cocktail reception about the décor, specifically why we place Lava Lamps in the laundry area of our gyms. Well, to tell you the truth, Lava Lamps have a personal family significance related to my grandmother. So does cheap beer. But beer is really bad for you when working with heavy weights, whereas Lava Lamps have a calming effect. They come in a whole range of colors and styles, well, actually, they basically all look the same. You can buy them in the back where we sell my book *The Bulgarian Training Manual*, which, like I said, won the Nobel Prize and it was also on *The New York Times* bestseller list for a gazillion weeks. If you go online, it is cross sold in the how-to, self-help, spirituality, sports, nutrition, wellness, Baltic studies, Edwardian literature, contemporary poetry, and cookbook categories. My agent wanted me to pretend I was a teenager so she could market it as juvenile nonfiction or young adult, but that would be unscrupulous.

Let's see, what else? Oh, yeah, my new project. I am writing a memoir, and I encourage all of you to consider writing a memoir because you all have a story. I heard some of your stories while we were scarfing down shrimp and pulled pork sliders during the cocktail hour. People like Nicky. Yeah, Nicky, that would be you. You got a great story. Don't worry, I ain't telling. Just keep me away from the margaritas later. What? You have to speak up. Yeah, yeah, all you guys, you know about Nicky. Who knew such things go on in, where are we?

Ugh. Nicky with the white shoes and stupid jokes who kept putting the moves on me whenever his wife went to the punchbowl. I hope he doesn't hang around.

Seriously, think about it: a memoir about your mother doing your laundry or maybe your first Maytag and how it changed your life. Actually, I'll do that one myself. *Eat, Drink, Wash.* Or better yet, *Eat, Train, Wash.* You see how it's done? And yes, you can use other people's titles; just change them around a little. But don't use that one. It's mine. Find something else, whatever floats your boat. The hardest book is the first, like anything in life.

Good. They laughed. A little.

I have to say, there is something awesome about being here. Who knew a bunch of people in a small town so far from New Jersey could be so chill? Somebody told me Oakbrook Terrace was originally called Utopia. That's amazing. I don't understand why you would get rid of such a great name except maybe it got to be old hat, like in New York, there's this highway called Utopia Parkway, but nobody drives it thinking it will be a Shangri-La experience.

I notice Cowboy standing in the back of the room. He didn't tell me he was coming. He catches my eye and winks. Reminds me of the day we met, when he gave me a lift in his truck. I look back at my notes, such as they are. Gotta keep focused.

Oh, um, I know you want to hear more about the laundry and gym connection, seeing as how this is the coin-laundry association.

Think about it: You are done working out. Your sweaty gym clothes reek so bad you hate the idea of putting them in your car. So you toss them in our machines and sit in the lotus position, watching the front loaders swish your shorts in one direction and then another. Or relax on a tanning bed with a cot and panpipes and get advice from our in-house hypnotherapist, Dr. Sadlyer. Take a nap while you're at it, because sleep is when muscles grow. Wake up and chow down on gluten-free communion wafers, made exclusively for us by nuns in Missoula and available in our vending machines for a buck. Remember, St. Catherine of Siena was said to have survived on communion wafers alone for seven years so there must be something to them, right? Ok, so she also drank the pus of the sick, but we won't go there. And by the way, our communion wafers are infused with patented growth supplements, extracted from arugula-fed snails, created by one of my business partners, a dude who looks like Crocodile Dundee. Yes, the guy in the back of the room. Let's not all look at once.

Ugh, he is waving. He catches me looking at him. I feel my face get hot and tingly.

I came up with this concept after an unexpected trip to Bulgaria. It's a long story. But I'll let you in on a secret. While I was in Bulgaria, I found out that my biological father is Arnold Schwarzenegger. Yeah, the real deal. Thanks. You don't have to clap but thank you. No, really, I didn't have anything to do with it, you know, the procreation, but I appreciate the applause.

Whew. Yeah, they love me. I'm good. What's Cowboy up to back there? He's smiling.

I'm telling you this not to name drop, but to let you know that to be successful you need to be well capitalized. I was lucky in that Arnold became a silent investor, helping us get off the ground. I'm technically not supposed to even talk about him because of the terms of our paternity agreement. DNA is a beautiful thing, by the way. So is the DNA test, which I am also not at liberty to discuss. Let's just say it proves there is a synchronicity in the universe and leave it at that. Even if it meant blowing up my fantasy image of my so-called father and my entire sense of self.

Cowboy is pulling a bouquet of roses from behind his back. What the –?

So, where was I? Yes, *The Bulgarian Training Manual* was on *The New York Times* best-seller list for 48 weeks. It is subtitled, *The Story of Me and Big Steve*. But let me make something clear. This is my story. Big Steve had nothing to do with writing it, but he had a lot to do with what happened in my life, including giving me a poorly conceived and bastardized precursor to *The Bulgarian Training Manual* at our gym. Today, Big Steve is also a business partner, selling books and filling out franchise applications. He used to be my boyfriend for about five minutes before he got into bodybuilding, and I thought I might want him to be my boyfriend again after Bulgaria, but instead old macho man took up with a guy he used to work with at the city dump. Yeah, right, a guy. Got it? Point is, Big Steve is living proof of the manual as a catalyst of change. I should have suspected something when Steve started philosophizing while wearing poet shirts. And I should have put two and two together when I found out he had memorized *Viva Las Vegas*. Woulda, shoulda, coulda.

It's true, my manual can change your life, but you won't end up in jodhpurs and flowing garments. Instead, you get the definitive word on bodybuilding, weight training, strength conditioning, wrestling, powerlifting and the whole mind-body way to live. I could have called it *The Way to Live*, but an ancestor of mine, Georg Hacken-schmidt, already wrote that in the early 1900s, and I would not want to step on anyone's toes, especially a dead person's.

So, I encourage you to buy it, and make sure you do not accept cheap counterfeits, as there are a lot of versions of *The Bulgarian Training Manual* circulating online and in gyms. Mine is a cut above, and that's not meant as a pun. One reviewer called my book the quote-unquote Bible of bodybuilding with the hipness of a *Rolling Stone* cover and the gravitas of the Dead Sea scrolls. The old and the new. Or the newly new.

Oh, before I forget, I am available for one-hour consulting sessions and even weekly coaching over the phone, which you can arrange with Big Steve. Or come to one of our gyms and check us out. We do poetry readings on Thursday nights for free. You wouldn't believe how many bodybuilders are into poetry.

I see a hand up. It's an old lady in a pink pantsuit and orthopedic shoes. I look at the moderator, who gives me a thumbs up.

Yes, I'll take your question. Can't really hear you. Can anyone else hear? Oh, oh, I get it. She says we should not be taking *The Bible* blas-phemously. Well, no offense but, what? She says she read the manual and it is nothing like the King James Version, but more like the, say again, what? NRSV? Uh, huh. New Revised Standard Version. No, ma'am, I'm not a Presbyterian. Let's take another question. Yes, the kid in the back. I see your hand up. You're asking if the Dead Sea scrolls are like seaweed? Are you fucking with my head?

OMG! I dropped the F bomb. Keep going. Just keep going. I'll call on the guy in the blue blazer. Is Cowboy smirking?

How did this change my life personally? Well, let's just say that I made so much money that Deno – he's an agent at a real estate office I used to work at – found me a fabulous condo in an elevator build-ing. And, by the way, I bought it with cash – I mean, I love Larry our mortgage guy to death, but they don't give away money like they used to. Oh, and I won the women's fitness championship at the IFBB – International Federation of Bodybuilding – so now Big Steve and me, we're in demand as guest posers at shows around the country. You can catch us tanned and oiled on our infomercial, if you stay up that late. We think there's a movie in our future, too. *Pumping Iron* with intellect. Recreate a winning formula.

Oh, I see another hand raised. Yeah, you, sir, with the Red Sox cap. I'm a Yankee fan but it's not a problem. What attracted me to the laundry business? Glad you asked.

I used to hang out at the Laundromat near my gym in Jersey City until just a few years ago, before my life-changing trip behind the former Iron Curtain. I'd go mostly to escape my awful apartment and my job. Besides, my clothes needed to be washed and nobody was going to do it for me. There was this older lady, Helen, who folded the best. But one thing about Helen, she don't like to separate. If you don't separate your stuff ahead of time, she throws all the clothes in together. I mean, if your stuff isn't separated and you ask her to do it, she will, but she charges extra. Yeah, go ahead and laugh. But she picks up some good coin from people just on separating. So, if that's all, then…

Oh, wait, another question? Sorry. I thought you were scratching your armpit.

Uh huh. Why do we promote poetry readings in our Laundromats? Great question! The poets are a vital part of the gym. You know, the *zeitgeist*. One-stop training or, as Mohawk, our corporate poet laureate, says: "Pump like a mother!"

Omigod, there you go again, Tina. Remember, you're in freakin' white bread land.

Well, folks. I see the moderator is holding up a little red card, which means I'm out of time. We have poets in the back of the room with Big Steve. Try out your latest haiku. Promise they won't laugh. And don't leave without a signed copy of *The Bulgarian Training Manual*.

Who knows? It could change your life.

I mean, just look at me.

I see one guy stand up and clap. Then another. In a moment, it's like they all get up at once. Cheering, whistling. A group on the left is chanting "Own the Rep. Feel the Burn." I see the lady in the pink pantsuit jumping up and down punching the air. I hear pulsating music, louder and louder and somebody screams "I'm a motherfucking beast!" It feels so familiar, so, well, Jersey Shore. Cowboy is slowly walking up the aisle, almost to the podium. I smile and peel off my blazer. An image comes into my head. It's Grandma, with a foot perched on her old TV, saying, "Ya did good, kid."

THE THREE LOMBARDIS

Luigi, Pietro and Frankie cannot agree on which archival/academic/intellectual/spiritual quote should be used to close the book. Rather than force a choice, the editors will permit each Lombardi to select his own concluding quote. The publishers look forward to feedback from readers, faculty (tenured at prestigious universities), and members of Tina's gyms, who receive a signed copy of the book with every one-year contract.

Luigi:

> They are mortal, these heroes, just as we are. They do not last forever. They fade. They vanish. They are surpassed, forgotten – one hears of them no more.
>
> JAMES SALTER *A SPORT AND A PASTIME* (1967)

Frankie:

I do not know why I write, but it definitely makes me feel good... Literature is about preserving your childishness all your life, keeping the child in you alive...

ORHAN PAMUK, NOBEL BANQUET SPEECH, DEC. 10, 2006

Pietro, with commentary:

Listen, just call me Pete. None of that Pietro shit, ok? Yeah, I know, Pietro is my legal name, but my parents were, you know, old school. Look, I get it, the platitudes to the noble profession of writing and all that. I appreciate it. But I think I would choose to end with something more, I don't know. Simple. To the point. My famiglia here, they disagree. But hey, it's a free country. So, here goes:

Someday we'll look back on this and it will all seem funny.

BRUCE SPRINGSTEEN "ROSALITA (COME OUT TONIGHT)"
1973, COLUMBIA RECORDS

ACKNOWLEDGMENTS

Works of fiction are informed by the totality of our lived experience, blending imagination, memory, and research. So it is with this book, inspired by countless people from all walks of life, some fleeting, others forever connected to my soul.

There is Steven A. from New Jersey, bodybuilder turned school teacher, who told me long ago about a peculiar Bulgarian training regime. The real Joe Fox from Hoboken, who no longer walks among us, but in his time loved scotch, flying aircraft, deal making, meatloaf, and Opera Without Words. And novelist Mark Leyner, who shares my interest in oddities, orange soda, and dive bars.

I would not have completed this journey without the folks at Stony Brook University's Lichtenstein Center for the Arts, who challenged me to immerse myself in all forms of literature, from fiction to playwriting to poetry, because each informs the other. Specifically: Program founder Robert Reeves, a gentle mentor whose advice and encouragement renewed my resolve and opened new paths. Novelist Meg Wolitzer, who, when the book was in its infancy, wanted to know what would happen next. (I had no idea, but knew I had to find out.) Poet Julie Sheehan, who introduced me to Bob Holman and the poetry slam world. Theater director Bill Burford, who convinced me I could write great dialogue. Novelist Helen Simonson, who urged me to send my characters "off to Bulgaria," and novelist/memoirist Kaylie Jones, a fierce advocate of brave writing who kept me going. Then there are friends who patiently caught typos and asked smart questions: among them Deirdre Sinnott and John Roynon.

I especially thank Leza Cantoral and Christoph Paul, founders of Clash Books, for enthusiastically embracing *The Bulgarian Training Manual* into their quixotic quest of growing an independent literary press.

Thanks also to coach Bill Pipes, for teaching me how to tame the eternal yammering that runs amok in our heads; Pete Lombardi, whose fervor for construction materials, gluten-free pasta and laughter is unmatched, and Prof. Susan Shapiro, whose belief in "good book karma" inspires her legendary parties honoring new and established authors.

Finally: Nothing is wasted, and everything counts.

This book is born of fear as well as deep joy. It could not have been written without both.

As Bruce Springsteen famously wrote, and a fictitious Lombardi repeated, "Someday we'll look back on this and it will all seem funny."

Indeed, it does.

hahahahahahahahahaha

PREVIOUSLY PUBLISHED

The Southampton Review: "Big Steve"
Winter/Spring 2018
Amy Hempel, fiction editor

The American Writer's Review 2023: "Stigmata"
D Ferrara, editor

ABOUT THE AUTHOR

Ruth Bonapace earned her MFA from Stony Brook University after a career in journalism, including two years covering professional sports for The Associated Press. Her work has appeared in many publications including *The New York Times*, *Newsday*, *The Southampton Review*, *Hippocampus*, and *The Saturday Evening Post*. She is a two-time finalist in the annual American Writer's Review. *The Bulgarian Training Manual* is her first novel.

Born in Brooklyn and raised on Long Island, where she attended an all-girls Catholic high school, Ruth is a former New York State Agriculture Writer of the Year who turned down a job with The American Dairy Association. Ruth believes her non-writing gigs as a real estate agent, mortgage banker, laundromat owner, mom of three and, of course, waitress, not in that order, inform her prose. Ruth divides her time between New Jersey and the Catskills. Do not ask how she finds time to write.

ALSO BY CLASH BOOKS

GIRL LIKE A BOMB

Autumn Christian

LIFE OF THE PARTY

Tea Hacic-Vlahovic

HOW TO GET ALONG WITHOUT ME

Kate Axelrod

WHAT ARE YOU

Lindsay Lerman

THE RACHEL CONDITION

Nicholas Rombes

AFTERWORD

Nina Schuyler

EARTH ANGEL

Madeline Cash

ALL THINGS EDIBLE, RANDOM & ODD

Sheila Squillante

THE BLACK TREE ATOP THE HILL

Karla Yvette

BORN TO BE PUBLIC

Greg Mania

WE PUT THE LIT IN LITERARY

clashbooks.com

FOLLOW US

IG

X

FB

@clashbooks

EMAIL

clashmediabooks@gmail.com